I0556040

First to Fall

Moonlight Rogues, Volume 1

Alexa Whitewolf

Published by Luna Imprints, 2018.

FIRST TO FALL

First edition. March 21, 2018.

ISBN: 978-1-9993839-6-1

Written by Alexa Whitewolf.

"I have been so long master that I would be master still, or at least that none other should be master of me."

Bram Stoker, Dracula

Author's Note & Acknowledgements

Since I started writing, I avoided the topic of werewolves because I thought it was extremely overdone since the days of *Twilight*. But in large part due to my upbringing and the stories I grew up with in Transylvania, I simply couldn't stay away.

And so started the series *Moonlight Rogues!* I meant it to be different from the start, dealing not only with werewolves but with different tales from across the world. I dug into Romanian folklore for this, doing my best to include different entities. These elements will continue throughout the series, and hopefully evolve into more!

Quick note about the historical authenticity: while some facts I mention are real, I've taken fictional liberty with everything, especially Dominic's lineage! ☺

I want to thank my family, specifically my mother, grandmother and uncle, for their invaluable input into the legends. Without my mom's encouragement to read when I was a child, I never would have devoured tales of werewolves, dragons and fairies, and that would have been a shame!

Huge thanks go to my husband, whose support in writing this book and caffeine providing for my all-nighters went a long way to helping me achieve its completion!

Zeus and Achilles, as always, were inspiration for any canine behavior you notice in the book and they're also my much-needed relaxing buddies.

The team behind this book who helped edit, design the cover, encourage me—you guys rock!! An extra hug to Y. Nikolova with **Ammonia Book Covers,**[1] who brought my vision of the cover to life with her awesome talent!!!

And last but not least, a huge hug to my readers!

Happy readings,

Alexa

---

1. https://mobile.twitter.com/AmmoniaCovers

∞ ∞ ∞

CHAPTER ONE

∞ Începuturi ∞

"The <u>beginning</u> is the most important part of the work."

-Plato-

Lucrezia

My feet crunch in the snow, and for the tenth time this morning I thank my lucky stars I invested in my fuzzy warm boots. It may have been money I didn't have, but with the way the winter is acting up, it will only get worse.

Rockland Creek, Wyoming, is renowned for its harsh winters—not that it's the real reason I ended up here. It was the most remote place near the border with Canada and having that quick escape possible eases the tightness in my back somewhat.

Memories of a much darker time linger at the edge of my consciousness, but I shake them off. Distance and months of breathing freely have made it easier to compartmentalize, and I'm determined to get in to work chipper despite the chilly Monday morning.

An icy gust of wind sweeps up, and I huddle in my coat, wishing I had grabbed an extra sweater underneath it.

Almost there. As if to spite me, Mother Nature throws in some nice flurries—and more wind. Gritting my teeth against it, I quicken my step towards Claws Auto Shop, which I see in the distance. I'm one of those lucky few who can walk to work rather than have to drive or bus, which keeps me in an overall nice shape and clears my mind most mornings.

Most times, it only takes me about half an hour to get there. It's a breeze in summer, but not so much in winter. I vaguely consider asking one of my colleagues for a lift for the rest of the season and then dismiss the idea. The last thing I want them to feel is obligated to protect the only girl in their pack.

By the time I finally reach the side door of Claws Auto Shop, where I work as receptionist, my cheeks are frozen and my fingers refuse to cooperate. I fumble with the key, dropping it three times in the snow, before I get the blasted thing open.

After taking off my coat and switching into some comfortable sneakers, I sit down at my small desk and get started on my day. Within the next hour, as I answer calls and confirm appointments, the guys pile in one by one.

Guys, no. These are *men* and so damn gorgeous my heart hurts every time I notice them. Unfortunately, other body parts I've neglected for a while also poke their head out. Normally, I have a tight control on my hormones. These last few weeks, however...

I tear my eyes away from them and focus on my paperwork, going through the previous week's sales and amounts for collection. Having studied accounting and business while in university, numbers always fascinated me. They make sense, more so than people ever do—to me, at least. But this time around, not even the dry accounts payable booklet is enough to keep me focused. With every ring of the bell announcing someone's presence, I glance up.

First Finn McConnell shows up, his mischievous green eyes twinkling already. With his mop of unruly dark hair and the lithe body of an athlete, he could easily be an actor or model. The lilt in his voice hints at his Irish background, and yeah it's sexy as hell. You would never peg him for a lawyer, but he once dabbled in the trade before leaving Ireland for the States—a long, long time ago like he says.

Next comes Tristan Cayne, brooding about another sleepless night, if the circles under his eyes are any indication. He's a war vet, honorably discharged from the Marines with PTSD—post-traumatic stress disorder. He lost his entire unit in an ambush in the desert and still has the nightmares about it. His skin is tanned even in winter, due to his Brazilian blood, but the man knows how to pull off jeans and a simple shirt like no other. With his shaved head, gentle hazel gaze and square jaw, he's the most aloof of the four.

Third in is Dominic Kosta, with blue eyes that capture me every time and the sinful body of Apollo. Dark blonde hair, clean-cut jaw and muscular build, he's the gentlest of the bunch. At first he told me he was born and bred here, but after many late evening conversations, he revealed he was adopted from a Romanian orphanage by an American couple who couldn't have children of their own.

The story answered a lot of questions about him, and it gave me more insight into this gentle giant who I've seen break more than one heart with all his womanizing. Despite it, there's a quiet confidence in him I respond to, and he puts me at ease in a way no other man has. I've been working here for the last year, but it's Dominic I connected with more than all the others.

His grin lights his face when he sees me, and he moves in for a hug. I squeal out of his grip, shivering at the wind drafting in with him. "Get away, you're ice cold!"

Dom picks me up snorting and twirls me around, before putting me back down. I'm still recovering from the closeness, when the last of them walks in.

"Already wasting time, I see?" Lucas Bianchi's remark would have stung, had it not been delivered with his side-smirk and glittering onyx eyes. The man is Italian to the bone, and his commanding presence tends to leave me shaking at the knees.

Lately, it's morphed into more than that. Whenever he's around, I lose my words—and I haven't crushed on anyone since high school.

"Morning, Lucrezia," he murmurs in his gravelly voice, and I smile feebly in return. To this day, Lucas is the only one who calls me by my full name, all the others having picked up on the nickname Dom gave me – Luz, for light.

As can be guessed, the mixed nationalities have definitely increased my vocab, at least where swearing is concerned. Both Tristan and Lucas lose it in their respective native tongues, and it's almost fun watching them when it happens.

With a nod to Dominic, Lucas heads to the back, already barking orders to Finn and Tristan. Two other guys help around the store in summer, but they're only teenagers from high school, learning the trade. Mostly, it's just us five – me on the paperwork and phones, and the guys tinkering and fixing the cars of Rockland Creek, and of the people passing through.

And I was the lucky one who got to work with them every week, day in and day out.

"Why the long sigh?"

Oops. I'm uncannily aware of Dom's steady gaze on me—and his keen sense of observation.

"Bah, it's Monday," I try to joke, but even I don't fall for it. I peek towards Lucas, who's now opening the doors of the garage—a tell-tale sign announcing they're ready for work.

The inside of their working environment has heat blasting so even with the cool air wafting in, they're comfortable. Not that it seems to matter to these four—they're so hot-blooded a hug from them will have you sweating in no time!

Thankfully for me, a transparent window and well-insulated door separates me from the garage area, and I get to stay indoors and enjoy the warmth.

My gaze is drawn to the two cars already driving in, one of which is a sporty red Mustang convertible. The other is a pickup truck that has seen better days. It's no surprise when Lucas walks over to the Mustang, with Tristan heading to the other car to greet the clients.

"Who the hell drives a car like that in winter?" My eyes narrow in annoyance.

The answer soon makes itself known. A leggy brunette steps out of the car, dressed in dark leggings, thigh-high boots with six-inch stilettos and a white fur coat. Even from afar, I notice her makeup is done to perfection.

Though I'm confident in my flaming locks and exotic features, I don't tend to flaunt my looks. Working with the guys gives me the perfect excuse for casual dress and flying under the radar in jeans and t-shirts.

It's better this way, the reasonable voice in my mind warns. *Remember what happened last time?*

A snort from Dom has me focus back on him, in time to see his grimace.

"What?"

"The girl," he rolls his eyes. "She'll be a handful. I better go, Lucas might need help."

I watch him go, trying to stifle an exasperated sigh—and failing. "You sure it's not *her* you want to get a closer look at?"

Dom turns around at that, a flash of surprise crossing his features. It's gone so quick I might have imagined it. He grins instead and winks. "Not with you around, Luz."

He's gone before I can figure out what he means, and I turn my attention to my regular tasks. At least until the brunette comes for payment. "I was told to come here to pay for the services," she says huskily, and I wonder for a second if she fakes that voice.

I force a polite smile, realizing how mean my thoughts are turning. "Of course. May I see their quote?" She hands me the paper—perfectly manicured nails, I notice—and I plug it into the computer and issue her a formal invoice.

Once she pays I staple a receipt to the invoice and hand it back to her. Eliza Porting is her name, and if it didn't fit her so classically I would laugh about it. She sounds so posh, dresses to a T, yet here she is in the middle of nowhere with a car that broke down.

You once ended up here in a similar way... I try to ignore the reasonable voice nagging me. A lecture would be bad right about now.

Oddly put off, I hand Eliza back the card and return to my computer. I figure this will be it and she'll go wait in the seating area, but she sees fit to hang around.

"How do you work with all that man candy around?" An annoying giggle follows her whispered words.

I track her gaze to the guys, for a moment detracted when Lucas bends down to check under the car, giving us both a perfect view of his, err, assets. Eliza's practically panting in delight, eyes glued to him solely now.

Mine, I want to growl, and hold back. This possessive nature is new for me, as is the jealousy. I have no right, but Lucas is that kind of man. The type you want to lock up and have your way with, day and night... *especially* night.

"Not sure what you mean," I mutter, focusing on papers that need no more organizing.

She turns to peer at me then—really looks at me, assessing me from head to toe—and smirks knowingly. "Oh, I get it. It's okay; I have nothing against people who play for the other team."

The diva goes back to ogling the guys lasciviously, dismissing me in the process. "More for me."

My palm itches, consumed by an almost insane urge to slap her. Just because I dress a certain way, she needs to label me already? *Bitch*.

I'm about to comment, when her next words hit me hard. "So, seen Tommy lately?" Her lips turn upwards into a sneer at my shocked expression, but those eyes are emotionless.

Shit. I thought I escaped this.

Dominic

I stare at Luz for who knows how long this particular time. At first, I tried to keep my distance. She was new, different, and mortal. But something in her calls to me as sure as the full moon, and the more I've known her these last months, the more I want her.

Unfortunately, she only has eyes for Lucas. She doesn't understand the reason for her attraction is linked to his status as chieftain of our pack. Nor that he officially took the lead as alpha in the summer, causing a hell of a lot of hormonal changes in his scent over the last weeks that affect even the most hardened females.

Then again, Luz also has no idea she's living and working in the midst of a town ruled by werewolves.

Some secret, huh?

We've kept it on the down low from the uninitiated—basically, people like Luz who think the world is normal. Her working for us was a complication at first. We were so used to joking around and acting like mutts in heat that needing to censor ourselves seemed like chaining.

It would have built resentment, were it not for Luz's open perspective on life. She quickly—and bossily—got us all in check, ordering us to treat her like one of the guys. It established a certain professional relationship.

Which is why I'm loath to break it. That, and there was something wounded about her when she first appeared in town. I still remember the day she got off the bus with nothing but a backpack, looking lost and so damn vulnerable it tore at my heart. I was in wolf form, and her scent acted like an aphrodisiac I had a hard time letting go of.

Not many humans are supposed to affect us this way. Not many *do*.

Except Luz.

Back then, despite morphing into my human form, I'd still struggled to quiet my wolf down. I can recall, even to this day, the anxiety in her expression when I first asked if she was new to town. After a few moments of awkward talk, I offered to show her around.

It might have been the loneliness or her quick assessment of me, but Luz agreed. Within the day, we ended up at a diner. No matter how much I tried to probe back then—and since then—the only information I got was that she recently moved to Rockland Creek and was searching for a job.

Before I thought things through, I was already telling her our mechanic's shop direly needed a receptionist. Lucas had been none too happy when I showed up with her in tow, but after some discussion, he relented. Luz was hired the next day, and Lucas has admitted on more than one occasion since that it was the best decision he ever made.

My thoughts of Luz must have intruded on my senses because my wolf is growling. *Danger.*

And no, I don't make a habit of hearing voices, at least not in the losing-my-mind way. But I do have a second facet to my personality, and that's my wolf.

He lives within me, like a subconscious part of me, not an alter ego but more… a voice of reasoning. On a regular basis, he pokes his head out only when strong emotions control me, luring me away from my more human side.

But this time…

I listen to the warning and look towards the reception desk where Luz's anger reverberates across the distance. The high-maintenance gal who's with her irks me, and she annoys my wolf.

"Don't," Finn mutters next to me.

I glance at my buddy, surprised he read me so easily. Then again, with Finn, you're an open book more often than not. That's the thing when you're around werewolves with special *gifts*, like I call them.

"You know she has feelings for Lucas." His eyes narrow in disapproval, darting from Luz back to me.

"And you know *why* she has them," I retort, going back to what I'm supposed to be doing— hammering back into shape a beat-up bumper.

Finn follows me to the long table meant for the task, not dropping the conversation. "You're assuming," he accuses, and I hammer the metal a little too hard.

My back muscles tense, and my wolf jumps to defense when I turn to him. "Back off, Finn."

He notices my glare, because after a few tense moments of staring at each other he steps away, hands held up in the air. "I'm only saying, mate. Keep in mind, Luz may have real feelings and more than a crush on our boss."

I don't believe that. *Won't* believe it, is more like it. And as I sense Luz's annoyance go up a notch, my wolf whines. *We can't sit by and do nothing.*

"Need a coffee." My mutter is barely audible, but I don't wait for an answer, instead storming toward the doors. I step through, and the gal from the city moves towards me like a cat pouncing on her favorite toy. Her overwhelming perfume makes me cough and I take a step sideways.

"Aw, poor baby's got a cold?"

I don't know what my face conveys at her idiotic question, but she backs away so fast she almost trips over her heels. "No, just allergic to perfumes, *miss*." I stress the term for professionalism's sake, before dismissing her and turning to Luz.

Luz's eyes flash towards the client and the scent of anger hits me again, something I seldom see in her. It makes the gold stand out against the green of her eyes, and the image of a cat superimposes itself for a moment in my imagination.

Cats and dogs don't mix, my wolf points out. I stifle a smile at that, and Luz stops glaring at the fake Barbie long enough to spare me a concerned look. "You okay, Dom?"

I fake cough this time and force a sheepish grin. "On second thought, I may be coming down with something. Want to make me one of your special teas?"

Whenever any of us is sick, we go to Luz. She has an insane knowledge of herbal teas and their best properties, which comes in handy. My eyes roam over her as she moves from behind the desk, noticing the jeans and long-sleeved purple top she's wearing. She's shorter than me by a head at least, but damn those curves have my mind wandering in a not-so-innocent way, one too many times a day.

Then Luz grins at my words, and it's quick and bright like the sun appearing after a morning of clouds. I swallow past everything else I want to add—this is not the time. Instead, I pout in supplication, hoping the ruse will work.

Luz glances over at the client, undecided and unwilling to slack on the job. "I'll watch her." My promise comes in a mutter, as I'm none too pleased about spending alone time with the snotty client.

After a moment, Luz bites her lip, but relents and moves to the back. "Her name's Eliza."

I'm staring in confusion after her. Why would she give me the useless piece of information? It's not like I'm planning to ask this girl out. Still, once Luz disappears around the corner, I turn to Eliza. "I'm not sure where you think you've landed, miss, but I would loathe rejecting your business because you're upsetting our staff."

She gapes, evidently used to getting her way. *Spoiled*, my wolf snorts, and I can't help but agree when she yells, "Upset your staff? How dare you!?"

The urge to roll my eyes is strong, but I hold back—barely. "In case you haven't noticed, we're a quiet town here. Tight-knit group of people. We notice when someone upsets one of us."

Eliza continues to scowl, but now there's a stubborn lift to her chin as if she's thinking of disputing my words. "Not my fault your girl can't take a joke."

A growl slips past my clenched teeth then, and she widens her eyes.

"Leave. Now."

"You can't do that, I already paid!"

"There is such a thing as a refund," I drawl, crossing my arms over my chest.

"I didn't even *do* anything!" She stomps her foot at that—I wish I was joking, trust me.

"Either you keep your mouth shut around Luz, or I kick you out." When I move towards her, she gives up and sits on the far couch. "Thank you. Now stay there until your car is ready."

I turn away, ignoring her glare, and follow Luz to the kitchen, determined to make sure she's alright.

Lucrezia

Dom's a sweetheart, and his actions warm my heart. Even if he offered to stick around so he could chat up little Miss Princess.

I'm aggravated with myself for caring, and even more so for not being able to let it go. Dom fools around, I know this. He's not a player per se, but he dates enough. In a small town like ours, he's known as a catch—in bed. But never for good.

Enough.

I go about making the honey and cinnamon mixture in the small kitchenette, adding some of the ginger root I keep in the fridge here. Once it steeps enough, I pour it all in a cup and am about to return to the reception area.

I almost smack into Dom, who apparently snuck up behind me and was watching me work.

"Easy," he cups my hands, grabbing the mug from them before it spills and burns me everywhere.

After placing it on the side cabinet, he turns his attention back to me. "You okay?"

I want to answer him, really I do. But I'm struck dumb by his proximity, now in my internal bubble, as I call it. Have I never been this close to him? Or have I only been blind to his charm until today? And why in the hell does it feel like I'm left staring at a real-life Apollo, instead of my best friend?

The broadness of his back seems to dwarf me, and every nerve in my body is aware of our secluded presence. *He could do anything...* My brain tries to backtrack, memories pushing forth, and I half-expect a panic attack.

Yet nothing happens, and that scares me more than the opposite. Either I've lost my mind, or there is something about Dom that makes me feel safe. *Maybe it's because I've known him for so long.*

If I was to reach out, I could touch the muscles of his chest. Even from where I am, heat radiates off him, and something in my stomach unfurls in response.

My breath turns shaky, and this time I can't tell if it's a panic attack, or emotions...or something else.

"Luz, you okay?"

I glance up at his worried tone and manage a nod that's too stiff. "Yeah, fine. Just...out of breath. Sorry."

He frowns then, those beautiful blue eyes warm and scanning me up and down. My skin tingles, and I take a minute to realize he's holding my elbow, as though afraid I'll topple over.

"You sure?"

"Mhm," is my only intelligent answer. Then, like a coward, I side-step him. "Your tea is getting cold," I mutter over my shoulder, and take off the minute he releases his grip.

Dominic

After the morning incident, the day goes by fairly smooth. Eliza leaves with her damn Mustang, and we get no more high class maintenance clients, only our regular clientele. Finn keeps his mouth shut, and I stay busy with as many things as I can take.

Despite my best efforts, I can't stop watching Luz. I see her blush when Lucas asks her out to lunch to go over the sales reports—which they end up doing on the couch in the reception area. I can smell the waves of arousal off her and want to rip his throat out.

Finn steps in at that point, not fooled in the least by my resenting silence. "He's our alpha, Dom."

I ignore how in my face he is, trying to keep my tone curt as I continue to fiddle with the timing belt. "I'm well aware."

"We promised him loyalty."

I throw the piece on the table, ignoring the clank of metal on metal that echoes. I face Finn, failing to appear calm. "He's still new as alpha. And if I recall correctly, I promised him my obedience as his beta, but not my allegiance—and not forever."

Finn glances towards Luz and Lucas, then back at me. "Pack law is clear, mate."

"He hasn't made a claim." The words are more than a growl, but enough to quiet even my wolf.

Then Lucas gets up to go in his office, and Luz watches him with longing. A thought strikes me and before I have time to reason it through, I'm already moving.

This is a terrible idea.

Or so I keep telling myself, even as my feet inch towards Luz. Before I know it, my mouth is running off again—without me. "I can help."

Luz turns those otherworldly eyes to me, the gold more clear up close, and I gulp. I've never had an issue with women, but hell, this one will be the death of me.

"Dom?"

I snap back to with a very unintelligent, "Huh?"

Luz laughs, and I rub the back of my neck.

"Help me with what?" Again, her eyes slide to where Lucas disappeared to.

"With him."

She turns so fast I'm afraid she got whiplash. "What are you talking about?"

"I can help you with Lucas." I drop on the couch, ignoring her stunned expression and those lips I want to kiss so bad my mouth tingles. "You like him, right?"

Her face falls as she whispers, "Am I that obvious?"

"Only to me," I answer truthfully. "But you *do* like him?"

She nods, her eyes big pools of uncertainty.

"Let me help. I know Lucas, we've been buds forever. If he has feelings for you, he may let rules get in the way. Guy always had a thing for not breaking them."

"What rules?"

I want to smack myself—the reference to our werewolf life slipped too quickly. "Dating work colleagues." I save face and change the subject before she inquires further. "Either way, nothing like dating someone to get him to make a move if he's interested."

"I'm not good at dating," she whispers, looking away.

My wolf points its head, sniffing her scent, which changed in a few seconds. *Fear.* I sense it, too. But of what? *Surely it can't be me.* Either way, this is a chance to find out more.

"It won't really be dating. We'll fake it for his benefit. If it makes you more comfortable, we can even put a time limit on it. A week, two weeks, whatever you want."

She glances back again towards Lucas as he steps out of his office and back into the garage. The longing in her expression crushes my heart, but I promise myself to rein it in.

"And what's in it for you?" Her gaze is wary when it meets mine.

I shrug. "A chance to annoy him." *And make you happy. And show you he's not the one for you.* That last part, I don't say out loud.

Luz is silent for so long, I'm sure she'll end up saying no. Besides, what am I thinking? Nothing except selfish thoughts. I want her first kiss, and I want her to at least have the memory of my lips imprinted in her mind before she ends up with Lucas. I want to stake my claim even if it won't be permanent.

"Okay," she surprises me by saying. "How will this work?"

I'm too stunned for a moment to react, but already my wolf is roaring in victory and a grin spreads on my face. "Leave it to me. Meet me tonight for drinks at The Cave, eight o'clock sharp."

When she nods, I lean forward and kiss her cheek, not even surprised when she jumps at the contact. "It'll be fun, you'll see."

And no kidding, I walk away whistling. Yup, like a poor sap who won the girl—not the one who promised to help her get the man of her dreams.

Bite me.

.

∞ ∞ ∞

∞ Reguli ∞

"You have to learn the <u>rules</u> of the game. And then you have to play better than anyone else."

-Albert Einstein-

Lucrezia

I can't believe I'm doing this. When Dom proposed the idea, it seemed ludicrous. A sure way to screw up our friendship and win Lucas' rage.

Yet, no matter which way I turn the problem over the next few hours of my shift, I can't deny its appeal. To know whether I can get a guy like Lucas, and to have my happily ever after... From any other guy, the proposition would raise my shackles.

But it's Dom. Sweet, gentle Dom who not only helped me settle in this town, but got me a job and has been a wonderful friend since. I trust Dom, and if this has to happen with anyone, I'd rather it's with him.

Plus, I've been out of the dating game for so long, I don't want to make a fool of myself if anything were to happen with Lucas. Dom can be my dating buddy, steering me through the murky waters of this new world of Tinder and hook-ups—without demanding too much in return.

After all, why not? Or so the crazy voice inside me keeps clamoring.

So that's how I find myself at The Cave that same evening. The rave bar is empty this early on, but I've seen it at its fullest before. There are only two of its kind in our small town, and you'll find anything from alcoholics looking for their fix, cougars way too old preying on the young, and then... Lucas' crowd.

The guys meet here for drinks every Friday night, their favorite pastime. Since it's Monday, no one we know is around—a fact I'm immensely grateful for. My eyes scan the area, falling in a darker booth where Dom's nursing a glass of amber liquid.

He took the time to change out of his regular work clothes, and he's now wearing a pair of black jeans and long-sleeved shirt, a leather jacket thrown carelessly to the side. His broad shoulders seem to take up the entire booth, and there's something about him that strikes me as tense.

I hesitate for a second, but as though sensing my gaze on him, Dom looks up. The intensity in his expression amps up a notch as he takes me in, then a corner of his mouth lifts in a smile and he waves me over.

Butterflies move in my stomach, and I'm halfway between a nauseous and excited mood. *Now what the hell is all this about?*

My feet move towards him, even as I gulp the lump in my throat. Like a perfect gentleman, he stands and lets me in the booth, then slides back in. We end up touching ever so slightly, enough to make me aware of his body heat.

"Are you running a fever?" I ask, frowning when he chuckles like I said something funny.

"No, why?"

"Well your skin, you're just so... hot."

He laughs out right at that, then bites back, "I thought you hadn't noticed."

The innuendo in his words is unmistakable and I shake my head. "I have a feeling this is a bad idea."

Dom stills at that, then turns to face me. "No, it isn't. First off, we know each other and you know I'll respect your limits. Second, it's all in good fun, right?"

Sure. Except this morning's events run through my mind, and my reaction to his proximity, and now I'm second-guessing the reason behind my eagerness for this. I thought it was just to get Lucas' attention, and maybe a week ago, it would have only been about that.

But now... I'm not so clear about it. My eyes roam his razor-sharp jaw, the cerulean eyes and determined expression. A lock of blonde hair falls across Dom's forehead, and my fingers itch to touch it. Pushing away the reckless idea, I meet his eyes again and nod. "Yeah, I guess."

"Perfect. So, what are you having?"

After I order a cheeseburger and a glass of wine, Dom taps the table to get my attention. I flush when I realize my mind wandered, yet here I have a perfectly sexy guy sitting next to me.

"Where did you go?"

I can't well tell him I was still thinking about Eliza's mention of Tommy, my ex-boyfriend, and whether he found me. Or, could I? I frown, trying to figure out if this is something that would fall in our... relationship.

"Earth to Luz."

I sigh, pushing the idea away. If this is to work, I better keep things light. "Just thoughts, is all. So, how exactly do we do this?"

Dom tilts his head as if trying to read me. For a moment, I fear he might say something, call me on my bluff. We've known each other for long enough to realize when something's wrong. But maybe because of that, he lets it go and sticks to the subject at hand.

"Well, first things first. How comfortable are you with touching?" At my obvious cringe, Dom's face turns serious. *I'll have to remember he doesn't miss much.* "I won't bite, I swear."

"Don't make promises you can't keep," I mutter, looking away.

His touch is gentle when he pulls my chin back towards him. "You can trust me. Have I ever done anything to make you scared of me?"

"No," I breathe, much too aware of his heat on my skin.

Those blue eyes peering into mine are almost my undoing, and my mouth parts to tell him everything. But old fears and shame rise just as quick, and I choke on the words, unable to get them out.

Dom's expression softens and he lets me go. "Good, then all is not lost."

After a sip of his whiskey, he says, "So, touching. Just to clarify, I mean holding hands, the occasional kiss—"

"Basically, PG-rated." I almost kick myself for my disappointed tone.

Dom laughs again, then nods. "Yup. Wouldn't have it any other way." Before I can ask him what he means, he pushes on, "Will you be comfortable with that much?"

I glance at his lips then, trying to imagine them on mine, and my cheeks heat again. When our eyes meet, Dom's have darkened by a few shades. He holds my gaze for a beat, letting me see it, then glances away and clears his throat.

"Yes, I will," I admit, but doubts nag at me already. "So that'll be it? Just pretend we're together, and Lucas will somehow drop to his knees and declare his undying love?"

Dom snorts, and I can't help a laugh at the idea. Lucas is nothing if not macho, so it's hard imagining him go to any lengths like that for a woman.

"I won't promise anything." Something in his tone grabs my attention. "Lucas is complicated, in ways you probably don't yet understand. But I know him well enough to say if you were to declare yourself to him, he'd shut down."

He does seem private, all right. In the one year I worked for him, I've never seen him lose his cool or control of any situation. The guys respond to that energy, treating him like more than a boss, more of a pack leader.

Dom's words drag my focus once more. "Lucas will respond to subtle threats, that much I can predict. But whether this will end up where you want it to or not... Well, all that depends on various factors."

I nod, having figured out as much myself. "You must think I'm pretty pitiful for resorting to this, huh?"

"Never." There's a conviction in his voice that lifts my spirits, enough so I can meet his earnest stare. "I think it's commendable you're going after what you want, albeit in a more roundabout way." His hand moves, grasping mine. "I'm glad you agreed to this, Luz. It's about time someone starts treating you like you deserve, and it seems like poetic justice that it gets to be me. Even if it's only for a pretend situation."

And there he goes again. This is what I most have trouble with, where Dom is concerned. The complete contradiction between the womanizer the town thinks he is, and the amazingly sweet man he is when around me.

Thankfully, the waitress chooses that moment to return with our food and my drink. I grab the wine glass like it's my salvation, taking a large gulp of it. It helps me swallow past the lump in my throat, and calms my nerves somewhat.

"I appreciate you saying that, Dom. But...I think we shouldn't go past a month with this charade, as it could lead to, um, complications."

"One month?" Dom takes another swig of his drink. I notice when he looks at me that his eyes are clear and not glazed like most guys who enjoy getting drunk. "All right, deal."

Then he extends his hand. I glance down at it and back up at his roguish grin. He really is too handsome for his own good.

"One more thing," I add, hand in his. "I know this will be all for pretend, but...you have a certain reputation. Please don't go being with other girls at the same time."

He smiles at that, then bends his head by my ear. "You have my word." When his lips brush my cheek, I inhale sharply.

Dominic

I release Luz's hand and go back to my whiskey, nursing it and thanking my lucky stars for the way the night is going. My new fake girlfriend is a complete contradiction, an angel and temptress all at once.

When she turns hers focus to the food, I chance another look at her profile, taking in her downcast eyes and fine features. I didn't expect the victorious feel in my stomach, nor the sharp pang in my heart at the thought I'm grooming her for another.

Still, I'm willing to take the risk if it's the only chance I get. It gives me a month to change her mind about Lucas or at the very least figure out a way to show her she's not in love with the guy, but in lust.

She still may want to get that out of her system. My treacherous mind points out, and my wolf bares his teeth.

I force my gaze back on Luz. Under my scrutiny, she tucks an errant strand of hair behind her ear. The rusty color is almost flaming under the dim lights of the bar, and I wonder what it would feel like to wrap it around my hand.

Luz looks up, her green eyes widening when she sees me staring. I do my best to hide the hunger I feel inside—and not for food—then take a big bite out of my burger.

After a moment, Luz follows my lead and digs into food. It's only once she's halfway through her burger and wine that she meets my eyes again. I can see the questions in her eyes, but she's holding back.

Since I've practically inhaled my food by this point, I lean back against the booth and focus all my attention on her. "What is it?"

She takes another nibble at the burger, then places it back on the plate with a sigh. "It's just.... I don't know if I feel right about doing this."

Oh no you don't.

"Luz, you're not hurting anyone. What we do will harm no one, only attract Lucas' attention. Which is what you want, right?"

Before she has a chance to answer, the door opens, blowing a gust of cold wind inside. As if on cue, Lucas steps in and Luz turns as if feeling him. I swear she stops breathing for a second.

Across the distance, Lucas is brooding, scanning the bar. Then he sees us and something flickers in his gaze. Next thing I know, he's striding over until he's hovering over the table.

"Late night snack, amici?" His tone is cool, but his eyes dart between us and his mouth flattens.

Nice trying to show you're cool, Lucas. But you're not fooling me.

As if hearing my thoughts, he directs his glare my way. I hold it for a few moments, then remember our pack rules and shift focus to my date instead.

"Not really. Just taking Luz out for a drink. It's allowed, no?"

Lucas glances between us again, then smiles. "Sure." He looks more like he's baring teeth than grinning, but I let it pass.

"You could join us?" Luz offers, and I catch the pleading in her voice.

Lucas, bastard he is, shrugs. "*Grazie*, but I'm here only for a quick drink. I'll be over there if you need me."

With a nod my way, he turns tail and heads to the bar. I hate it when he starts dropping Italian words, even more so when Luz's eyes follow his rigid form. "You think he's mad?"

"Let him." At her startled expression, I amend my statement—mostly, my bitter tone. "He'll get over it, Luz. Lucas just doesn't like surprises."

I notice her sharp intake of breath and reluctantly turn towards my alpha. A leggy blonde by the bar made her way to him, and she's now leaning close enough to touch and for him to see down her shirt. Lucas barely gives her a glance, but Luz's turmoil is plain.

Rather than tell her he's not interested in girls flinging themselves at him, that he likes his chase, I amp up the conversation.

"You realize tomorrow will be exactly one year since you came to this little shit hole?"

That gets her attention, and those green eyes turn back to me. Something like a smile tugs on her lips, and I grin back. "Cheers to that little anniversary."

She clanks her glass to mine, and we each take a sip. When it looks like her gaze is drawn back to Lucas, I keep going. "What did you think of the bunch of us when you first saw us, all together?"

Luz's eyes twinkle. "I thought you were the most rambunctious, big children I ever set eyes on." A gulp of wine, a blush, then, "Also, the most good-looking."

I laugh good naturedly at that. "Damn straight!"

She shakes her head, almost as if not believing her admission. "But you guys come from different parts of the world. I never quite understood that. Quite a big coincidence to have you all converge here, in Rockland Creek."

"Mm," I sip from my whiskey, debating how much I can tell her. "Well, you already know I was born in Romania.

Orphan by the time the wall came down between East and West, I was adopted by a nice couple and brought here."

Lucas is all but forgotten as Luz leans across the table, resting her hand on mine. "I remember you telling me that."

I turn my hand so our palms touch and squeeze hers, then continue. "My parents were nice, and I lived the good life, but I was always restless. I dropped out of veterinarian school, and told them I didn't belong, that I needed more. They accepted my need to leave, even if they didn't quite understand it. A few months later, as I was traveling, I got word they died in an accident, and that was the last of my strings cut. I roamed the country until I landed here. Met Lucas. Stayed."

She tilts her head to the side, silently encouraging me to continue. It's a good thing her attention is no longer on Lucas, seeing as the blonde is practically in his lap. *Can you get a room at least?*

My annoyed thought is shot telepathically, not quite sure if Lucas will listen. Depending on the type of werewolf, communicating wordlessly while in human form is not the easiest thing. In my case, it only works with the alpha, otherwise it's pretty much a shot in the dark.

"And Finn? He's Irish, right?"

I nod at Luz's question, noticing Lucas tries to shrug his companion off again. "Aye, the old bugger." My bad imitation of an Irish lilt has Luz chuckling. "He and Tristan joined us within six months of each other, and my arrival. Lucas was already here."

Rather than ask me about Lucas like I half-expected her to, Luz throws me for a spin with her next question. "Do you miss it, Romania?"

"I was young when I left." I shrug, trying to shake off visions of mountains, valleys and everything in between.

Luz takes another bite of her burger, brow furrowed in concentration as she mulls my words over. "And you remember nothing?"

Nope, more like I remember too much. I sigh, looking away.

"I'm sorry, I didn't mean to push." Luz's contrite tone is the final straw that brings forth my honesty.

"You didn't. I remember snippets, but only a little. I can close my eyes and see mountains, tall enough to blind the sun. Their peaks are dusted with snow, dense with forests, full with wildlife. I ran through them countless times, in the care of a family who took orphans in."

What I don't tell her is the first bite of my vârcolac heritage, nor my first time morphing into a wolf. "Though I was young, and we didn't have much past the basics, I can still taste the fresh milk, the smell of baked bread in the house...The fresh air outside and the wildlife calling."

I trail off, assailed by other memories. My first kill was a doe, her death swift by my canines. I carried her carcass home as human, but the couple saw me for what I was. They were not fit to deal with me, nor I with them past that stage.

I must have zoned off, but Luz's tentative touch on my shoulder brings me back to the present. Her green eyes glitter with emotion, and my wolf quiets, nuzzling closer, lulled by her presence. He chose her that day, a year ago, before I even had a chance to realize what was happening.

Me and the guys, we're as different as werewolves come, each battling different demons from the past. Lucas is what you'd expect in one of our kind, a shifter and leader. Me, I've got a rebellious streak that more often than not gets me into trouble. Finn and Tristan, well, they've got their own stuff going on.

But what really separates us is the way we pick our mates. For a vârcolac, it's not a choice made by the human side, but rather by the wolf. Once that part of me zoned in on Luz when I first saw her, I was lost whether I agreed or not. And if by the end of this month she doesn't see the connection...

The moment is broken when the door slams open and three men stomp in. Dressed in leather and studs from head to toes, chests bare, heavy boots, they're your basic trouble crowd. Except I know them—and so does Lucas.

Luz glances over, then shifts closer to me instinctively. I wrap my arm around her shoulders, but my focus is on my alpha. At the bar, Lucas pushes off the blonde hanging on him and turns his body halfway to face the intruders.

Their leader, Jared, we're all familiar with. With a half-shaved head and ring piercings in his nose and ears, he's the ruler of a small territory in the west. Incidentally, he's also the werewolf alpha of a pack called the Reapers.

Yeah, you can tell how this might be a problem in such a small town. But mostly, they stay away from us. They don't like our mix of different werewolf bloods, it makes us too volatile. Plus, past skirmishes in the past ended up with losses on their side rather than ours.

Which is why their appearance in a bar that is *our* known hangout is, for the least, surprising. My gaze latches onto Lucas' and his imperceptible nod towards Luz.

Get her out of here.

What about you?

My question goes unanswered when he straightens his back and Jared spots him. "Well, well. The alpha himself is here."

I cringe, but no one seems to notice the slip. They probably assume he's talking about Lucas' natural macho attitude. See, the Reapers don't go by our rules—they don't care if humans know of our existence or not. In fact, they'd prefer it, as it would ensure their rule as the predator.

They also hate humans. Which is why Lucas wants me to take Luz away. The only problem is, any movement at this stage will have their eyes on us faster than you can say run.

Turns out, my worries are right on spot. Because even though we don't move, my arm around Luz's shoulders draws Jared's attention on his way to Lucas.

"What do we have here?" Eyes flashing, he changes directions and heads to our table. His guys stay by the door, as if to stop anyone from leaving.

Luz tenses under my hold with each step they take closer, and I brush my lips against her temple. "It's alright. Just trust me." My words are a whisper, intended for her ears alone, and she relaxes.

Jared is now next to our table, glaring down at me with his icy gaze, then at my closeness to Luz. He dismisses her with a sneer, and speaks only to me. "I get the appeal, brother, she's pretty enough. But why a mutt?"

I grit my teeth at the derogatory term they use for humans, clenching my free hand under the table. It wouldn't do to start something with them here, in front of witnesses.

As if sensing my agitation, I hear Lucas in my head. *Keep your cool.*

Easy to say. Much harder to actually put into practice. Still, I settle for narrowing my eyes to Jared, daring him to say more. To my surprise, before he can, Luz explodes from under my arm.

She jerks to her feet, fists clenched at her side and cheeks flaming. "Are you freaking kidding me?"

Jared does something I don't expect – he actually looks her in the eye. Normally, the Reapers consider all humans beneath them, a weaker species created only to be dominated. But Luz's outburst draws his attention, and I'm not sure that's a good thing.

"In this day and age, you dare to dress up like motorcycle thugs and waltz in here, ruining perfect dinners and saying nasty things? So what if Dom is an outsider, you have no right being an ignorant prick!"

My jaw drops at her rant, but I don't have time to correct her. Jared wasn't referring to me as the mutt—but her.

Protect!

My wolf roars just in time, sparking me into movement. Jared takes a step closer, flushing and looking ready to strangle her. I jerk to my feet, simultaneously tugging Luz so she's behind me. In the small booth, it's a tight fit but I'm ready to go to war if need be.

Lucas, however, has other ideas. He walks over to Jared, tapping his shoulder to get his attention. "I believe your problem was with me. What is it you want this time, Jared?"

I can't believe his bored tone, considering what nearly happened, but I push my anger down. It would not do to let my wolf out right now—especially in front of Luz.

Jared glares at Luz for a moment longer, then he smiles coldly. Something about it makes the hairs on my neck stand, and judging by Luz's shiver, she feels it too. I pull her against me, hoping my heat will help somewhat.

Lucas zeroes in on the touch, and a muscle ticks in his jaw. *Too bad, buddy.* He focuses back on Jared, his eyes shooting flames. "Still waiting."

"See, I thought you had a tight leash on your pups." I cringe again at the animal reference, but Luz is too enraptured by Lucas' show of force to catch it. "Yet here I find them hunting on our territory."

Lucas' eyes narrow and meet mine in silent questioning. He must read my surprise, because he widens his stance and crosses his arms over his chest. "I have no idea what you're talking about."

"Sure you don't." Jared scoffs to his two followers, then steps closer to Lucas. They face off, bodies tight with tension. "If I catch them, they're dead meat."

With one last sneer our way, the Reapers take off, and the entire bar breathes freely. "I thought I would have to call the cops."

Lucas chuckles to the bartender, but we both know human police would be way out of their league in dealing with Jared and his cronies. I watch as my alpha puts the humans around him at ease with a joke and smile here and there, then motions to a corner.

I ask Luz to wait for me, making sure she's settled in the booth, then follow him to the quiet area.

"Do you know what he's talking about?"

I shrug, glancing towards the door where the Reapers disappeared through. "Jared must be deluded, as always."

"Maybe... But have a whiff around town tonight. Then meet us by the borderline at midnight." His gaze flickers to Luz, then me. "Unless you have other plans."

The steel in his tone is unmistakable, but it only makes me straighten and meet his glare head-on. "No plans, *chief.*"

His eyes narrow at the sarcasm in my tone, then he moves past me. "Good. I'll bring Luz home."

"No need. I will." I'm blocking his way, so close I could shove him. Lucas' glare burns holes in me, and I feel the imprint of the wolf wanting to submit. Still, I stand. "She'll be safe with me."

"Bene." His agreement is more of a growl, but under the circumstances, I'll take it.

I step back to Luz, drop cash on the table for the food and we collect our jackets. Then we head out into the cold, the biting wind not bothering me, rather helping to clear my head. The walk to her small condo is short, but with each step Luz moves closer.

Our hands brush, and I grab hers into mine. "Cold?"

Her red nose confirms it as much as her nod, and she burrows deeper in her jacket. "This winter's chilly."

Wordlessly, I pull her close by the waist and she leans into my side, soaking up my heat like a cat. When we get to her place, she pulls away, taking her time.

"Thank you for walking me home. And.... for everything. Back there."

Luz glances down, shuffling her feet. There's more she wants to say, and I want to hear it, but my wolf is distracted by the previous confrontation and wants to patrol around town.

Still, the night is ending on a good note, and I'm grateful for that. I lift her chin with my finger, searching her gaze. Her lips part open, in response to whatever my expression is communicating. But instead of taking what she willingly offers, I press a kiss to her forehead. "Sweet dreams, Luz."

She blinks, then nods weakly and steps away, heading inside.

"Lock your doors tonight."

My warning gets through, but I still wait until I see the light turn on a few floors above, before leaving her side.

Lucrezia

I listen to Dom's advice and lock my doors, then head to the window on an impulse. He's still below my apartment, seemingly waiting for something. Once I turn my lamp on, Dom turns and walks away.

My eyes follow him until he turns the corner, disappearing out of my sight. I lift a hand to my lips, blaming my need to kiss him on the wine I indulged in. And yet he hadn't picked up on my silent plea... I shake my head, moving away from the window.

This whole evening was nothing I expected, and my head feels like it's swimming in feelings and doubts as I undress and get ready for bed. By the time I slide under the sheets, it's Dom's eyes I see under my closed eyelids, his touch I feel when sleep takes me.

And above all, one thought spins round and round... *What the hell did I just get myself into?*

∞ ∞ ∞

CHAPTER THREE

∞ Animale ∞

"We can judge the heart of a man by his treatment of <u>animals</u>."

-Immanuel Kant-

Dominic

I'm still riding a high after the dinner with Luz and trying to get my head straight. It won't do to get lost in the game, but at least I have one month to show her who she belongs with.

And if her demeanor tonight is anything to go by, she may develop feelings for me. With each step, my mind drifts to what could be. It's not that I don't think Lucas and her would be great for each other. It's that I know I'm better for her, period.

Mine, my wolf growls, then steadies. It draws my attention to something else in the air. The hairs at the back of my neck prickle in warning, and a putrid scent hits me at once. I stop dead in my tracks, trying to identify where it's coming from.

My wolf rises under my skin, and I let him take over. Lucas once told me that watching me change compared to how his morphing occurs is different. And in a way, I guess he's right.

The vârcolaci come from the deep mountains of Transylvania, there where legends still exist and mists conjure up old wives' tale galore. I'm not sure of my entire history, only that my genes are different from the werewolves I've seen here. I get the canine body, the canines and the strength. But my bite cannot turn someone into a werewolf unless my blood drips in their wounds.

Neither can silver bullets kill me, only a stake through the heart will do. As far as that goes, it makes me pretty happy. Lucas, born in the Americas to Italian parents, is prone to both silver bullets and his bite alone can turn someone. He's your regular werewolf, but he was also in this territory long before any of us, which accounts for his alpha status—among other things.

Either way, as I shift, a soft light envelops my body and my limbs shorten. Sharp pain runs through me, but I've done it so many times I no longer scream in anguish. I grit my teeth like a good soldier, and before long I'm in full wolf shape.

My fur, in this form, is dark like coal except for a white line running from my forehead all over my back. I've never known why, but it was the shape I had even as a youngling. My eyes change color to a pale gray, the irises surrounded by blue. Though I am bigger than the regular wolf, I'm still average enough to pass as an extremely large Alaskan Malamute. Unless people look closer... which, in these parts, they've learned not to.

Now my wolf is loose, taking over my subconscious more than the human part of me. I let him lead, picking up a rotting scent and following it at a trot. I'm taking the backseat on this, at least until we get to the targeted destination, and I stop in shock.

In a corner filled with garbage is a dog—or what's left of it. It looks mature enough, some mix between a retriever and something else. Its mouth is open in shock, long tongue drooped to the side, lifeless. But the worse is lower. Its stomach is gutted open, deep enough I can see his ribs.

The human in me wants to throw up at the sight, but rage fills my wolf—and a need to tear into something. It overwhelms us both until we can only see red, and the urge to kill overcomes everything else.

Dominic.

A howl in the distance pulls my sight from the corpse, and tugs on my human mind. Lucas' call is enough to throw me back in charge, and the primal part of me moves to the back, whining in displeasure.

With one last look to the poor corpse, I follow the call to the borderline of our village. To protect the people of the town, Lucas asks to meet outside, keeping our wolf scents to the borders. It ensures no visiting packs try to make this their new permanent location.

I get to the meeting spot and three other wolves sit in a circle. Two of them face a larger, rusty-colored one, and I recognize Lucas' angry scent.

Same as me, each wolf has their own characteristics. Tristan and Finn are smaller than Lucas, but only by a few inches. It would be the difference between a German Shepherd and an Alaskan Malamute. If, you know, those dogs were supercharged twice their regular size.

Either way, I recognize Finn by his calm demeanor. He's the wolf sitting on his hind, eyes trained on the leader. His obedient nature comes as much from his human career—he used to be a lawyer—as his status in the pack. His eyes shine bright, his fur a mixed gray like snowy mountains with ash, except for a crescent moon on his left shoulder. All black, it stands in stark contrast to the rest of his fur, a marking from his past.

Tristan, on the other hand, is the paranoid of the group. Even sitting, his eyes dart around the place, expecting the worst. We always joke he has half a mind on the environment, a quarter on himself and the rest on everyone around him. It's also why he's so silent, not that he can be faulted after what he endured in war.

In wolf form, he mirrors Finn but with darker spotting, more charcoal than white. His eyes are the same color as in human form, and he's the only one of us who can change appearance at will—growing larger or smaller—not that he's ever told us how he manages.

Which brings me to Lucas. The alpha faces Finn and Tristan with bared teeth. His canines are huge, and his body is larger than mine. Though I'm broader in shoulders, Lucas is longer in body, giving the overall impression of towering over us. His rusty fur is mixed with hints of white and dark. A while ago, it had been pure red, but I guess being our alpha means he pulls some of our characteristics.

Or so the story goes. His hackles are raised and the snarls coming from his mouth are anything but friendly, drawing my entire focus. He stops when I appear, jerking his head my way.

What's going on?

The way we communicate, it's hard to explain. It's not telepathy per se, more of a thought being pushed out, connecting with everyone I choose to let in. Lucas' eyes flash and he takes a step closer.

Did you see the body?

Yes, I admit. *Why?*

An attack, Finn steps in. Whether consciously or not, he puts himself between me and Lucas. *Whoever did it did not rip into the body, only cut it open. Someone is doing something to these animals.*

Animals? I blank at that. *There's more than one?*

Where's your head been at? Lucas growls. *Two more bodies showed up last weekend.*

I don't recall ever being told. And I'm not about to take a hit for something I didn't know.

Tristan shakes his head at my tone, but Finn saves the day—again. *I told Lucas when I found the first, and Tristan fell upon the second shortly after. Lucas wanted to investigate further before calling a meet.*

Lucas growls, now pacing from one end of the clearing to the other. *I thought they might have been kills by someone passing through!*

But they're not, those desgraçados. Whoever is doing this lives around here. That piece of good news comes from Tristan, whose tone is only outshined by the blank look in his eyes and his venom when he snaps into Portuguese and calls them bastards. He's seen more than all of us put together, and it's obvious this whole mess brings back bad memories.

I think back to the body and shake my head. *The cut was surgical, not gutted.*

Says the vet among us. You took what, two years of veterinarian schooling before dropping out?

I snarl at Tristan, taking a step forward. *What is up with you, man? The facts speak for themselves. It must be someone with medical background, and once we figure out whom, we can drag them to justice.*

Well, your job should be easy in that case, meu amigo. There's only one legit doctor around here. I snort at Tristan's suggestion, which isn't taken well. But Arthur Morris, an eighty-year-old doctor almost going on blind but with a heart of gold, is unlikely to be our criminal.

You have a better idea? Finn pushes, turning on Tristan.

Sim, claro. How about another beast, like us?

We each share looks, having not considered the option. *What makes you say that?*

For one, why would a human do such an act?

Finn shakes his head, already refuting the point. *I worked long enough as a lawyer and can tell you, human minds can get sick. Extremely so.*

Possivelmente. But I've also been around the world longer than any of you, including to mountains where legends still live, and so do monsters.

Tristan's gaze never wavers from mine as he speaks. A shiver runs up my spine, and I tilt my head. *Are you talking about my home country?*

Tristan gets off his hide, moving closer, his every muscle rippling. *Not only yours. Greece. Eastern Europe. Your kind is not alone.*

I look at Finn, then Lucas, but both seem as epically lost as I am. In contrast to our stunned stances, Tristan is pacing from side to side, unable to sit still. His eyes dart around the meadow, ears flattening on his head in agitation.

Care to untangle your riddles, mate? Even Finn seems to have lost his patience, but Tristan passes by me and seems ready to take off. Only Lucas' order stops him.

Tell us what you know, amico, and your reasoning.

Tristan stops dead in his tracks, his entire body rigid as if he's fighting with himself. I know full well what he's feeling—the struggle between his desire to leave, and the alpha's orders. But he's a better wolf than me, and despite the slight tremor running through him, he turns around and faces us.

I knew when I met Dom that he's a vârcolac. It was one of the reasons, if you recall, that I gave him such a hard time. His words vaguely bring back memories of us fighting over everything and nothing, but I shake them off to focus. *But from what he's said, he has no idea of the two kinds that exist.*

Lucas looks to me for confirmation, but I only shrug and sit down. *This looks like it'll take a while.*

Finn nudges me with his muzzle, but I don't budge. Try as I might, my thoughts are a jumbled emotion. Somehow Tristan knows more about my kind than me. Only one question remains – how?

As if guessing my mind, Tristan glances my way. *I traveled a lot, with the army. They took us to remote locations, hot spots...* He shakes his head, his gaze growing haunted. Guilt ripples through me for making him relieve an obviously bad memory, but I need to know.

After another shuddering breath, Tristan bends his head and continues. *In Greece, there's this little village no one's heard of. You can't even find it on the map. We were passing through, but needed a spot to sleep. Short of rooming with the locals, my buddies and I slept under the starry skies. At night...*

His pause is not theatrical, but to ground himself. We can all feel the memories tugging at his mind, his heart rate increasing. I expect Lucas to move, but when he doesn't, I do in his stead. I place my paw over Tristan's front one, meeting his gaze. *You're in Rockland Creek, buddy. You're safe here. What happened that night?*

The shadows in his eyes, the obvious pain and fear rake through me and I stumble back, unable to hold his gaze. Tristan's words reach me through a fog, like it's not really me they're addressing.

They call them vrykolakas over there, your kind. And though you're normal—I don't know how—they were... monstros, Dom. Como vampiros.

My shocked gaze lifts to Lucas, but despite Tristan having announced the monsters were like vampires, there's no surprise in his expression.

They gutted open the entire village overnight, a pack of them. Tristan stops again, inhaling to rein his emotions in. *We didn't hear a thing. It was the smell that woke me up—alone from my regiment. I caught the last few and tried shooting at them, but they wouldn't die. One of them almost had me when this old man drove a stake through his heart. It was... He saved my life, and died in my arms shortly after from his own wounds.*

Why not tell us? Finn pushes forward, agitated. *Shouldn't we have known we have a vârcolac—vrykolakas—whatever you want to call it, in our midst?*

My wolf growls, hurt and angry. *I've always been honest with you. This story, this... I never knew my kind could be like that. Nor do I know why I'm different.* My eyes shift to Lucas, pleading with him to believe me. *I've never felt the need to kill such, you have my word.*

Lucas stares at me hard for a few moments, but it's Tristan who breaks the silence. *That's because you have a soul, and they didn't. They were undead, Dom.* He must have read the questions in my eyes, because he adds, *I couldn't feel their heartbeat, even as I tried to kill them. When I returned back home, I did a lot of research, and that's how I separated the two in my head—the vârcolaci, like you, and the vrykolakas, the undead.*

Great. So if Dom dies, he becomes one of them? Finn's question takes me by surprise, but it also angers me. Before I can do anything, he pounces at me and we roll in the grass.

I never would have expected the obedient one of the bunch to throw the first punch, and I guess that's my mistake. Finn seems perfectly ready to kick my ass, not that I'm about to let him. Bunching my legs under, I throw him off me, but not quick enough to avoid a scratch to the face. Finn shakes himself off a few feet over, but doesn't seem ready to back down.

Really, mate?

Just making sure your anger doesn't trigger some kind of hunger we didn't know about. His easy tone has me hold back from escalating the fight—barely.

How about we focus on the real issue here, considering I have no intent to die? I head back to stand by Lucas. *With Tristan's information, we have a new suspect to consider. But if these killings are done by other vrykolakas, make no mistake. I stand with you.*

You better, Finn snarls.

Basta! Lucas stops our bickering when he shouts, standing to his full height, his voice firm and authoritative. A current runs through us, and our entire focus turns to the alpha, unwavering.

We will find whoever is behind this and bring them to justice. Lucas' gaze falls on each of us in turn. *Pack justice.*

Our howls echo his, and the wolves in us are ready to pounce.

Lucrezia

I've been minding my business today. The guys are quiet, focused on three jobs they're working on. Even Dom only graces me with a smile before heading in, ducking his head and keeping his distance.

Close to lunch hour, he comes and towers over my desk. I peek up with a smile, but it falls off when I notice the scratch on the side of his face.

"What happened?"

I move around the office and raise my hand to his cheek, trying to inspect closer. He flinches when I touch it, but it's not too deep and looks like it's healing already.

I'm about to ask again what happened, but the minute I meet his gaze, I'm rooted to the ground. His blue eyes darken, and there's a hum between us akin to energy I can touch. It's like what happened the night before, when I almost kissed him.

The thought of his lips draws my gaze to his mouth, and mine part in response. This is the second time in less than a day that my reaction to him puzzles me, and it's enough to melt the brain cells in my head.

"Darling," Dominic drawls, "you may want to watch your acting skills. A man could fall for this."

I jerk back at his tone, hoarse and filled with... hunger. Something clenches in my stomach, and heat spreads through me as I blush.

Before I can move farther, Dom's eyes flicker over my shoulder and he steps nearer, his mouth to my ear.

"Lucas is coming." I tense at his closeness, unused to having a male—especially of his bulk—in my personal bubble.

Sensing my rigidity, he wraps an arm around my lower back and plays with my spine, running his hand up and down. "You're all right, beautiful. You're safe with me."

Then his head is dropping, and I fear he might kiss me. Something flashes in his eyes and at the last minute his lips move to the side of my mouth, kissing the corner. Rather than go for the full prize, he trails down my jawline, and right under my earlobe.

I gasp aloud at the sensation, feeling like I've been electrocuted. His sweet words broke my walls, but his touch—dear God, his touch!—makes my knees buckle.

As though sensing it, Dom's arm around my waist tightens. His nose nuzzles my skin, causing further shivers, and I tremble against him.

Then he bites it—a nibble only—but it's enough to make me jump, squeaking, moving further into him. Dom chuckles against my neck, and it rocks his strong chest, vibrating every muscle that now surrounds me.

Whether my lust-fogged brain wants to admit it or not, Dom is good at what he does. Too good. Which is why I give in, unable to resist the sheer temptation of his heat—both literal and figurative.

I melt in his embrace, which somehow makes me even more aware of the muscle hiding under the simple black shirt. There's no rhyme or reason to how I'm acting, but a primal part of me responds to whatever vibes he's sending out.

There's a safety in in arms, a sense of belonging. It's not the first I've felt it near Dom, after all he's been my best friend—my only close friend—for a year. But this is a new development that confuses me.

My enjoyment of his unexpected attention lasts until Lucas' growl ruins the moment.

"Che cazzo è...What the *fuck* is going on here?"

Disappointment crashes over when I realize Dom was only trying to get Lucas riled up. That it's the only reason behind his actions somehow leaves me....bereft.

I try to move, but he won't have it. Dom finishes nuzzling my neck, and lets me go at his pace, so I can face Lucas, but still be under his shoulder.

"Um..." To be honest, I've never heard Lucas be quite that explosive in his swearing before. I may not speak Italian fluently, but even I know *cazzo* is the worst word he could have picked. With that in mind, I can't really talk under the fire of his gaze, so I peer helplessly up at Dom.

I'm not ready for this! My silent plea is answered, albeit not in the way I expected.

Dom is grinning a bit too smugly when he announces, "Luz and I are dating."

Lucas' gaze heats even further if that's possible. He glances between us, brow furrowed as though not believing it. His question, when it comes, is more of a growl. "Since when?"

"Since last night." Dom's revelation has the effect of a bomb dropping. Both guys grow silent, staring at each other with increasing intensity. With each passing second, Lucas' expression hardens, yet he never so much as looks my way.

I glance up at Dominic, noticing the muscle ticking in his jaw. His hold on me tightens. Just when I'm about to say something, he speaks.

"It's not against the shop's rules, so back off, *boss.*"

The words make me frown, as if I'm missing the key to decode this particular riddle. Yet I'm distracted when I hear a legit growl from Lucas—or so I think.

When I tear my eyes off Dom's face to confirm, all I notice is his stoic expression. "Don't let it get out of hand. Be professional."

Without a word, he turns and steps away.

"Yes, boss," Dom salutes mockingly to his back, then kisses my temple.

I fall against him in relief. "That was... intense."

"It was bound to be." He doesn't seem affected, instead playing with a strand of my hair.

The words I want to say are on the tip of my tongue, as is the certainty I owe Dom honesty. Whatever that was, earlier, scrambled with my brain when he was barely trying. Though there's a legit possibility this crazy plan will succeed and get Lucas' attention, I'm starting to fear what I'll lose in the meantime.

"I don't think this will work."

Dom doesn't stop his movements, only smiling in amusement at my uncertain statement. "And why not?"

I open my mouth once, twice to say something that makes sense, but nothing comes out. Dom chuckles and kisses my cheek.

"I beg to differ. Lucas was ready to throttle me, that has to count for something." He drops his arm from around me and walks back to the garage, leaving me staring after him.

I guess giving it some more time can't hurt....

∞ ∞ ∞

CHAPTER FOUR

∞ Inimă ∞

"The human <u>heart</u> refuses to believe in a universe without a purpose."

-Immanuel Kant-

Dominic

The night is silent around us, giving a fake illusion of peace and tranquility. Finn and I know better as we move in the shadows in wolf form. While I blend in with the darkness, my buddy is all but a target with his snowy fur.

This damn full moon isn't helping things. His mutter echoes across my own thoughts, and I snort my chuckle.

Stick to the shadows and we'll be fine. I angle my head, trying to catch scents but failing. Since our last pack meeting, Lucas has us patrolling the grounds at night—every night.

Needless to say, I've spent little time with Luz between work and pack life.

Over there.

Finn jumps ahead and I snap to and follow him. As wolves, we have a sharp sense of smell in general, but my Irish buddy combines that with an innate extrasensory perception that comes in handy when we hunt.

As a Celtic werewolf, there are many things I still don't understand about him, and much more he refuses to tell us. But no matter what secrets we each hide, I've come to trust these guys with my life.

So when I follow Finn, it's without doubt, my senses honed in trying to see whatever had him spooked. We run a few blocks, sticking to the shadows, before reaching a restaurant. The alleyway behind it bears the distinct stench of werewolves, and I recognize the aroma of the Reapers. Since they tend to consume most of their food as wolves—meaning they hunt and kill it while morphed—it sticks to their skin.

Sure enough, when we turn the corner and step closer, two wolves are going at it hard enough to saturate the air with the smell of blood. I wrinkle my muzzle, throwing a look at Finn. In the darkness, it seems like he shrugs.

We approach silently, sticking to the shadows, our hackles raised and ready for action. When we're only a few feet away, the dark brown wolf whirls to face us, and I recognize his empty gaze.

Jared. What are you doing here? It's probably not a good idea to drop my mental barriers to communicate with him, but there's not much choice if we want answers.

The Reapers' alpha scoffs, stepping back from the wolf he's fighting with. Half his size, the tiny black animal seems pitiful in comparison. One ear is bleeding, torn to shreds, and his muzzle has a deep gash.

Beating up pups again? My taunt raises a growl out of Jared, but the other wolf only backs away in a corner, trying to make himself scarce.

Whatever's going on here, we can't intervene. Each pack has a set of rules, and if Lucas was here, maybe he could influence Jared to show more mercy. As it is, nothing I do will help, only aggravate the situation for the other wolf.

Dom.

Finn's call snaps me out of doing something stupid, and back to our purpose here. I glance around, but catch nothing. There's garbage bags everywhere, broken bottles on the ground, and even human excrements—but nothing of what we need.

My eyes fall on Finn, who shakes his head. *I thought I smelled something, but it must have been only his blood.*

His gaze lands on the wolf cowering in a corner, and I think I recognize the dirty fur as one of Jared's lieutenants. *Having a hard time controlling your pack, Jared?*

He snarls, inching closer. The man always had a temper, and it doesn't take much to rile him up. Finn knows as much and moves by my side, ready to back me up. Lucas would frown on us engaging Jared in an open fight, but then again the man is on *our* territory, which means it's free hunting time.

I don't budge, despite him getting so close we're muzzle to muzzle. He's smaller than me in wolf form, but it doesn't stop him from being the most aggressive of his bunch.

I said it's none of your business.

My gaze drifts around again, scanning the surroundings. I don't know what I'm searching for, but something tells me Finn had it right and we're missing a clue.

That's when I see it—a piece of fabric peeking out from a garbage lid. There's nothing special about it, but the minute I focus on it I get the uncanny sensation this is *it*. I head towards the area, dismissing Jared's grumbles and trusting Finn to have my back if he's stupid enough to attack. The closer I get, the scent assails me more.

What is it? Finn senses my agitation and takes a step towards me.

I throw a look over my shoulder, stopping him in his tracks. *Stay with Jared. Don't let him out of your sight.*

If the roles were reversed, I would have snapped at being ordered around by anyone besides the alpha of our pack. But Finn knows the rules, and he's a stickler for following them. I don't have to look again to confirm he's taking my command to heart and keeping his attention on Jared—I know he is.

Instead, I stalk to the garbage, scanning the area to make sure nothing's hiding in the shadows. When I reach the lid, I grab the cloth and pull on it until it's free. It's a pair of old jeans, washed out and holed. But the scent off them... I stick my muzzle closer, inhaling and committing it to memory.

Then I grab the pants and walk back to Jared, dropping them at his feet. If I was expecting a reaction, I'm disappointed when he only looks at me with an inscrutable gaze. *What the hell is this?*

You tell me. You're the one in our territory, injuring a wolf, and near a telling piece of evidence.

Evidence? Jared scoffs, almost rolling his eyes. *You're delusional. Come on, Tiny. Time to get back home. Rabid dogs can be contagious.*

Before I can rationalize my next step, I'm directly in his path and block his way. Probably not my best move, considering he's an alpha in his own right, and I'm only second-in-command. Normally, this would mean I bring the evidence to Lucas and let him decide.

But then I think of the dead animal, and whoever is out there, and all I see is red. Jared steps to the side, a rumble building in his chest. I tense my muscles, getting ready to fight him if need be.

Finn, the ever-peacemaker, moves between us and separates us. *We're not looking for a fight, Jared.*

Speak for yourself.

He ignores me, instead keeping a calm tone. *Someone is targeting animals on our territory, eviscerating them like nothing. We think it may be a human or someone like us, so we've been patrolling the area. Tonight, it led us here.* He nods to the discarded jeans. *To that. Did you see anything?*

Jared's gaze falls on the jeans again, then back to Finn and me. For a moment, I almost think he'll be helpful. But all he does is push past us. *Tiny, I said come!*

The smaller wolf scurries after him, leaving Finn and I alone. *Damn. You think he has something to do with it?*

Much as I want to say yes, I shake my head, not quite believing it. *I couldn't smell anything off him. But there's definitely something going on with the Reapers.*

Finn turns to face me, tilting his head in surprise. *You caught that too?*

Caught what?

Rather than answer, Finn stares at Jared and Tiny's departing forms. The smaller wolf is trailing way behind the alpha, seemingly afraid to get anywhere near.

Jared wasn't just beating his lieutenant up, Dom. He was trying to get information out of him.

Of course Finn read more into the altercation than I did. *You sure you're not grasping at straws?*

I'm telling you, that had all the markings of an interrogation, not a beating. Lieutenants may be low on pack hierarchy, but in a grouping like the Reapers, they'd be the one carrying out daily operations like food supplies, targeting humans... He trails off, meeting my stunned look. *And territory patrol.*

His meaning dawns on me, and I glance to the jeans. *You think Tiny might know who's behind this?*

At the very least, he saw something. Why else would Jared be so focused on him?

Another thought pulls at me, and I scratch at my muzzle in annoyance. *There's something else. When I was at The Cave with Luz, and the Reapers walked in... Jared accused us of being on his territory.*

You're saying he thinks we're behind this?

I nod, picking up the jeans in my mouth. *We should probably bring the jeans to Lucas, and tell him all this.*

That's... new.

Finn's tone has my attention. *What do you mean?*

For a second there, you didn't seem to care much about Lucas' authority, considering you nearly started a fight with a rival alpha.

I can't explain my contradicting feelings to Finn, so I move instead out of the alleyway. *Let's just go.*

Lucrezia

I finish typing up the sales report Lucas wanted, print a copy and head towards his office at the back. He's been acting distant since Dominic revealed we're dating, and normally it would worry me. But I catch his onyx eyes every so often lingering on me, and the tingling it gives me makes the lie worth it.

My boots clack on the floor, and I cringe. The snow melted in the last few days, and I thought it safe enough to wear a pair of boots with heels. The discomfort I've been experiencing all morning has me now rethinking my decision.

I'm almost at the door when I hear voices—Dom's and Lucas'—and they don't sound happy.

"I'm getting mighty tired of your antics," Lucas is saying, and through the half-open door I see him leaning back on his chair, hands crossed behind his neck.

My mouth waters at the sight of him, recognizing the sex appeal he exudes. But then his high and mighty tone makes me frown. *Antics?*

"I thought you might." Dom sounds annoyed, and I can see half of his back through the crack, tense with emotion. "But we both know you didn't send me out there only to patrol. So why don't we cut the bull?"

Lucas' eyes narrow, though his pose remains casual. "What are you going on about, amico?"

"You *know* what. You don't want me near Luz, and this was the perfect excuse to keep me at bay."

His words root me to the ground as I try to wrap my head around the implications. Lucas didn't want Dom around me? But that would imply he's bothered by us dating. The realization should give me more of a thrill, but other than my mouth watering at the sight of his body, I don't feel any of what I had expected.

Rather than react to the jibe, Lucas' face gives nothing away, other than further frustration with Dominic.

"Why don't you admit it?"

Oh Dom...

"None of this has anything to do with Luz, but with your disobedience. I'm the boss, and you can damn well start acting like you respect it!"

"As I recall—"

Lucas lifts his hand, stopping Dom halfway. "Come in, Lucrezia."

I couldn't have ignored his order if I wanted to. My feet, frozen until he spoke, shuffle one in front of the other. Then I'm pushing the door open the rest of the way, wondering how the hell he guessed I was outside.

My eyes dart between Lucas to Dom, and sure enough my assumption was correct. Dom's gaze is darkened with barely held-back fury, his lips pressed together. I linger on his mouth, remembering it against my neck, his body close to mine...

Lucas clears his throat, and I jump guiltily to face him. His face is hard now, no longer relaxed, and his nostrils are flaring. "I, um..." Faced with such an obvious reaction, I lose my voice.

"The sales report, *draga mea*." I throw Dom a grateful look—noticing his now amused expression—and dump the folder on Lucas' desk.

"You asked for the budget figures until now. I, um, I'll be at my desk if you have questions."

Then I turn tail and run out of there, cheeks flaming. On a sharp corner I run smack into Finn with enough force to stumble back. Without his arms wrapping around me, I would have fallen straight on my ass.

As it is, his body heat seeps into me and I meet his confused gaze. "Sorry."

He chuckles, releasing me. "All good, love. What were you running from?"

My glance to Lucas' office gives me away, and Finn goes, "Ah."

"What's going on with Dom and Lucas?" I don't mean to pry, but... He *is* a guy, and has known them longer than I have. Surely he has some insight.

Finn grimaces, shaking his head. "Those two have been at each other's throats for ages, don't worry about it."

I nibble on my bottom lip, not reassured in the least. "Lucas seems very, um, set on obedience, huh?"

"You could say that." There's a playful smile on his lips, not unlike the Mona Lisa's secretive smirk. I can't help feeling like something's going over my head here.

"Know what helps two guys in a pissing contest?"

I'm about to contradict him on the contest, but only end up asking, "What?"

"Sugar."

I blink in surprise, thinking he's playing some joke on me. But Finn grins instead. "I promise. Doughnuts, croissants, you name it. Think you can bring us some while I go disarm whatever situation is unraveling back there?"

My lips mirror his grin and I nod. "Sure. It's lunch time, anyway."

As he passes by me and heads to Lucas, I move to my desk. Imagine my surprise when I find Tristan, of all people, leaning over the counter.

"I... Can I help you?" I like Tristan, same as all the others. But he's the most quiet and reserved of the bunch, and not the most talkative. Which, basically, means he intimidates the hell out of me.

Seeing him all relaxed and charming crookedly throws me off. And then I have the uncanny sensation I'm like little Red Riding Hood amid a pack of wolves.

"Here's a question for you, beleza."

His endearment is new—calling me beauty—but it's the semi-amused tone that makes me snap out of my thoughts and my entire attention on him. "Yeah?" I'm not sure I want to answer any of his questions, but then again, it doesn't look like he'll give me much of a choice.

"Blue or green?"

My jaw must have dropped because he throws his head back and laughs like it's the world's funniest joke. "I... What?"

"Relax, Red. I don't bite."

His words only leave me shaking my head, and I move behind my desk. His unnerving gaze keeps watching me, even as I log into the computer and save the last files I was working on, before gathering my coat to go out.

"Seriously, Tristan... What do you want?"

When he says nothing, I look up. He searches my gaze, but for what, I don't understand. His only comment is, "I can understand what Dom sees in you. But be careful, Luz. Not every wolf sheds his skin."

My skin prickles at the warning, but Tristan up and leaves before I can ask more. If he wanted to unsettle me, mission accomplished. Because his words echo my thoughts too closely.

Shaking my head, I zip up my jacket and step out the door. There's a small bakery two blocks down the street, owned by a nice elderly couple. With the way the day is going, some sugar and baked goods seem to be the perfect idea.

With the still frigid weather, I practically speed-walk there and it takes me less time than normally. Inside the bakery, fresh smells of croissants and baked goods assail me, and my mouth waters.

"What can I get you, sweetie?"

A busty, round woman walks behind the counter, watching me with twinkling brown eyes. Her hair is white, pulled back in a ponytail. She pats her hands full of flour on the dirty apron she's wearing, and her wrinkled expression immediately puts me at ease.

"I hope so," I laugh. "I have four guys to feed." When her eyes widen at my statement, I hasten to add, "My coworkers, I mean!"

She nods at that, and points to a side display of goodies. "You'll want some of these! Any grown man will go for them."

I take a bit of everything, as much as I can afford while on my salary. Just as she's packing it all up, a young woman about my age steps from the back. Her face is flushed, making her hazel eyes stand out more. What I can see of her hair is chestnut brown, and tied in a bun.

"Grandmama, the oven broke again!"

By her whine, I can tell it's not the first time this particular issue has come up. The elderly woman rolls her eyes good-naturedly. "Heavens, Elle, can't you see I'm with a customer? Pick up the phone and call the usual guy, he'll come by and fix it soon as he can."

Grumbling under her breath, Elle does as she's told and walks to the back, nearly stomping her feet. I catch myself thinking she'd be a good match for one of the guys... Then shake my head at the errant thought. *I doubt they'd appreciate me playing matchmaker.*

"Here you go, dearie." The elderly woman hands me my package and I pay for the treats, then head out. Elle's pretty face still floats in my mind, even as I'm mentally inventorying the guys' qualities to see who she'd be best fitted with.

I'm pushing the door open while trying not to drop my package when a bulky body walks in.

"Well, well. Look what the dogs dragged in."

I know that voice...

I glance up to see a man, a few inches taller than me, with a shaved head and cropped beard. He's handsome but aloof, in a cold type of beauty reminiscent of an untouchable panther. A scar cuts across his eye, ruining the pretty face aspect and adding a hint of danger. While some girls might find him hot, I barely retain a shiver.

"Sorry, I almost knocked into you." I back off while talking, wanting to put some distance between us. "I work next door and was coming in to get some treats..."

My nervous babble stops when another man follows him in. He'd been the one speaking, and I recognize the biker from the bar the other night, Jared. His gaze narrows on me like on an unworthy insect. I stop talking at that point, squirming under their scrutiny.

"You're their recruit, aren't you? Lucrezia something?" The new guy's voice is hoarse like a smoker's, his tone snide and snotty.

I nod, unsure where this is headed—and not liking it.

Dom....

His name echoes in my head, but I can't fathom why. The bearded guy tilts his head to the side, smirking now. A glance to his boss, Jared, then he turns back to me. His hand lifts and tucks a strand of hair behind my ear. I jerk out of his reach, scowling.

"You've got spunk, I'll give you that. I'm Aiden. Do me a favor, little girl. Tell *Dominic* I say hi, won't you?"

Something snaps in me at his condescending tone and I straighten my back, no longer avoiding his glare. "Tell him yourself."

Without pausing, I push between them and head out the door. I hear curses behind me, but I don't stick around. Instead, I move as fast as I can—without actually running—towards Claws Auto Shop.

Dominic

After Luz leaves, Lucas' anger skyrockets a notch. I'm amused by it, if slightly confused by her behavior. For someone who wants Lucas, she's sure acting like my lips are the sole focus of her existence.

"You need to be careful."

I cross my arms over my chest, widening my stance and Lucas' gaze narrows at my obvious defiance. To my surprise, he sighs and pinches the bridge of his nose. "I know you think I'm trying to sabotage your relationship, but I'm only looking out for you. I like having you as beta, Dom, and would hate for anything to break the balance. Capisci?"

Yeah, I understand all right. "Nothing will." So maybe my answer comes out through gritted teeth. I never said I'm good at masking my emotions.

Finn walks in at that point, reading the situation with a sweeping glance. "Luz is on her way out to grab us some sweets. So what do you both say to cutting the pissing contest and focusing on the problem we have? Serial killer, anyone?"

Lucas and I glare at each other for a bit longer, then I uncross my arms. "Finn's right. We're too old for this shit. What do you think of the jeans we brought you?"

For an alpha, Lucas sure knows how to defuse fast. In the blink of an eye, he's standing and pacing the office, thinking out loud. "I caught the same scent you all did—of murder. But there have been no sightings of bodies. I even listened to the police scanner this morning on my way in... still *niente*."

"What about our theory of Jared being involved?" I'm kind of happy Finn's the one who asked, seeing as I still feel the tension between me and Lucas.

"You may not be far off... The newfound jeans make me seriously think we're looking at a werewolf. But Jared's interrogation of one of his own seems weird, to say the least."

"So let us talk to him." Lucas faces me, nodding to indicate I can continue. "If you go accusing Jared, it'll start a turf war. Let me find Tiny on my own and ask him a few innocent questions."

"You and innocent don't mix, Dom."

I glare at Finn, but sadly, he's right. Lucas seems to realize the same thing as he shakes his head. "You're too impulsive, and I can't condone something like this. If it blows up in our face..."

"You have plausible deniability."

Lucas glances to Finn, then runs a hand over his face. "I cannot agree to this." I'm about to argue, but he raises a hand to shut me up. "However, Tristan and I will take the next few nights of patrol. If, at any point during that time, two members of my pack were to meet up by pure coincidence and run into Tiny on their way to grab a drink..." He shrugs, smirking. "Not much I can do if you chat, sì?"

I laugh, clasping his back. "Quite right, boss."

Lucas rolls his eyes, but the tension is now gone and I finally feel like we're moving forward. Tonight, we can find out who's behind this. My excited gaze meets Finn's, and I can read the eagerness in his expression.

"One of you should meet up with Tristan and me after to share what you found out. We can't do anything until we know what we're dealing with."

I nod, but my mind is no longer in it. For the last few moments, my stomach's been in knots and I can't figure out why. When the bell rings, signaling the door opening and closing, I storm out of Lucas' office.

Luz is by her office when I get to her, a box of goodies on her desk. "Damn, that smells good!"

She jumps at my voice, almost dropping her jacket. "Is everything alright?"

Her nod only confirms my suspicions, as she looks distracted. She meets my gaze, biting on her bottom lip, then the words pour out. "Um, I ran into a friend of yours.... Aiden something? He said to tell you hi."

My teeth nearly snap with the force I'm using, but I manage to keep a lid on it. Aiden is Jared's beta, and the fact he was near Luz bodes nothing good.

"That man is no friend of mine."

Luz sighs at my admittance, shifting on her feet. "I thought as much. Jared was with him." When I only clench my fists in response, she steps closer. "What's going on, Dom? Who are these guys?"

Out of the corner of my eye I see Lucas approaching, followed by Finn.

"Everything okay here?" He echoes, but his eyes are only on me.

My admission comes through gritted teeth. "Aiden says hi. Ran into Luz at the bakery."

To his credit, Lucas doesn't even blink. Instead, he says, "We'll take care of it." He turns to Luz, and she almost becomes a puddle at his feet when he touches her shoulder. "Stay away from that guy in the meantime."

She nods, and in that moment I can't decide who I want to kill more, Aiden or Lucas.

The day goes by more or less smoothly from there, though my wolf won't quiet down. Each time the bell rings, my head snaps to Luz, checking to make sure it's none of the Reapers. When the end of shift comes by, I could scream in relief.

Luz is putting on her jacket by the time I change and head out of the garage. "I'll walk you home."

"Does that fall under your duties as my fake boyfriend?" There's a smile tugging on her lips, but her eyes are wary.

I lean against the wall, crossing my arms and watching her closely. "Maybe, maybe not...but it's *definitely* part of my friend duties." Pushing off the wall, I step closer and bring my hand up to her cheek. "Regardless of what this is, Luz, I'm first and foremost your friend. And your safety is my priority."

For a moment, I'm afraid she might say no, looking as skittish as a doe in the headlights. But whatever runs through her head seems to decide her, and Luz inclines her head in assent. "I'd like that."

Finally.

I hold the door open for her, and lock up behind us. Lucas and Tristan left a while ago, at sundown, to start their patrol.

And Finn said he had something else to do, so we're the only ones left.

Lucas thinks whoever is behind the killings is nocturnal, so it stands to reason we don't want to miss a second of darkness. Human police will never bother investigating animal crimes, but we don't intend to let this psycho go by unpunished—not by a long shot.

Luz's hand slides into mine, and I glance down in surprise. She doesn't acknowledge it, only steps closer. "You called me something today, in Lucas' office."

"Draga mea," I repeat. "In Romanian, it means my darling."

Considering her last comment, I half-expect her to say it's not normal in fake relationships to be using endearments. Instead, Luz only says, "It's sweet. I like it."

Something in me melts at her tone, but all too soon we've reached her door. Luz's grip on my hand tightens, pulling my attention to her.

Her eyes are downcast, and there's a faint blush to her cheeks that takes me by surprise. *What I wouldn't give to read her mind...*

When she finally looks at me, her green eyes are dark with emotion, but I don't have time to search their depths. Luz rises on her tiptoes and kisses my cheek, then pulls back quickly. "Thanks for walking me home."

She's gone before I can say another word, leaving my wolf and I restless, and unsaid words in the air. Once her light turns on, I walk to my place in silence.

∞ ∞ ∞

CHAPTER FIVE

∞ Vechi Prieteni ∞

"Old friends become bitter enemies on a sudden for toys and small offenses."

-Robert Burton-

Lucrezia

I wake up the next morning feeling at odds. Last night, Dom's sweetness got to me and I almost kissed him—not that I think he noticed. I'm having a hard time understanding my own feelings, and this new attraction to Dom rather than Lucas.

Still, the dread I feel has nothing to do with that particular drama. The sky outside is gray, and overnight we were blessed with freezing rain. It's enough to make my walk to work precarious, and I curse and slide all the way there.

Somehow, I make it in without falling on my ass, and open the shop. Lucas sent me a few emails the night before on more reports he wants to run, so I get started on them.

An hour later, the guys file in one at a time. There's a line of three cars outside, so Dom only stops for a hug, then heads straight into work. For the next few hours, I go through the motions of entering quotes in the system, taking payments and answering questions from each client. The remaining two customers leave their cars in overnight, and before lunch I find myself alone at the front.

It's normally not something that bothers me, but between the freezing rain and the morning, I'm even more unsettled. Outside seems deserted, no one out messing with the bad weather—not that I blame them.

I busy myself with filing away receipts by month and fall upon Eliza's. The image of the bitchy model from days before runs through my head as do her words. *Does Tommy know you're here?*

Between agreeing to the façade with Dom and running into those bikers, I've forgotten all about it. How did she meet my ex? And worse, did she tell him where I was?

The door rings open again and I mutter, "Be with you in a second."

A silence, then his voice freezes me. "Take your time, babe."

I shoot to my feet, knocking over my chair. It can't be him, but sure enough, a few feet away Tommy stands. His blonde hair is slicked back with gel, his brown eyes cold and unfeeling. He smirks at my obvious surprise, stepping closer.

My eyes slide to where the guys are, hoping they won't notice him. One thought runs on a loop in my head. *I can't believe my dickhead of an ex is here.*

"What the hell are you doing here, Tommy?" My question comes in a hiss, but I'm happy to hear there is no weakness in it. I don't want to be alone with him, so call me selfish but I don't move out of the shop—implications be damned.

"You're a hard little bitch to track down." He's now in front of my desk, leaning over. I'm still too close, but my feet won't budge. When he extends a hand towards my face I cringe, moving out of his reach. His smirk widens and my heart starts pounding an all-too-familiar panicked rhythm.

Dominic

His stink hits me first, and I drop what I'm doing. I glance towards the reception desk and see a guy with Luz. He's standing way too close for comfort, which alone has my wolf in a frenzy.

Then I notice her body language, the way she's putting as much distance as possible between them, and all my attention zeroes in on them.

The prick reaches for her, and I growl low. Luz moves away, avoiding his touch.

Without even realizing it, I've stepped forward. A hand on my shoulder stops me, and I look at Lucas. Tristan and Finn both went out for lunch, so it's only me and him in the garage. Despite his restraining grasp, his darkened face is also fixated on Luz and the stranger.

"Who is he?"

He doesn't sound too happy about the newcomer, and I want to snap. *What the hell do you care?* Sanity returns before I say anything stupid, and I realize that this is what we wanted, me and Luz, to get him to care.

"Don't know."

Movement draws our attention again, this time when the stranger goes around the desk, invading Luz's personal bubble.

"Let me go." It's not a request, but Lucas frowns at me.

"He's human. You can't go in there and act your usual hothead self, Dom. Relax."

In a split of a second, the stranger grabs Luz's arm. She freezes, then her cheeks flush and I can see the anger in her—but my wolf also smells fear.

"What the fuck did this guy do to her?" I don't realize my words are aloud until Lucas tightens his grip. Without his iron hold, I would be across the room lunging for the guy.

"Dom..." Lucas' tone is a warning.

"I get it!"

But still my eyes linger on them. When he takes a step closer, I yank myself out of Lucas' grasp and move. By the time I reach them, storming through the doors linking the garage with the reception area, Luz got herself out of his grasp. I smell something metallic—blood—and a quick look confirms the scratches on his arm.

"Draga mea."

Luz turns to me, emotions flashing across her face—fear, surprise, but above all, relief. It makes my heart squeeze, but that's short-lived when a river of lava boils within me.

I step around the guy, pushing him out of her working space. My arm goes around her shoulders, pulling her into my side. Off balance, she has to rest her hand on my chest, and I relish the light touch.

Not once taking my eyes off the stranger, I kiss the side of her forehead. "Who's your friend?"

She releases a shaky breath, and with it, an introduction. "Dom, meet Tommy."

Lucrezia

I'd have to be a fool not to sense the testosterone in the air. And I don't mind it. Yes, Dom is only pretending, but it's a good act. Tommy is too busy staring at us with hate to realize how much trouble he walked into.

"Didn't know you had a new boy toy." His smirk is still on full-force, and I don't bother answering. What's the use, when all he wants is to rile me up?

"Hey, I'm talking to you!"

I glance over in surprise. Is he daft to try this in front of Dom? A bubbling laughter escapes me at the thought, but Tommy doesn't appreciate it.

"You crazy little—"

Dom moves with an agility I did not expect. One minute he's my big cuddle bear, the next he has Tommy grasped by the throat, flattened against the wall and a few inches off the ground. Tommy whimpers, and turns a nice shade of crimson.

"Dom," I whisper, "Let him go. He's not worth it."

For a moment, I fear he won't listen. Then he cocks his head as though listening to music only he can hear. A sixth sense has me turn, and I see Lucas across the distance. His face is as dark as Dom's, features hardened by anger.

The air itself is stifling with heat. Tommy is losing breath, his face turning an ungodly shade of purple now.

"Enough."

It's a vibration, a rumble... Whatever it is, it's coming from Lucas—yet he never spoke. Then, as if that alone was the magic order, Dom lets Tommy go.

He glares at Lucas, breathing heavily, and turns back to my ex. Hovering over him, Dom scowls, his tone heavy with malice. "Get out of here, scumbag, while you still can. If I ever see your sorry ass around Luz or this place again, I *will* finish this."

The last part is said in something close to a snarl, and Tommy goes pale as a ghost. He gets up on shaky legs and we watch him leave, but not before throwing me one last dirty look.

Once he's gone, Dom stays frozen for a few moments, breathing through flaring nostrils. I glance around, but Lucas vanished. I must have imagined that, there's no way...

I shake my head, but my thoughts are derailed when Dom turns to me. His eyes are a soft blue again, and he holds out his palm to me.

"Let's take a drive."

After a brief hesitation, I grasp it and follow him out the door. I have no doubt what he means, nor can I avoid the questions in his gaze. It's time to answer them.

Dominic

Being around Luz calms my wolf, but at the same time stirs him up in different ways. A complete contradiction, but as euphoric as any drug. The drive is silent at first, then we chat about insignificant stuff while I take us into the mountains.

After an hour or so, I worm my way to the subject gently—or as much as I can. "We might have made progress today."

"Hm?"

I would give anything to know what she's thinking about.

"Lucas." It's a near growl, my wolf way too near the surface. I mentally pet him down, calming him, before continuing, "He was watching earlier, seemed concerned about you and Tommy."

"Oh..."

Her tone is distracted, almost disappointed, and definitely not as exhilarated as I expected.

"What's wrong? I would have thought you'd be happier."

"I am! It's just... sorry. Lots on my mind."

"About Tommy?"

Luz is quiet, but it's an unnatural stillness. I pull the car over while she gathers her thoughts, then exit and open her door.

It feels old-school when I offer my hand to help her out, but she takes it with a secret little smile. She pulls her scarf tighter and we walk along the cliffs, our feet crunching in the snow.

"I know a nice spot a few miles off, if you feel up for a hike?"

Luz nods blindly and I take her hand in mine, leading us upwards. Whatever is going on in her head, I have a feeling she needs time to process it and to figure out how— if—she wants to share it.

I keep quiet while we walk, lending a helping hand when needed but otherwise restricting my touch only to holding her hand. With each passing hour, the wind picks up as the sun drops in the sky, until it's close to sunset.

Luz stops mid-step, her eyes darting around. I can read the uneasiness in her expression, and squeeze her hand in reassurance. "We're two minutes from shelter, and I promise you're safe with me."

Her reaction is, like everything else, a complete contradiction. While her expression softens, her body is still tense with wariness. Hoping to ease it, I point over my shoulder. "There's a cave off to the side of this path. It'll give us some shelter from the wind, and it has a pretty awesome view."

Curiosity seems to win over her hesitation and Luz nods, then we're moving again. Just as I said, within minutes we move off the beaten path and to what first appears like a wall of solid rock.

I drop Luz's hand and move around it, pushing off the boulder that's actually masking the entrance to the cave. Luz's eyes widen at the discovery, and she takes a few steps closer of her own volition.

"How did you find this spot?"

I shrug, dusting off the rock in the middle of the entrance. "We go on a lot of hikes, me and the guys."

Satisfied the flat top is now clean enough for her, I gesture to it and Luz takes a seat. I shrug out of my jacket and drop it to the ground, flopping onto it with a grunt. Whatever Luz has to tell me, it'll be hard enough without having me in her personal bubble. This way, I'm close enough to touch but not enough to distract.

"You're not cold?" Her breath comes out in white puffs of smoke, but I grin.

"The hike warmed me up."

After lingering on my profile for a bit, Luz finally glances downhill and a sweet little gasp escapes her. My body tightens with images of other ways I could elicit that sound from her lips, but I grit my teeth and shake it off. *Now is so not the time.*

My wolf disagrees. *Mine.*

While Luz takes in the breathtaking frozen lake below and snowy mountaintops, I spend all my energy trying to wrestle my counterpart into submission. Eventually, he relents and moves to the back of my mind, and I release a frustrated breath.

With the blood red in the sky, water at our feet, the entire world covered in a blanket of snow...everything stills. Then the peace shatters with Luz's confession.

"Tommy assaulted me."

Lucrezia

Out of the corner of my eye, I see Dom turn abruptly but refuse to look at him.

"We'd been dating for a bit. Three months to be exact. He thought he was entitled to something, but I wasn't ready. One night, he took me for a drive, and tried to rape me in his car. He would have almost succeeded if it hadn't been for the crowbar I found. I smacked him in self-defense over the head, then ran."

Memories of that night tug at me, increasing my heartbeat. I try to focus on my breathing, like when I used to have panic attacks. Without even realizing it, I start picking at the skin around my fingernails—until Dom rests his larger hand over mine.

I'm still avoiding his gaze, but I turn my palm upwards to grasp his, then draw in a shaky breath. "A nice old man picked me off the side of the road and drove me to the police station. I filed a report, they took pictures of my bruises. Tommy showed up later wanting to press charges against me. He might have gone to trial, but I didn't want to stick around. I'm a foster kid, I come from nothing, and him... Well, his parents were loaded. I left town to start a new life and ended up here."

I'm surprised at how easily it all rolls off, and the relief overcoming me at telling Dom. And for the first time since it happened, I don't feel ashamed. No more. The mantra I've repeated over and over since that day sinks in – *it was not my fault.*

Lost in my thoughts, I don't catch onto Dom's stillness until he whispers something.

"I'm going to kill him."

When someone says that, it's easy to believe they're just words. But as I turn to him, taking in his clenched his fists, his flaring nostrils, and the pure rage in his eyes... There is no doubt in my mind that Dom means what he says.

I tug on his hand, in an effort to ground him. "Dom, he isn't worth it."

"Luz..." At a huge cost to himself, Dom inhales deeply. "You don't understand. I *have* to kill him."

"That's crazy talk!"

He takes another deep breath at my outburst, then his free hand caresses my cheek. Despite the anger still in the rest of his body, he's so tender it brings tears to my eyes and a lump in my throat. No man has ever touched me with such reverence.

"It's stupid," I whisper as tears drop, one after the other. "I only now realize what a dick he was. I blamed myself for so long, for what happened, thinking I had led him along, because I was a virgin and I hadn't been with a guy in that way.... As if I would be stupid enough to give it up to the first guy that came!"

In my rant, I don't realize Dom's frozen again. Not until I sniffle, then look up and notice the most peculiar expression on his face.

"Um... Dom?"

His hand grasps my chin, searching my eyes.

"You... are amazing," he half-whispers, half-growls, then drops his mouth to mine.

It catches me by surprise, but not for long. His kiss is as tender as his touch is, not once pushing past a barrier he has erected himself. That, more than anything, makes me realize what the kiss really is.

There's no seduction in it, though the man is pure sin and his mouth knows what it's doing. Rather, there's a sweetness to the way his lips move against mine, giving me all the time in the world to pull back.

When he stops, I blink and fall into his ocean-dark eyes. This isn't fake. There is no Lucas around, no need to pretend. But what I feel, the tugging in my heart, in my body, it's impossible to restrict.

For months after the incident, I blamed myself. Nights on end, after first moving to Rockland Creek, I had nightmares of Tommy's hands on me. Now that the truth is out there, that I've told another person, I realize it's time to forgive myself, to break free of the limitations I set upon myself.

Not giving in to the kiss would have been letting Tommy win, to forever have control over my reaction to a man. So I do the exact opposite, and press my lips to Dom's again. At first taken aback, he snaps out of it quickly enough and takes over the kiss.

Rather than pull back, I let him. *I deserve to have a hot guy kiss me, and to enjoy it without feeling guilty.* Vaguely, I hear myself moan before I give in completely, no restraints, and stop thinking altogether. I trust Dom, and I know he'll respect my boundaries when the time comes.

Dominic

I'm only semi-aware of my hands moving to Luz's hips, gripping her tighter against me. I couldn't resist her now if I tried, and I would lie down and die at her feet if she asked me.

She cannot understand what her confession—what Tommy did—does to me. How can I explain to her the million deaths I've already envisioned for the bastard? My wolf is ready to pounce—to hunt. To make right what was done wrong.

Only her plea held me back as strong as Lucas' order to let Tommy go. I meant the kiss as comfort. Then she surprised me by kissing me back, and now I'm drowning, and the ocean's name is Luz.

My light. Calling me out of the darkness.

I break the kiss, panting, stirred beyond imaginings. She told me too much, but she doesn't understand that. She's completely, innocently unaware of how much my wolf wants the innocent that she is, not just to claim but to protect and forever keep safe.

She is the purest snow, meant for me alone. But Lucas...

I shut out the thought. Lucas won't go near Luz unless he proves he is worthy. I won't let anyone near her... myself included.

"Dom?" Those emerald eyes stare at me in wonder and confusion for stopping the kiss.

I run my thumb on her bottom lip, then whisper, "You were nowhere at fault with Tommy. A man has a choice to control himself. To treat a woman like a lady. He chose not to. And I swear to you, Luz, he *will* pay."

With a huge effort, I put some distance between us, reining in my desire to kiss her again. I want to do right by her, and my wolf is much too present in my subconscious mind to trust that he won't try to take over. So I do the reasonable thing and grasp her hand in mine. "Let's enjoy what's left of the sunset."

As she drops onto the jacket, leaning against me, I make a single promise with the blood-red sunrise as my witness. *Pack justice will prevail, and Tommy will pay. Whether or not Lucas agrees.*

∞ ♦ ∞

Later that evening, I drive Luz back home, holding her hand the entire way. It feels soft, precious in my larger one, and infinitely more fragile.

When the car comes to a full stop, I turn in my seat to face her. She seems reluctant to leave right away, and I'm not sure I'm ready for her to either. "What you told me today, you have to believe me when I tell you how precious your trust is."

I caress her cheek, and she nuzzles into my palm. "I know."

"And I will never betray that, Luz, believe me. But I need to tell Lucas." Panic flares in her eyes, and I scoot closer. "I will not tell them what happened, not unless you agree. But I have to at least let them know Tommy tried to hurt you and that he's dangerous. We will protect you, you have my word."

And I will seek justice for this. That part, I keep to myself. No sense scaring her with statements she cannot understand.

Luz bites on her lip, looking so damn vulnerable it's all I can do not to rush her out of here onto some deserted island, to make sure she's never harmed again. Still, my brave girl ends up nodding. "Okay. You can tell them Tommy is a slime ball... But please don't reveal everything he did unless it's necessary."

Her trust in me warms my heart, but words fail me. So I express it the only way I can. My hand moves to her neck, pulling her mouth to mine. I intended the kiss to be soft, but Luz leans further into me, demanding more until the seat belt digs into her chest.

She pulls away with a gasp, her eyes glazed and lips red from my ministrations. I smile, tucking a strand of hair behind her ear. "You should get going, you need rest."

Instead of moving, she stares at me, her brow furrowed in concentration. "Why do your kisses feel so right?"

Because I'm right for you, not Lucas.

I swallow past the words stuck in my throat and instead grin. "Because I'm a great kisser?"

Her features ease into a smile. "You had best stop kissing me when we don't have an audience, then. A girl might fall for your acting skills."

Before I can retort, she unbuckles her seatbelt and shoots out of the car. At the door, she turns around one last time and blows me a kiss. I wait until she's gone upstairs and am about to start the engine when I notice a dog crossing the street.

No... Not a dog. It's larger, and the back is hunched like it's disfigured. In the darkness of the street, the creature turns and I see yellow gleaming orbs, and a foaming mouth.

My first thought is something like, *What the fuck?* The second, quickly following, is that this must be the creature behind the killings. But it's the third one that has me rooted to my spot, heart pounding.

What is it doing near Luz's place?

The creature finishes crossing, then disappears into the crack between houses. I throw off my clothes, glancing around to make sure there's no human. When I'm satisfied I'm alone, I step out of my truck—naked—and lock the doors. Then I tuck the key behind my tire and morph into a wolf.

The scent hits me, causing me to retch. It's pungent and heavy, enough so to bring tears to my eyes like onions would if I was human. I shake my head, inhaling deeply to neutralize its effects on me, and follow in its stead.

I spend a full hour doing the tour, checking every nook and cranny, without finding the blasted creature. Dejected, I refuse to leave Luz alone for the night, so I do the next best thing. Still in my wolf form, I climb on the fire escape and squint through her bedroom window.

Mate, you free to go find Tiny?

Finn's question takes me by surprise. He must be in wolf mode already, and I feel slightly guilty turning him down. But there's no way I'm leaving Luz alone.

Not tonight. Tomorrow.

She's sleeping by now, a blanket thrown over her body. I will let nothing happen to her. In wolf form, I fall asleep in a corner. If anyone plans to come by, I will have their hide.

∞ ∞ ∞

CHAPTER SIX

∞ Confruntare ∞

"If you avoid <u>conflict</u> to keep the peace you start a war inside yourself."

-Buddha-

Dominic

I'm pacing back and forth in the bit of forest, unable to sit still.

What's gotten up your ass? Tristan's rumble is easy enough to recognize, even before he shows up. He's followed by Finn, whose eyes are fixed on me.

Nothing.

Yeah, right. My Irish buddy throws his thoughts on the matter, making a show of getting closer and sniffing me. *You stink of anger—and Luz. What the hell happened?*

I said nothing! My wolf growls, even as I step backwards. I don't want to hurt my pack, but this is beyond their comprehension. Tristan's wary eyes follow my every moment, probably out of fear I'll turn like the vrykolakas.

But it's not thirst for blood that has me close to manic. It's the need for revenge. The more I try to rein my nature in, the more I want to let loose—and find Tommy.

Who's Tommy?

Lucas pushes in, his massive wolf body corded, tense. He tilts his head to the side, showing me his teeth in a low snarl. *I asked you a question.*

Finn nudges me from the side, and his unspoken plea is clear as day. *Don't start something. Answer the leader.* Yet I have an issue listening to him. Instead, I push forward and get as close to Lucas as I dare.

He's Luz's ex. Did you know about him? About what he did?

The snarl builds up, but Lucas doesn't make a move. That is more sign of the truth than anything else, and I reel back in shock. *You knew!*

Certo che sì! I smelled the fear on her the first day you brought her in our midst. I don't know the specifics, but I know he hurt her. That's why I agreed for her to stay... He shakes his head, then closes his jaw. *She's safe with us, Dom. Why are you intent to ruin it?*

Would either of you care to share? Finn's irritated voice crosses all our minds.

I stare at Lucas, and he glares at me. We stay like that for long moments, and I know he's waiting for me to back down. And normally, I would... On any other day, I would break eye contact and step away, pushed by his alpha attitude and the rules of our pack.

Today, I cross every line and step closer, ignoring Finn's whine. *He hurt her and was never caught. He would have continued hurting her... That's why she ran away.* Only my promise to Luz, my loyalty to her, has me holding back on the full truth.

Through the connection linking us all, I sense my pack's shock, then quick burst of anger—none of us can stand for a woman being hurt.

But Lucas being Lucas, he tampers his emotions down quickly. *We cannot exact vengeance for something that happened before Lucrezia was with us.*

My wolf demands it.

Lucas stares me down, and I know he catches my meaning. *You're not mated, so that request is useless. Stand down, Dom. I order you—as your alpha. Do not touch the human.*

Then he turns away, dismissing the whole thing. *We have bigger problems. I ran across another dead animal on my way here. After what I saw... I really don't believe it's a human doing the work.*

This peaks Tristan's interest. *Then what?*

Un demone.

I don't miss Lucas' side-glance to me when he says demon, and bare my teeth in response. He ignores the disrespectful gesture, instead saying, *Finn, have you and Dom found Tiny yet?*

No, I've been...distracted. Sorry, boss. I'm surprised he's taking the fall for this, and grateful considering how pissed off Lucas is with me already.

Go now, then. We need answers.

Finn nods, then walks over to me, prodding me with his muzzle to move back. *Let's go before you dig yourself into a deeper hole.*

∞ ◆ ∞

We're on the outskirts of town, having picked up Tiny's scent near a motel. Finn sticks to the shadows like last time, but luckily there's no full moon tonight. After another mile of tracking, the scent stops.

What the hell?

Finn steps out of the darkness, turning in a circle. *Where did he go?*

Before I can answer, a ball of fur shoots out of a bush, aiming straight for Finn's neck. He ducks the direct hit, but they roll on the ground a few times. I wait until they stop, then lunge across the distance and slam into the attacker's body.

Dom, wait! Finn's plea stops me mid-hit, as I'd been about to smack the wolf over the head. Instead, I recognize the bleeding muzzle and torn ear, and back away. *Tiny?*

The small wolf groans, getting up to his four paws, and glances between us. *What's it to you?*

Why did you attack us?

You were following me. I have to protect the pack. Can't have intruders nearby. Tiny scratches the back of his good ear, his tongue lolling out of his mouth. It would have been comical, but I realize his mouth is like that because Jared seriously beat him up, enough to screw up his jaw.

And is that a sign of their protecting you? He notices my gaze is set on his bleeding flank, and looks away.

A misunderstanding.

I'm about to shake some sense into him, but Finn throws me a warning glare and steps closer, bowing his head in submission, appearing as harmless as possible. *Tiny, we want nothing to do with your pack and we definitely don't want to harm you.*

His eyes dart between us, then he stills. *So...what, then?*

We need information. The other night, when Jared was beating you up... Was it because you knew something? Maybe about a creature running loose around here, killing animals?

Tiny gulps audibly at that, and starts crawling backwards. *I know nothing about that!*

He turns tail to run, but I jump over and land behind him, blocking his path. *Tiny, we don't want to hurt you. But we need this information.*

His head moves from side to side, the pitiful torn ear flopping in the breeze. *I can't say nothing! Please!*

My gaze shifts over his head to Finn, completely disarmed at this poor thing's dilemma. *You're calmer, want to take over? I'm obviously scaring him shitless.*

Finn nods and steps closer. *Tiny, how about a trade?*

He whirls back to Finn, but continues glancing over his shoulder at me, plainly not trusting me at his back. *What kind of trade?*

Answer a few of our questions, and I'll personally escort you out of town. You can leave the Reapers, find a better pack.

Run...away? There's so much hope in his tone that it leaves me wondering how old Tiny really is.

Yeah, mate. Not all packs are filled with wankers like yours. Sure, they'll be cross you took off, but you're not important enough on the food chain for them to chase after you.

Tiny gulps again, and his voice is even quieter this time. *You promise you'll help me get out?*

I will personally, I give you my word. In that moment, I realize why Finn had such high statistics of getting confessions. There's nothing his gentle tone wouldn't get him, short of the truth.

Another glance over his shoulder, then Tiny nods. *O-okay. What do you want to know?*

Whatever you know about the creatures.

Tiny shifts, then scratches the back of his ear again. *Jared's scared. He's been losing pack members to it.*

Finn's gaze moves to mine, then back to Tiny. *What do you mean?*

We've found three of our guys dead, killed like the corpses of the other animals. At first, Jared thought it was you guys, trying to clean up shop. But once he started losing his tougher, most loyal guys, he's come to realize there's too few of you to pull it off. He thinks it's a rival pack.

No way in hell.

Tiny jumps at my assertion, eyes darting around everywhere in panic. *I swear it's the truth!*

Easy, lad. You did all right. Finn throws me a look meant to shut me up. *What else?*

W-what d-do you mean?

That's not all. The deal was you tell us everything. Though he sounds calm, Finn's voice firms up enough to flatten Tiny's remaining ear on the back of his head.

I did! I promise I did!

Finn shakes his head, and I make sure I'm placed in a good position in case Tiny gets it in his head to run. *No. You told us everything except why Jared was trying to beat you up. What do you know?*

Tiny's head moves everywhere, then a pitiful whimper escapes him. *Don't make me say this, man. Please.*

We can get you out of here, I vow it. But you need to tell us everything.

The little wolf paces to the side, then back, and finally bows his head. *I saw them. The... The creature and a...a wolf. Talking about...sharing. And the wolf, it was one of ours.*

A Reaper?

I...I can't tell for sure, I swear that's the truth. But I told Jared after he beat me up... Said Aiden told him I was hiding something and... He sniffles, and I shake my head. This wolf's a cub, not a damn soldier. *Jared still wonders if you're involved, but mainly he's trying to keep us from being killed.*

Finn nods then, and steps closer to Tiny. *All right, mate. You did good. Let's get you out of here while we can, shall we?*

With a last nervous glance to me, Tiny follows Finn into the bushes and on the path out of town. I hear the echo of his thoughts before he disappears. *I'll have him somewhere safe, then I'll meet up with Lucas and debrief him. Stay on your guard.*

You too.

With one last scan of the area, I head back to the shop. After what I just heard, there's no way I want Luz alone.

Lucrezia

I jerk away from Tommy's hold, not in the mood to deal with his crap. Not even five minutes ago, I headed out to grab a late lunch—more like dinner, since the sun is close to setting—and this prick was waiting for me at the corner of the street. Before I could even see him, he grabbed my hand and dragged me to a more secluded spot.

"You're an idiot, you know that?" Something about telling Dom seems to have released all the anger I feel at his attack, and rather than fear Tommy's presence it makes me want to bash his head in.

"You better watch what you're saying, princess." His eyes glitter and I'm pretty sure a muscle's ticking in his jaw. "There's no one around to save you now."

"Fuck you." Rather than step backwards, I move closer and shove him away. "I am done being afraid of you, dumbass."

"Well, well, the human speaks with intelligence. What a surprise."

I whirl around, and my eyes fall on Jared—and he's not alone. Two other guys just as bulky and scary-looking flank him on each side.

"Jared, remember?" He grins, as if I needed the reminder.

I offer a weak smile. His cold glare settles on Tommy behind me. "Well what do you know? Two mutts in the same day."

I frown at his words. *Who the hell is he calling a mutt?*

The two guys flanking him chuckle, but their inexpressive stares only make me shiver. I realize my precarious position all too soon – I'm stuck between my ex who almost raped me and a trio of thugs, with no backup and away from the public eye.

I should have eaten lunch at the office.

Despite the dangerous—understatement of the year!—situation I find myself in, and the fact I know none of the guys are at the office, I raise my chin. "What do you want?"

Tommy, idiot that he is, chooses that moment to side-step me and get in Jared's face. "I was here first, buddy. Get in line."

Jared looks at him like he's an insect he's ready to squash, not that Tommy clues in. He shoves the leader, and I hold back a gasp.

His acolytes move as if to hit Tommy, but Jared waves them off. He stalks towards Tommy, his jaw set and eyes glaring. Rather than back away, Tommy widens his stance. Next thing I know, Jared's fist slams into his face so hard I hear a crack.

Tommy falls backwards, landing in a pile of garbage. His nose is bleeding, and a part of me can't help feeling a little satisfaction.

"You inconsequential little shit." Jared towers over him, apparently very ready to continue. "You dare put your hands on me? Do you even know who runs this town?"

Tommy's answer is an unintelligent garble if words, not that it stops Jared. He lifts his heavy booted leg and slams it down Tommy's stomach with force.

My ex bends in two, his entire face contorting in pain. Jared smirks, then follows it up with a kick. No matter how Tommy tries to move, Jared's foot is there, unforgiving.

"Stop it!" The scream escapes me and I move between them, pushing Jared away.

He didn't expect my movement, as I actually manage to unbalance him. Then the same superior gaze lands on me. "Take a turn, little girl. This won't take long, then you can have all my attention."

I gulp past my terror, widening my stance like I learned in my self-defense classes. It's not obvious, only a shifting of the hips, but it's enough to ground me in case he tries to take a swing at me.

"What is your problem?"

Jared laughs, and again the noise makes me shiver. "This guy was bothering you. I figured a little quid pro quo, I scratch your back you scratch mine." Another laugh, this one darker. "Of course, we can start the scratching now."

He moves towards me, and I prepare myself for impact.

"We have it handled."

Lucas' voice is the salvation I hadn't dared hope for. I sneak a glance past my shoulder, where he conveniently appeared with Tristan. "Leave us, Jared."

Something akin to a growl leaves the other man, and I take a step backwards towards Lucas. Jared's flash of teeth tells me he saw it, and a shiver runs down my spine. "We'll finish this another time."

I feel Lucas' presence behind me, hard and unyielding. "No, you won't. She's with us, Jared. *Off limits.* Surely your thick head gets that."

Jared snarls at him, baring his teeth. Something about it makes me want to run for cover, but without a glance my way or Tommy's he pushes past Lucas and Tristan, and disappears around the corner with his two guys.

Once he's gone, I focus on Lucas, whose glare is set on Tommy. "Need any help, cara?"

It's the first I hear him use the endearment, but it's too little, too late. "I have it handled." I face my ex one last time, gaze narrowed on his pitifully beat-up form. "Get lost, Tommy, while you still can."

I turn to leave, but a scuffle behind me has me whirl around. Tristan is holding Tommy by the bicep, his knuckles white from the force he's applying. Lucas stepped between me and my ex, and judging by his posture, Tommy had been about to lunge for me.

"Leave before I change my mind."

I've heard Lucas angry before, but nothing this close to losing control. My entire being wants to be as far removed from him as possible. Whatever Tommy sees on his face, he gets the same idea because he pales and takes off like a terrorized rabbit.

My gaze shifts to Lucas, and he turns to face me. Tristan's been quiet the entire time, and something tells me he's only here as the backup.

As if noticing my attention, Lucas' eyes dart to Tristan. "Meet us back at the shop. There's something I need to talk to Lucrezia about."

I can tell myself my pulse is racing because of the aftereffects of adrenaline after what I survived. But with Lucas' full focus on me, it's hard to dispute the fact I am still drawn to him.

What about Dom? I quiet the treacherous voice at the back of my head, and instead cross my arms over my chest, grabbing onto my elbows. "Thank you... for your help with this."

Lucas stares at me for a beat, clenching his jaw. Then he inhales and runs a hand over his face, all the tension escaping him. "There's no need for that, Lucrezia. You have our protection, no matter what."

He glances at the garbage bags Tommy had fallen on. "Who found you first?"

"I'm sorry?"

"Did Tommy, or Jared?"

I bite my lip, and despite being near Lucas now, all I want is Dom's arms around me. Shivers are running over me, and I don't know if it's a delayed effect of shock or what, but my mouth is pasty as hell.

When I don't answer, Lucas' expression softens and he seems to realize my mental state. He steps closer, opening his arms as if to hug me, but I balk.

My body might be drawn to him, but there's nothing familiar about those arms. Rather than comforting, I see them as restraining and step away, shaking my head without really thinking about what I'm doing. "I... I'm good, thanks. It was Tommy. I went out for lunch and he grabbed me at an intersection, dragged me here. Jared and his guys showed up when we were fighting."

The surprise—at my rejection, I suppose—leaves his expression, replaced by fury. There's a flash of something too quick to interpret, but I can feel his agitation when he speaks next. "Did he hurt you?"

I don't know how much, if anything, Dom told him, but I strive for evasive honesty. "No. Jared inflicted more damage on him."

Lucas sighs, rubbing the back of his neck now. "That's what I was afraid of. You need to stay away from him, Lucrezia—"

A spark of anger runs through me, and I speak without thinking. "It's not like I actively seek them out, Lucas! Trust me, the last thing I want is to be around Jared and his crew. Not that he seems to care."

Whatever he's about to tell me gets swallowed up as his attention shifts. Another flash of annoyance crosses his expression, and it's enough to get me curious.

I turn in the direction of his glare to see Dom entering the alleyway, his expression filled with something I can't quite decipher. He comes to a stop, glancing between the two of us, noticing my defensive stance and Lucas' surprise. In two strides he's by my side, and his arms wrap around me without a word.

A sense of comfort and peace surrounds me and I burrow myself in his embrace, forgetting all about Lucas and Tommy and Jared and anything else that could go wrong. Dom places his chin atop my head, squeezing tighter. "I got you."

Those words are enough to quiet my shivers, at least for the time being.

"Tristan told me what happened." He's not asking me to retell the story, but answering some unspoken question from Lucas.

The silence is enough to make me pull out of his hug, at least enough to peek at Lucas. He's watching us with an unfathomable expression, then he focuses on Dom.

"Jared has a thing against you two being together. Be careful, Dom. It'd be better not to poke that particular wolf."

Dom says nothing, and with one last glance at me Lucas takes off. It's only then I look up at my fake boyfriend's face. "What are we doing, Dom?"

His expression tells me nothing, instead searching mine with an intensity that brings back my shivers. He runs his hand up and down my back, then kisses the tip of my nose. "We're doing what feels right, Luz. I'll be anything you need me to be—friend, boyfriend, fake boyfriend. Take your pick."

My heart squeezes at his honesty, but my mind can't respond in a neutral way. So I bury my face in his chest, asking the only thing that makes sense. "Take me home?"

Dom kisses the top of my forehead, squeezing me. "Sure thing, draga mea."

∞ ∞ ∞

CHAPTER SEVEN

∞ Duşman ∞

"If you know the <u>enemy</u> and know yourself you need not fear the results of a hundred battles."

-Sun Tzu-

Lucrezia

I jump awake in bed with the uncanny sensation I'm no longer alone in my condo. Call it a sixth sense, but I never thought things would be over with Tommy after the way things ended two days ago with Jared. I saw the hate in his eyes, and I know him enough to realize he won't let this go.

So when I wake up to some undetermined sound in my place every nerve on my body is going haywire. Despite the urge to unplug my phone from where it's charging and call Dominic, I fight it off. Tommy is my business, as stupid as it is to say that. I can't be running to my fake boyfriend to fix all my problems for me, especially not when it will land him in trouble with Lucas.

Plus, a part of me—albeit a really stupid part of me—wants to overpower Tommy on my own. So I slide out of bed and pull on a pair of sweatpants, breathing deeply a few times. I've been practicing self-defense for the last months, and though I'm no black belt, I should be able to take care of myself.

At least I hope so.

I move past the door to my bedroom into the dark hallway that leads to the living room. A cluttering noise comes from there, and I step on the balls of my feet, avoiding the creaking boards.

When I enter the living room, my eyes scan it but there's no one. I'm about to drop my guard, thinking I must have dreamt it, when I feel his presence behind me.

"Evening, beautiful."

I whirl around, taking a few steps backwards for good effect. Tommy is standing there looking all shades of blue and purple, with a split lip. He shuffles towards me as if he's in pain, and his breath comes in short gasps.

"See what your little friend did to me?"

I scowl, forcing myself to stop moving away. "Jared's not my friend. He's a bully, like you. And I'm not sorry he gave you some of your own medicine."

Tommy laughs, but it comes out more like a wheeze and forces him into a coughing frenzy. "You're going to pay for this, Lucrezia."

I know he wants to see my fear, so I force my heartbeat to slow down. *Deep breaths.* I only speak when I know my voice won't quiver. "And how is what happened to you my fault?"

Rather than answer, Tommy pulls something out of his sweatshirt, and I know now why he's been so calm all along, despite his frail state. In his hand is a gun, and judging by the safety he takes off, it's loaded and ready to shoot.

"If not for you, I never would have ended up in this shit hole. I wouldn't have had to chase you down on some lead from a girl I fucked once, nor would I have become a punching bag for some guy who's got it in for you. So yes, this is *all* your fault."

"You're delusional." I can't help my sarcastic laugh, no more than I can help my next words. "You called all this on yourself, Tommy. How about you own up to it for once?"

I guess it's the wrong thing to say. With a shaking hand, he aims the gun at me. "How about I don't?"

People will tell you having a gun in your face is enough to make your life flash before your eyes. When Tommy pulls the trigger, all I can think of is Dom—and how I wish I'd told him how he makes me feel.

But no bullet escapes it—by some stroke of luck, it jams. Without giving Tommy a chance to react, I launch myself at him. I aim my punches to the side of his ribs where I saw Jared kick him. He howls in pain and while he holds his sides, the distraction is enough for me to wrestle the gun out of his hands.

We fight over it, moving across my living room and knocking things over. He elbows me in my side, enough to knock the wind out of me, and follows it with a punch to my stomach.

I drop to the floor, wincing as my knees hit the hardwood. *This'll leave a bruise.* I glance up, and Tommy has the gun aimed at my head again. "Stupid second-hand shit."

Not sure if he's referring to the gun or me, but either way, I don't waste another second. I duck under his wrist and punch his groin, grappling for the gun and throwing it away. I don't want that kind of temptation around me—I've seen way too many movies of how it would end.

Tommy surprises me by recovering over the last hit and throwing himself on me. His entire weight pins me down, and his hands go for my throat.

A million self-defense moves run through my head, but all I can focus on is his breathing—and the hard-on pressing against my belly. Flashes of that night pass behind my closed lids, and my breathing goes haywire.

My lungs can't draw enough air, and all I can see is that night, his weight on me, his hands everywhere, my pleas to stop...

He smiles like a maniac above me. "Maybe before I kill you, I can finish what I started that night."

Hell. Fucking. NO.

His words are a much-needed cold shower. I swore to myself I would never let another man get control of me, and this is no different. I grit my teeth, then reach up and sink my thumbs in his eyes as deep as I can.

Tommy releases me, howling in pain. I kick him in the nuts for good measure, then scramble away to the gun. *Screw being righteous.*

When he next looks at me, I have the gun leveled at his face. "Get the fuck out of my house."

"You wouldn't dare."

I take the safety off, but I think what's more telling is there is no shaking in my hands nor my voice. "Try me, Tommy. Just fucking *try me.*"

He backs away, hands held up in mock-defense, and takes off out my balcony and down the fire escape. I lunge at the door, locking it behind him, and drag a sofa in front of it for good measure.

Then I walk to my bedroom in a daze and dial Dom.

Dominic

In my experience, it's never good news when a phone rings in the middle of the night. Which is why I answer without checking the caller ID and am greeted by empty air.

"Hello?"

There's more silence, followed by a single whispered word. "Dom."

I'm wide awake at Luz's voice, and everything she's not telling me. "Where are you? Home?" There's a whimper, enough to take as confirmation, and already I'm throwing on clothes. "I'll be there in a few."

Going as a wolf would be faster, but I have no patience for the ruse it would require. So I hop in my car and blow every red light between our places until I park nearby in a screech of tires. I glance up towards her fire escape, and I can smell Tommy even from here.

My wolf pokes his head, demanding we follow the scumbag and rip him to pieces. But I can hear Luz's heartbeat inside, and it's enough to center me. I run up the same fire escape until I'm near her bedroom window and keep my touch light as I knock on the door.

"Luz, it's me."

I take in her curled up form on the bed, the panting I can hear even from here. When she turns to me the second time I knock, her eyes are pools of panic. "Let me in, draga mea."

Luz slides off the bed and pushes the sofa blocking the door. With painfully slow movements, she opens the door, standing there as if waiting for instructions. It's only then I notice the gun in her hand. I reach for it, but she backs away, shaking her head.

"Luz, it's me. Darling... Look at me."

My wolf urges me to seek retribution, and despite not knowing what took place here I want to listen. But first I need to make sure she's all right.

"Luz?"

She meets my gaze then, her eyes filling with tears. I open my arms, hoping she will come of her own volition, and somehow my prayers are answered. Luz throws herself in my embrace, grasping onto my shirt like I'm an anchor to her drowning.

I wrap my arms around her trembling frame, absorbing all her sobs and vowing Tommy will bleed for each and every single one. Gently, I take the weapon out of her hand and place it on the dresser. We drop into an armchair in the corner, and Luz curls up on my lap.

"Please don't leave tonight."

I glance down at her in surprise. Her eyes are closed, cheeks wet with her tears. Her hands clench my shirt, her entire body tense.

"I won't, iubirea mea. I swear I won't."

She relaxes against me ever so slightly, and I chance running my hand up and down her spine. I wish nothing more than to stay like this forever, but it's killing me not knowing what happened. "Luz..."

She understands my plea though she doesn't speak right away. It takes another quart of an hour before she admits

Tommy broke into her place. Once the full story comes out, my wolf resents me suppressing him, and tremors are going through me.

Despite my best efforts to mask them, Luz catches my agitation and peers up at me with concern. "Are you okay?"

The fact she's checking on my well-being after what she went through makes me choke for very different reasons. I clear my throat, trying to explain myself. "I'm angry, sweetheart. So fucking angry that if I didn't have you on my lap right now, I would be tearing shit up with no remorse and going after Tommy to rip him apart."

A deep breath later, I cup her cheek. "Why didn't you call me from the beginning? Don't you trust me?"

Tears fill her eyes again and I feel like the world's biggest jackass. "Of course I do. But I didn't want you to have issues with Lucas and, Tommy is my problem. It's only fair I handle it."

My jaw hurts from the force I'm clenching it with. "Luz... Hear me, I beg you, when I tell you this. I am here for you whenever. Forget Lucas, forget everyone else. *I'm here.* Please never hesitate to call me."

She searches my eyes, so fragile in my arms that it tugs on my wolf even more. Then she nods, and it quiets my panic.

"Can we stay like this?"

I smile at her soft-spoken question, nodding against her head and pulling her closer. "As long as you need."

Luz is silent for a beat, and her voice is sleepy when she asks, "What does iubirea mea mean?"

Thankfully, she's asleep in the next breath. Because there's no way I can tell her that I just called her my love. It'll have her running for the hills, and all I want is her in my arms—where she's safe.

Lucrezia

I wake up the next morning in my bed. Once my brain jostles me awake with vivid images of the fight with Tommy, I blink my eyes open and scan my surroundings, half-expecting him to pop out of a corner.

But it's only me in my room, and the handsome beast of a man who apparently spent the night playing martyr.

Dom is on the armchair, legs spread and mouth slightly open. He looks so cute I can't help a slight chuckle—but the noise itself wakes him up.

He glances around, eyes alert for any danger, then his gaze falls on me. His expression, hard before, softens considerably, even more so at my next words.

"You could have slept on the bed."

Dominic gets off the armchair, stretching like a cat. His shirt rides up and my mouth waters at the expanse of abs I see. He turns too quickly and I don't have time to hide my expression of longing.

But rather than comment on it, Dom kneels by the bedside and tucks a strand of hair behind my ear. "You weren't awake enough to give me permission, and I wasn't about to intrude."

His words, spoken in a voice roughened by sleep, almost bring tears to my eyes. "And now I'm making you cry. Why?"

I shake my head, burying it in the pillow. After a few moments of him rubbing my back, I turn back to him and wipe my face. "You're too much, Dom. You have this player reputation yet all I see is the committed guy—to a fake relationship, for crying out loud!—who keeps me safe and makes me feel all kinds of things. The fact you're not pushing any boundaries, it's..." I trail off, incapable to finish.

Dom smiles and steals a kiss off my surprised lips when I least expect it. It's a slight brush, a quick touch, yet it sends tingles all the way to my stomach. "It's what makes me so endearing."

Then he stands, moving by the window. I don't have to ask, I know he's checking the area to make sure Tommy isn't lurking around. He glances over his shoulder, rolling one arm to stretch the muscles. "Are you taking a day off today?"

"No. If I stay I'll be thinking over what happened, and I'd rather keep busy. Why?"

"I need to talk to Lucas." Something about the way he says it tells me it won't be a light chat. "Think you can get ready in half an hour?"

I'm already halfway to the bathroom before he's done talking. "Even faster!"

Less than twenty minutes later, Dom drops me off in front of the shop. He parks illegally right across from it and follows me in, his hand on the small of my back.

"Wait here."

He disappears in the garage, then comes back out after a minute and heads to the kitchenette and Lucas' office. By the time he's back, the tension in him eased somewhat. "No one else but us here."

"So go talk to Lucas, I'll be fine."

He frowns at me, disliking the idea. "Not a chance. When one of the guys shows up, I'll go. But not before I leave someone I trust with you."

As luck would have it, Tristan chooses that moment to walk in, throwing off his sweater and a bunch of fresh now off it. "Que merda tempo!" Which, roughly translated, says something unsavory about the shit weather outside.

When we don't answer, Tristan looks up. It takes one sweeping glance from me to Dom, and his gaze hardens. "What's going on?"

Dom leaves my side and pulls him away. In hushed tones, he gives him a summary of what happened. To my surprise, Tristan grows tenser by the minute, until at the end all I can hear from him is what appears to be very vivid cussing.

My fake boyfriend leaves his side and kisses my forehead, then my lips. "Tristan will stay with you, and the fates help whoever chooses to be on his wrong side today."

With the cryptic warning, he takes off and I'm left with Tristan. At first, there's an awkward tension, so I decide to at least get answers.

"Why did Dom go to see Lucas?"

Tristan freezes like a deer caught in the headlights. It's such an unlikely expression on him that I can't help but burst out laughing, which only leads him to frown. When I calm down enough to speak again, I try to explain myself. "You looked so funny, like you got caught in a lie or something."

He snorts, moving closer. "You're an odd bird, you know that, beleza?"

I sober up despite his calling me beautiful, more aware of my weirdness than I'd care to admit. "So I've been told."

"It's not a bad thing." He's smiling when I glance up, and I return it, thinking there's nothing intimidating about him now. "As for your question, it might be best if you asked Dom."

"But Dom's not here right now."

Tristan shakes his head, moving away as if not trusting himself. He stands with his back to me, and I can't figure out why such a tiny question has such an impact.

"Tristan?"

"Foda!" His swearing in Portuguese doesn't surprise me, but the vehemence behind it is, at the very least, amusing. Then Tristan sighs and faces me once more. "Dom went to ask Lucas for permission."

"Permission? To do what?"

"To get rid of Tommy once and for all."

Dominic

When I get to Lucas' place, the sun is up and Tristan's been with Luz for about half an hour. I hope to hell he's not telling her things she can't know. He always was compulsively honest—maybe too much.

I push past the fence and walk in on Lucas' workout. He's hanging off a tree, wearing little other than sweatpants, and pulling himself up over and over. He doesn't glance my way, continuing the countdown under his breath.

"Careful with that training of yours. One of these days, you'll give some poor lady a heart attack."

Lucas snorts, landing on his feet and straightening up. "I doubt that's what you came here for at the break of dawn, amico."

"You're right. Tommy attacked Luz last night, broke into her apartment. And I want retribution."

To his credit, my alpha doesn't waste time with idiotic questions. Only one passes his lips, heavy with meaning. "How is Lucrezia?"

"Shaken up, but otherwise unharmed. She took him on herself because she didn't want to cause trouble for me." I move closer to him until we're an inch apart. "Enough of this crap, Lucas. Let me go after him."

Lucas stares at me for a long moment, then inclines his head. "Bene. Permission granted, but only to run him out of town. Force is at your discretion..."

I'm already out the backyard when he adds one more thing. "But no killing him."

Can't promise that, boss.

I'm standing outside the flea bag motel, leaning against my pickup truck. It's taking every ounce of willpower for me not to move and head in there to rip Tommy's head off.

Tristan comes out of the reception area—a dirty entrance, a desk and some poor sucker who got roped into doing the job—and I straighten up. I texted him after the talk with Lucas, and he waited until Finn got to the shop before taking off, leaving Luz in his capable hands.

I vaguely wonder if Finn told Lucas about what we gathered from Tiny, but then all thoughts of pack problems leave my mind when Tristan reaches me.

Most people think Tristan's aloof, and to outsiders he is. But the last year he warmed up to Luz, and there's a new edge to his glare. I know behind the sunglasses he's close to spitting fire, if his clenched jaw is any indication.

"He's in there all right," he growls, stopping a few feet from me.

The itch in me nags more. "Good." I take a step forward, but Tristan grabs my forearm.

"I want to rip his head off as much as you do, and the *pinto* deserves it, but we have to wait for Lucas." A few minutes after we got here, I received a text from Lucas saying he would check on Luz, and join us. He also ordered us not to do anything until his arrival.

My mouth is dry and I taste sandpaper, then metal, only to realize I've bitten through my lip. "She's my girl, man. And this dick, like you call him, needs to learn she's off limits."

I glance up in Tristan's stony gaze, and we stare at each other. After a beat, he nods and lets go of me. "Bem, meu amigo. I have your back."

"What room?"

"11."

I'm not walking towards it—stomping, more like. If anyone sees us head in, they say nothing, instead watch us and keep their distance. Once we're facing the door, I bang on it with my fist repeatedly until Tommy opens.

His eyes bulge out of their sockets as he takes us in. "What are you—"

We don't give him a chance to answer, instead moving into the room uninvited. "Let's talk."

∞ ∞ ∞

CHAPTER EIGHT

∞ Trecut ∞

"Sometimes you don't get <u>closure</u>. You just move on."

-Unknown-

Lucrezia

I smile at the elderly man as I hand him the invoice, and watch him walk away. Mr. Embers is our longest-standing customer, with his old-school Mustang. It was his wife's, he'd told me once, and he doesn't have it in him to get rid of it.

But as the antique keeps breaking down, it's been costing him a pretty penny. Unknown to him, Lucas has been fixing the car on his own money, only charging him half of the labor. It basically amounts to paying around twenty-five percent of the repairs.

"Was he happy?"

I jump, then turn to see the devil himself staring at the closed door.

"Yup, as always."

I try not to read into Lucas' coming closer, and the stare I feel on me. My skin prickles at the attention until I can't stand it any longer.

"Did you need something?"

Lucas opens his mouth as if to respond, but Finn barges in looking as panicked as I've ever seen him. "You need to come. *Now.*"

"What is it?" Lucas turns to him, none too worried.

"It's Dom and Tristan."

I drop my pen and they both turn towards me. I flush, but don't cower in front of them. "What happened to Dom?"

Something passes in Lucas' eyes—annoyance?—but I'm too focused on Finn to try and decipher it. "Finn?"

With one glare from Lucas, he shakes his head and says nothing. They both take off, leaving me fuming and biting my nails.

Dominic

My fist connects with Tommy's face and I hear a satisfying crunch. It's one of many, but Tristan doesn't stop me.

We're not animals. I offered Tommy to fight me like a man, but it seems he only likes picking on defenseless women. His pitiful cowering form, curled up from my last hit, almost makes me stop.

Then I remember Luz's tears, the panic in her gaze, the trembling in her body...

Like I said, *almost.*

I pull my arm back, aiming for another punch, when the door bursts open. Lucas takes in the scene, his fists clenching at the obvious disobedience he sees. After a deep breath, he stalks in followed by Finn. My Irish friend glances down at Tommy, then at me and Tristan.

"This isn't how we do things."

My wolf snarls, agitated, but Tristan's arm on my shoulder holds me back. "Lucas approved this."

Our alpha bares his teeth, onyx eyes glittering with anger. "I never agreed to *this*. I told you to run him out of town."

"You can be damn sure I have with this." I move towards him, ready to pick him up, but Lucas steps between me and Tommy.

"Finn and I will handle this. Go back to Lucrezia, or for a run. Whatever it is, do something that gets your mind off bloodshed."

I glare past him to Tommy. His face is a mess of bruises and blood, but he's still breathing. Way too fucking much for my taste.

Finn, with Tristan's help, pulls me out of the room and into the fresh air. "You've both crossed a line."

"Spare me, man." Tristan pushes me down the stairs, scowling at Finn over his shoulder. "You would have done the same—have, in fact, done the same. So stop being a hypocrite."

I know he's talking about what landed Finn here, in a remote town, rather than the lush emerald pastures of his native country. He had a good firm, a good practice as a lawyer, once upon a time. Before he threw it all away by taking justice in his own hands.

It's why he's such a stickler for rules, the best among us. Still, he's out of my head as soon as we get in my truck, and Tristan drives straight for the shop.

Before I get out, I shake his hand. "I owe you one."

"Trust me, it was my pleasure." Something flashes in his eyes, a confirmation he got as much out of the justice we handed out as I did.

Luz is already halfway out of her chair when I enter, and she jumps in my arms. There are no customers around, so I take no shame in digging my hands under her ass and hoisting her up in my arms.

She squeaks, but her arms wrap tighter around my neck as she buries her face in my chest. Moving us backwards, I place her on top of her desk and pull back, remaining between her spread legs.

"Miss me?"

She smacks me lightly, trying to scowl but failing. "You scared me!" Her cheeks are flushed, eyes sparkling with something akin to relief, and suddenly I don't care about games or fake relationships.

I drop my mouth to hers, not asking permission but taking. Luz moans against me, pulling me closer as she opens her mouth to my plundering. My hands move to her waist, feeling the heat of her skin through the top she's wearing, and desperately wanting to touch bareness.

My wolf rumbles, agreeing with my needs, but I know it's too soon, and too fast. So instead, I do the next best thing and kiss her like she's the sweetest wine, getting lost in it.

Lucrezia

When Dom entered the shop, I thought my heart would burst in relief. Now that he's busy kissing me like the world is ending, I no longer care about my questions, only that he's okay.

Someone clears their throat and we pull apart guiltily—me more so than Dom. He seems annoyed if anything, scowling over his shoulder.

"This better be important."

I peek past him to notice Tristan entering, closely followed by Lucas. The latter takes one look at us and storms back out, slamming the door behind him. My gaze shifts to Tristan, then Dom. "I caused this, didn't I?"

"*Nu*, draga mea." I love how his voice grows deeper when he speaks Romanian, and his endearments bring butterflies to my stomach. "That's just Lucas being Lucas. I'll take care of it later."

I push him away, and jump off the desk. Dom wraps an arm around me as naturally as breathing, but it's not enough to detract me. His comment reminded me of one very important question.

"What happened? Lucas and Finn took off here like they were being chased by the devil himself."

Dom shares a silent look with Tristan, then peers down at me. "We stopped by Tommy's motel. I may have gotten a little too carried away with emphasizing how he needs to stay away from you."

I bite my lip, frowning. The last thing I want is him to get into trouble on my behalf. "Dom…"

He places an index against my lips, and follows it by a kiss on my forehead. "Lucas is touchy because I got there first, and might have gone overboard. Don't worry about it."

"Don't…What about cops?"

Dom snorts, and it's picked up by Tristan. "Trust me, they won't be an issue. You really shouldn't worry."

I bite hard on my lip at the impossibility of what he's asking me, trying to rephrase. "I really don't want you getting into trouble."

"I won't." Dom kisses me again—this time to shut me up, I think—and Tristan clears his throat again.

"Ai, que amor... You guys are sickly sweet, you know that?"

I pull back from Dom, and another thought enters my mind. This whole thing started as a way to get Lucas' attention, but it's no longer that for me. If nothing else, the panic I've felt while waiting for him to return is a pretty good sign that things have progressed.

Is that the case for Dom, though? I try to search his gaze, but can't read anything past his amusement at Tristan's tone.

Lucas doesn't come back that day, but Finn shows up right as we're closing. He dusts the snow off the sweatshirt he's wearing, then glances in the garage where Tristan and Dom are tinkering with our latest client's car.

Tristan is the first one out the door, followed by Dom. By the time the three of them are in the reception area, the air is stifled with tension, and it's making even me uncomfortable.

After another beat, Finn lifts his hands up in mock surrender. "You know why I told Lucas, mates. No hard feelings?"

Tristan looks to Dom, whose gaze darts to me. Then he faces Finn. "What happened with Tommy?"

Rather than answer him, Finn walks a few steps towards me and takes my hand. His eyes are gentle, but there's a scathing tone to his voice I know he reserves for the likes of my ex. "Luz, Tommy will never touch you again. I dumped him at the police station of the closest town, along with enough evidence of crimes to keep him locked up for the rest of his life. I waited around until they booked him and spoke with a cop on duty. He's gone, Luz. For good."

I blink back tears, and manage a whispered, "Thank you."

As if my words were the absolution he needed, Finn turns back to the guys. "So? Forgiven?"

Dom takes a step towards him, pulling him in a man-hug and patting his back. Tristan is next, and now all three are grinning like maniacs. "Forgiven, brother."

Boys...

It's not long after that Dom drives me back home, dropping me at the entrance and taking off only after my lights turn on. After a shower, I change into sweatpants and a top. I'm about to get into bed when my buzzer rings.

More than curious, I head over to the door and press it, wondering who the hell could be calling on me this late at night.

"It's me."

I stare like an idiot at the speaker, recognizing Dom's voice, but not the need reverberating in each syllable.

"Can I see you?"

It's only been about twenty minutes since he dropped me off, but there's no way I can deny the longing in him—and me. Before I can change my mind, I press the buzzer to let him in, and by the time I open my door he's already at the top of the stairs.

His eyes take in my outfit, but there's an intensity in his gaze that tugs at me. When he gets closer, I rise on my tiptoes and kiss him without second thoughts.

Dom being Dom, he takes over the kiss and pushes us back inside the apartment, his tall frame towering over me, both his hands at my hips. I pull him closer, wrapping my arms around his neck and tugging him down, only to hear his muted groan.

Rather than take me up on my offer, he pulls back, panting. "I... Sorry, Luz. I couldn't leave you alone, after last night and..." He trails off, shaking his head.

He's about to back away, maybe even run, but I place my hand on his forearm. "Stay the night." His eyes flare, and I smile at him. "Just hold me? I'll feel safer knowing you're around."

There's a brief hesitation in his eyes, but when I grab his hand and shut the door behind him, I know he's mine for the night.

Dominic

I'm going to kill that bird.

It's the middle of winter, yet outside Luz's apartment there's a freaking bird that won't shut up. It woke me up about two hours ago, not that I really minded. I got to stare at Luz sleeping, draped over my chest.

When she dreams, her lashes flutter against her cheeks, and her breathing either deepens or grows faster depending on what she's dreaming. I also found out she hogs the blankets, not that I care since my body temperature is much higher than a regular human's.

Still, that damned bird is about to wake her up and ruin my view.

As if on cue, Luz shifts, burying her head in my chest. She inhales, and a secret little smile tugs at the corners of her mouth. The next minute, she's gluing herself closer, her mouth moving up from my chest to my jaw, then my lips.

I know what's happening. In her sleepy state, my wolf is linking with her. Like a mental energy, it's tugging on her baser instincts, encouraging her to act on her most primal desires. Of course, if Luz is responding like this, it means at least a part of her truly wants me.

Biting back a laugh, I sit back and humor her, kissing back, all the while wondering how long it'll take her to realize what she's doing. So for the time being, I go with it—I never said I was a saint.

Luz kissing sleepily is an aphrodisiac I could get used to. Her body melts against me, her mouth soft and pliant under my kisses. The only problem? The raging hard-on she's giving me.

Against my body's advice, I push her away and kiss her forehead. "Wake up, draga mea. Before you start something we can't finish."

She blinks awake and her eyes go wide as saucers when she realizes I'm in bed with her. For a moment I'm scared she forgot she gave me permission to be there. But Luz only flushes to her roots, then covers her face with her hands. "Did I just...?"

I can't help finding her embarrassment adorable, not that I can really explain to her what happened to make her act like that. "Mhmm."

Luz peeks through her fingers at my smug tone, smacking my chest. "This is your fault, you know. I don't do this kind of stuff!"

I laugh, pulling her hands away and kissing her, all while trying to ignore a very obvious secondary effect—I never said I was a saint.

One more touch, and I breathe against her lips, "Don't worry, I forgive you."

She glances down at my problem and smirks. "Does *he*?"

"He'll learn. Now get out of here while I make us breakfast. Apparently, I'm needed in the shop."

"But it's Saturday!"

I shrug, and avoid mentioning it was a direct order from Lucas. He's doing it to put some distance between us, not that I'm about to allow him.

"Fine," Luz grumbles, stretching next to me. I try not to pant like a damn dog in heat. "If you go, I'll come with. Catch up on paperwork or something."

Not about to argue there, draga mea.

Whether Luz realizes it or not, my wolf speaks to her. That's what this whole morning make out session was about. She's responding to my own desires, and I'll be damned if this bond gets broken by her lust for my alpha.

I watch as she gets up and grabs a change of clothes, then sneaks into the bathroom for a shower. By the time she's out, I whipped us some toasted bagels, cream cheese and coffee. She wraps her arms around my waist, hugging me tight, before we both dig into breakfast.

"You didn't have to, you know?"

"I know."

Luz munches around a bite, then her eyes drop to her plate. "I mean, this being a fake relationship and all."

I freeze, but force myself to swallow the now ashy bagel. "So we're still doing that?"

Her eyes search mine for an answer that should have been easy to see. "Aren't we?"

I want to talk about this, but before work is not a good idea. So I tell myself tonight. Tonight I'll tell Luz what I can and let her decide what she wants—*who* she wants. It's nowhere close to the month I promised her, but my patience where Lucas is concerned is gone.

Without giving her an answer, I clear my plate. Only once I know I'm calm enough do I return to her and kiss the side of her head. "How about we talk tonight? I don't want to get into this before work."

She bites her lip, looking like she wants to say more, but ends up nodding. "Okay."

Half an hour later, we arrive at the office and I lose track of her. Lucas has a pile of shit he assigns me to sort through while Finn and Tristan get to have the weekend off. I don't bother arguing with him, instead taking it all in stride.

Still, by the time lunch comes around, I'm wired with impatience. If I have to talk to Luz tonight, I'd best make it a memorable enough day for her not to forget what she feels about me.

Poking the bear—Lucas—is not the best idea. So technically I shouldn't be trying anything while we're in the shop. But after the rough time he's been giving me and Luz, I figure it won't make much of a difference.

So when I see Luz get up and make her way to the kitchen, I drop my stuff and follow her.

Luz is by the sink, cleaning the mess the guys left behind yesterday. I make a mental note to tell them to clean up after themselves. Then I move in, putting my hands on both her sides, caging her in.

I'm rewarded for my efforts when she doesn't even freeze, whether recognizing my cologne or my beige sweater, but she laughs instead. She turns around, but stops the minute she sees my expression.

"What...?"

The confused frown is my undoing. My mouth drops to hers with all the grace of a tornado. And as our lips move together, she melts against me.

"Excuse me."

I take my time lifting my head and glancing over my shoulder where, sure enough, Lucas is glaring at us. "What is this?"

"What's it look like?" I shoot back.

"Do it on your own time."

He moves to the fridge to put his lunch back in and drops the dish in the sink. When he seems ready to leave, I snap. "I am. It's lunchtime, smartass. And learn to pick up after yourself, Luz has been doing everyone's dishes."

Lucas' anger abates a little at that, and he glances down at Luz, still under my arm. "You have?"

Luz shrugs, then nods, "If I didn't, we'd have rats in no time."

Lucas glances between her and me, then rubs the back of his neck in contrition. "Grazie, I... hadn't realized. It's not part of your duties, nor should you be expected to do it because you're the only woman around. I'll talk to the guys."

Her small, "Thank you," falls on deaf ears, as Lucas already escaped.

Lucrezia

I'm following Lucas with my eyes, not to check him out but because his behavior is frankly annoying me. When Dom grabs my hand in his and tugs me after him, I stumble over my feet.

"Come on."

I meet his mischievous gaze and lose my train of thought. When their blue hue sparkles like that, he's kind of endearing.

"Um..."

"I'm taking you out to lunch."

Once in his pickup, Dom surprises me by driving to the bakery down the street. Bemused, I follow him inside, where he starts picking out treats to bring with us.

This time, it's not Rose who helps us out but her granddaughter, Elle. With every choice Dom makes, her cheeks flush more and I bite back a laugh. She must be young, to be so shy. Then again...

I try to check out Dom like a stranger would, taking in his tight blue jeans, beige shirt that emphasizes his broad shoulders, and casual attitude. A few locks of dirty blonde hair fall on his forehead, and his mischievous gaze keeps darting between me and the food.

"Dom, seriously!" I tug on his hand in a vain attempt to slow him down. "That's way too much food for lunch."

He shrugs, turning a disarming smile to Elle. "You wouldn't happen to have some of those sandwiches your grandma makes sometimes?"

She nods, mumbling something that sounds like an agreement and heads to the back. I shake my head at Dom and he notices it.

"What?"

"Nothing." A chuckle escapes me despite my best efforts, and finally I admit, "I think Elle might have a tiny crush on you."

Dom arches an eyebrow, glancing between me and the closed door to the kitchen. He shrugs. "Too bad, I only have eyes for one." Then his mouth descends on mine, and I lose track of what I was saying.

When he pulls back, I lick my lips and whisper, "Don't you think she'd be perfect for one of the guys?"

Dom squeezes me tight, biting back a rumble of laughter. "Trying to play matchmaker, draga mea?"

I want to deny it, but Elle steps out in that moment with another box that smells positively amazing. Dom pays for everything, picks up the food and we head out. Once outside, he throws me a side-glance. "You're right, she'd be perfect for one of them."

"Really? Which one?"

Dom shakes his head, refusing to answer as he sets the food inside the truck, then helps me in my seat. Despite my best efforts, all I get out of him is a knowing smile.

∞ ♦ ∞

Turns out, Dom's idea of lunch is an hour-long drive until we're amid wilderness, with enough takeout to last us a lifetime. Today's warmer outside, and the sun is shining brightly.

Though it's not warm enough to have a picnic on the snow, we get out of the pickup and hop in the cargo bed of the car, spreading our food over a blanket. Over the next hour, as we eat, Dom is a perfect companion, asking me about my childhood, my schooling, anything and everything.

I don't even see time pass by, nor the food disappear, until we reach dessert. As we dig into a lemon meringue pie, he reaches over and wipes a corner of my mouth. A zing of electricity runs from the tip of my head to my toes, leaving me slightly dazed.

As if nothing happened, Dom takes another bite of the pie and continues regaling me with stories.

My mind shifts back to this morning, and the subject of our relationship. *Tonight*, he'd said. Without even realizing it, the memory of his promise has me staring at him. Dom's blue eyes are sparkling, and he's invested in a story about a childhood hike in the mountains of Romania, and I smile.

There's no doubt about it. Regardless of what I wanted before, this whole ordeal has only showed me that what I most desire has been right in front of me all along.

I open my mouth, about to tell Dom everything, but growls interrupt me. Dom stops talking, instead crouching low and moving to shield me. I peak over his shoulder and see three wolves emerge from the thick bushes around where we parked.

"Dom..."

He throws a glance over his shoulder, but his eyes are no longer all blue. They're rimmed with grey, fierce and alien. "I'm sorry."

I can't even begin to understand his apology before my world—my reality—shatters.

Dom's entire form shimmers, a golden halo surrounding him. His body bends over until it's almost in a curled-up position, and a groan escapes him, followed by a sound I can't identify but that's halfway between a snarl and a scream of pain.

Under my bemused gaze, his limbs retract, claws and fur emerging from the previously human skin. His features, the same ones I'd been staring at merely minutes before, change and elongate into a muzzle. Razors-sharp canines elongate in his mouth, and another agonizing noise escapes him.

In less than ten seconds, what's left in front of me is not a human...but a wolf.

CHAPTER NINE

∞ Adevăr ∞

"Three things cannot be long hidden: the sun, the moon, and the <u>truth</u>."

-Buddha-

Dominic

Everything was going great. Luz was relaxed, and I even forgot about Lucas' glares today. For the first time, I had her all to myself without some kind of revelation hanging between us, and was enjoying the sparkle in her eyes.

And then *they* showed up.

I should have felt them coming, seeing as my senses are way sharper. But I was so engrossed in Luz, it was only when I heard a branch crack that I caught the danger.

By that time it was too late to take flight, so fight was the only option left. Switching to wolf form was a no-brainer. If I wanted to protect Luz, it was the only way. Plus, this wasn't just any pack of wolves—it was Aiden and his shadow trio.

So that's how I find myself on four paws, panting from my transformation, and still on the cargo bed of my pickup. A quick glance behind me confirms I've shocked Luz to her core, as she's staring at me with her mouth open and wide eyes.

There's no way I can communicate with her in this form, so I jump off the car instead and land in the snow. I angle my body in the perfect position to watch the wolves approach, while keeping my back close to the truck.

I'm the only obstacle between the attackers and my truck, where Luz is staying hidden. I can't even think how I'll explain this to her, or Lucas.

We have strict rules about showing off in front of humans. Mainly because each one of us was hunted, in the past. There's no elderly council or anything that enforces the law, only a consensus to adhere to the priorities Lucas, the guys and me put into place when we first bound ourselves as a pack.

Jared, Aiden and the rest don't have the same qualms. Plus, their kind of werewolf is the type whose bite turns you into one. Same as Lucas, they have venom in their canines, and any human they turn becomes one of them. At first, they're only able to morph under a full moon, but Jared does a good job teaching them how to shift at any point in time.

How do I know? Because I saved a few poor kids from his influence and helped them be on their way. One of the main reasons I have beef with Aiden – he loves biting humans. Which is why it's even more imperative I keep him away from Luz.

All this goes on in my head for about three seconds before Aiden's growl gets my attention. I drop my mental guard in time to catch the last bit of his rant.

You frolic with a human, here in our woods?

There's no point correcting him or his wrongly superior view of the world. *Please. Since when do these parts belong to the Reapers?*

Aiden glances at his followers, signaling them, and they move closer. *Since a month ago.*

Then you should have informed my alpha and I would have stayed out. Now let us go, Aiden. We both know you don't want to start something you can't finish.

Technically, he can't touch us. But it wouldn't be the first time the Reapers broke a rule, only to ask forgiveness later. And I'm not ready to bet Luz's welfare on Aiden's word.

I straighten to my full capacity, snarling their way until they stop moving. It's a useless gesture, but I throw my head back and howl as loud as I can, putting all I can in it. If any of my brethren hear my call, they'll come.

With my next breath, I focus on Aiden. In dark gray with cold black eyes, he's the epitome of nightmares. A jagged scar runs over his right eye, a remnant of a battle he lost—I know because I put it there.

One of his buddies jumps, trying to pass over me and hop to where Luz is. I raise my paw and smack him over the muzzle, watching as he flies back and lands close to ten feet away, smacking into a tree. And this is where vârcolac power comes in handy—not only am I strong, but I'm stronger than your average werewolf.

Except maybe Lucas.

Still, my particular gifts are enough that I can hold the fort if faced with only these four. The Reaper I knocked down stays put, whining as he tries to center himself. Another breaks formation next, but I block his path.

Think twice before you do this.

He glances past my shoulder, sniffing the air. *I think I will enjoy this. It's been a while since I've had a human as succulent as yours.*

When he jumps, I'm done being merciful. I lunge with my muzzle first, biting into his neck and not letting go until he tears himself from me. I spit part of his fur—and skin—aside, then face Aiden and the remaining Reaper.

How about you face me alone, Aiden? Unless you like being a pussy and having your men fight your battles for you.

His snarl echoes in the area, and it's answered by a few more. I back away uneasily. Fighting them, I have no problem with. But Luz... She's like honey for their explicit tastes.

I turn to the truck, but to my surprise she's on the edge of the cargo bed, holding a crowbar of all things. She glances at me, frowning as if to make sure it's me. I nod my head, not sure what to expect.

Though technically she'd be safer up there, away from their coveting glances, I should have known my girl wouldn't sit still. She slides off, landing on her feet next to me. "Who wants a piece?"

Luz bends at the knees, centering herself for better access. When Aiden's last wolf jumps towards her, I want to knock him out. But Aiden chooses that moment to attack as well and pushes me away from Luz.

I hear a cracking sound and narrowly avoid Aiden's teeth while trying to peek at Luz. She must have knocked over the wolf by herself, because he's whining a few feet away and she's looking mighty victorious.

The wolf in me howls his approval, but Aiden blocks my view—again. *You're really pissing me off.*

Get in line.

We jump and scratch at each other, each protecting his neck. He gets in a good smack on my back, drawing blood, but I hit him hard enough to spin. Just when I think we might catch a break, more wolves emerge from the forest.

And they circle us, making all escape impossible.

"Um, Dom?" Luz's voice is firm, but I feel her heartbeat increasing. "Got any ideas?"

I wish I did. If none of the guys are here by now, it means they're too far away to hear me—or they got delayed. Either way, we're screwed.

I'm about to shift and tell Luz to run off, when the stench hits me. *Fuck no.*

Sure enough, to the left of the Reapers another bush parts, only this time it's not another wolf that passes through. It's the large black-haired creature, its back hunched over, canines dropping drool and yellow eyes glowing.

Its beady glare settles on me, but rather than jump me, it lunges at Aiden's pack.

Their terrified howls draw my attention. More creatures emerge like insects, and then they're everywhere. For whatever reason, they spare me and Luz, avoiding us and concentrating on the Reapers.

Without wasting a beat, I nudge her towards the truck, and she seems to get the gist as she hurries and locks the door behind her.

I run to the other side, morphing human as I go. A nearby scream of pain pulls my focus, in time to see one of the monsters jump a Reaper. They roll on the ground, and the creature sinks its fangs into the wolf's neck. A sizzling sound escapes from the bite, even as he shrieks to the skies.

The hair at the back of my neck rises at the sound, something I've never heard before. *What the hell are they doing to these guys?*

There's no time to investigate, and no time for me to get dressed either. I hop naked in the truck, grabbing a blanket to dump in my lap—for Luz's modesty, if nothing else. After a quick glance at her to make sure she's strapped in, I'm gunning the engine like our life depends on it.

Which, it kind of does.

We drive in silence for close to half an hour. My eyes dart to the rear-view mirror every few minutes to make sure we're not being followed, but it doesn't seem to be the case.

I breathe easier when we pull over in front of Claws Auto Shop, back in familiar territory. "Go inside and wait for me. Please."

Luz opens her mouth as if to say something, but ends up nodding and listening. Once she steps inside, I lean my head back against the seat and inhale deeply, trying to gather my thoughts.

What the hell was that all about? Why did the creature let us go? I know I have to report to Lucas about Aiden's breaking the rules, but I also need to talk to Luz first.

I pull a pair of sweatpants from the back on, then head into the shop, not bothering with a shirt. Lucas is deep in the garage, but Finn is with Luz, frowning at her pallor and muteness.

"I got this."

He glances up at me, brow furrowed. "What happened to you?"

For a moment, I think he means I'm hurt. A quick check of my chest and back in the entrance mirror confirms that's not the case, but I also realize what Finn meant. There's darkness in my face, and a haunted look to my eyes that he can probably see right through.

Shaking my head, I turn back to face him. "I said I'll handle this. What are you doing here, anyway? It's Saturday."

Finn glances between us and says, "Lucas called all hands on deck. Didn't explain why."

Gritting my teeth, I take a step towards my girlfriend. Finn inches away, his frown deepening. "Watch the back," I order him, "and tell Lucas we need to talk. But we're using his office first."

My gaze clashes with Luz's and I hold my hand out to her. She glances at it, then me, and air rushes out of my lungs. I could drag her there, but if my transformation repulsed her, I don't want my actions to traumatize her any more than what she already witnessed.

When she reaches out and grips my hand, I breathe again.

Lucrezia

Dom stalks to Lucas' office, almost dragging me with him. The entire time, I'm clinging to his hand going over in my head through what happened.

He turned into a wolf.

We got attacked by wolves.

And saved by some... creature.

For crying out loud, I should be freaked out, right? I mean this kind of stuff happens only in books.

Dom lets go of my hand once we're inside the office, and takes a few steps away. He paces back and forth, running a hand through his messy hair and over his face. I'm reminded of how he looked at me, his hand extended. Like he was begging me not to reject him, to give him a chance.

Like I might be afraid.

And in all due truth, I should be. Despite this, the main thing unfurling within me is an undeniable and possibly misplaced curiosity.

I have questions, tons of them. But nothing I saw changed the way I think of Dom. Or Lucas and....

My mind trails off. *They must be wolves too, right?* The way they all act, thick as thieves, almost reading each other's minds.

Yet I've been with them for a year and not once did I think....

"Please say something."

I glance up at Dom, noticing his pained expression. He's tense, and not in a good way. His mouth is down-turned, brow furrowed, eyes flat.

He's clenching his fists as if to stop himself from touching me. I'm distracted again, recalling the grace he morphed with, the way he fought. There's something primal about what I witnessed, despite the danger.

And yeah, it was hot as hell.

So perhaps the reason I have such an easy time with this whole werewolf thing is because of the books I've been reading.

Or maybe I'm just weird.

Or insane.

Yet when I look at Dom, at the wariness in his eyes like he expects me to go running, I can only shake my head and laugh. "Well. That definitely explains your heat factor."

I see his eyes widen and I smile, taking a step closer.

"You're not...." He stops, struggling to find his words. "What, exactly, are you?"

I tilt my head, moving closer. "Curious. I'm... really curious."

Dom gapes, searching my expression as if not believing me. "Curious?" A beat, then he shakes his head, muttering in Romanian under his breath.

My feet continue to bring me closer to him. "I'd like to understand, at least, what you're saying."

A short laugh escapes Dom, followed by a wry chuckle. "I'm trying to wrap my mind around why you're not running for the hills."

I guess that's fair. The question is, do I even know? And then, in a flash, I realize I do know, and it's the simplest explanation of all. "Because I know you, Dom."

His expression grows even more bemused, if that's possible. By this point, I'm close enough to wrap my arms around his neck, which I do while he doesn't move a muscle, and seems to be barely breathing.

"For the last year, you've been my friend and confidant, always there when I needed someone. Seeing you change into a wolf, while it was extremely unexpected and quite literally surprised the shit out of me, doesn't take away from the fact that I. Know. You."

When he frowns, I untangle one hand and smooth down his brow. "It's no different than if I'd found out you were a drug lord, or a spy or..." I shrug, running out of options. "This isn't some delayed reaction situation where I'll be screaming murder as soon as I can wrap my head around it. Have some faith in me...like I trusted you."

Dom's gaze, which has been focused on my features the entire time I was talking, softens and he closes his eyes, breathing in relief. When he opens them again, the blue is brilliant and full of life once more and I smile.

"Can you talk about it? With me, I mean."

He makes a face that tells me he shouldn't, but follows it with a shrug. "I've already morphed in front of you, so not much more trouble I can get into."

"Were those other wolves as well...?"

"Yep. That was Aiden, whom you've had the pleasure to meet. Jared wasn't there, but three more of their gang were. Which, by the way, you handled superbly."

He rewards me with a light kiss, and I grin up at him. "Thank you. Were you born like this or?"

"Born. As far as I can remember, to be honest."

"And you're a werewolf? That's the correct term?"

Dom grimaces again, almost as if debating to reveal something. After a beat, he says, "I'm a vârcolac."

"A what?"

"Vârcolac. It's a Romanian werewolf that lives deep in the Carpathian Mountains. Legend has it we could bite the moon to get power, which is what led to a blood red moon." He chuckles, shaking his head. "As cool as that would be, I'm afraid I only get the extra strength and ability to shift at will. Plus, I do have a certain affinity for moving faster across distances during a time of full moon."

I gape, trying to wrap my mind around all this. "That's cool." An understatement as far as those go, but my brain is swimming in questions. "Will your bite turn me?"

Dom's face darkens at that. "No. The only way you can become a vârcolac is by carrying the gene as I do, or if a vârcolac mixes their blood with yours. However, Aiden's and Jared's bites can turn humans—that's how they create their wolves."

The mention of blood brings another, more important, question to mind. "You were hurt, weren't you? What happened to the wounds?"

Dom glances down at himself, noticing the lack of scratches. "When I turn back to human, the transformation regenerates my skin and I find myself naked, but without a single scratch on me."

I frown, distinctly recalling he'd been hurt, once. "But that morning, when you came into the shop and you had that scratch on your cheek..."

He thinks for a second, trying to remember, then his expression lightens and he chuckles. "Oh, that. Courtesy of Finn. We had a, err, skirmish the night before and he got in a lucky swat. His blows don't heal as quickly."

When I open my mouth to ask why, he places an index on my lips. "I will only say the reason behind that is related to a particular ability of his, but I cannot explain further. It's not my secret to tell. And on the topic of my buddies, neither Finn nor Tristan's bites can turn you, but Lucas' can."

"Lucas?" I can feel my eyes at the confirmation. "So him and Finn, Tristan..."

"Yep, they're all like me."

"And they're all vârcolaci?" I try to wrap my mouth around the unknown sounds and manage to replicate the way Dom said the word.

"Nah, they're different."

"How different?"

"Lucas is a regular werewolf, like Jared. Finn and Tristan...." He trails off, shifting in place and avoiding my stare.

After a beat, I nod in understanding. "I get it. I'll ask them directly." His relief is palpable, but I'm too wired to stop with the questions. "Jared and Aiden then, what's their problem with me?"

"The Reapers are what you'd call fanatical werewolves. They don't like mixing of bloods—wolf and human—and can get nasty about it."

"Wonderful.... Racist werewolves."

He shrugs, accustomed to the notion. And if I plan to date a werewolf, I'll have to deal with it, too. I search Dom's expression, trying to look past the tangle of questions in my head and ask myself the one that really matters.

Do I actually plan to date a werewolf? Because something tells me this isn't going to be one of those light and easy relationships you see in Hallmark movies.

It dawns on me in that moment that we didn't quite have that talk we promised, about our relationship. I'm about to bring that up, when the door bursts open and Lucas stomps in.

He takes one look at us, then jabs a finger in the air. "Porca miseria, Dominic, you *told* her!? Are you insane?" The swearing, if not the tone full vibrating of anger, clues me in that Lucas is seriously pissed.

Dominic

Damn Lucas and his bad timing. I can't believe Luz is taking all this in stride, but his interruption is not helping our case.

Still, I refuse to let go of Luz. "Relax, Lucas. We got attacked in the woods by Aiden and his crew. Kind of hard to defend her as a human, don't you think?"

He scowls, clenching his fists. "Then maybe you should have run your little picnic plans by me first. This could have all been avoided!"

"Sure, so you could shoot me down?" I scoff, knowing full well I'm not doing myself any favors.

Something burns in his glare, and I know if Finn was here he'd tell me to shut up. But right now, with my wolf secret out, all I know is I want to be honest with Luz in all aspects, including telling her about him.

"You've crossed many lines, Dominic. But you're getting closer to a limit you won't be able to return from." Lucas spares a glance to Luz, before directing his glare to me. "We'll finish this later."

I wait until he leaves, then place my hands on Luz's shoulders and push her slightly away.

"About this relationship... And how it started."

In retrospect, I should have let Luz talk first. Instead, I follow my statement by kissing her senseless—then quite literally shoot myself in the foot.

"You can't like Lucas."

Luz freezes under my touch, frowning up at me. "Excuse me?"

"Lucas is the alpha of our pack, Luz. Since we pledged our allegiance to him, it activated some kind of pheromone and it attracts any woman to him. This entire time, that's why you lusted after him."

Luz frowns, shaking her head. "I would know my own feelings, Dom. I'm pretty sure it had nothing to do with your wolf thing."

"But it did. It *does*." Her emerald eyes that previously shone are now narrowing my way, and I know I should stop while I'm ahead.

She takes a step back, crossing her arms over her chest. "You're telling me I can't differentiate between my feelings and some spell?"

"No, that's not—" I run a hand over my face, ready to kick myself. "It's not a *spell*, Luz. It's deeper than that, like basic, primal attraction that will continue to call out to you until you act on it."

Her face flushes at that. "So you're saying I've been a virgin all this time but now because of some wolf crap Lucas is pulling, I'll just fall in bed with him? Wow, Dom, thanks for the vote of confidence!"

I'm moving towards her before I can stop myself, unable to shut up. She's missing the point and panic is welling inside me at the thought of losing her, so close to having her. "I'm not contesting your virtue, I'm trying to tell you that it won't matter."

"Don't tell me what will and won't matter in my life, Dom!" Her eyes flash, and there's both hurt and irritation in there.

"But it's the truth! You've fallen into a world you don't understand, and if you don't listen to me you might do something you regret. This, you and me, it started because of your so-called love for Lucas. But you don't love *him*, it's this whole alpha shit that has you twisted!"

She purses her lips, her cheeks flaming now. "Stop. I know what I feel, and nothing you say can affect that."

"Luz—" *Shit. How did this conversation go so haywire?* I try to put my arms around her, but she jerks out of my reach.

"No, don't!"

And yet I do. I grab her anyway and crush her mouth with mine until I feel her sweet surrender, and her arms wrap around my neck. I continue my assault on her lips while her entire body leans against mine, pliant and practically melting against me.

In that moment, I pull back and meet her bemused glare with one of my own. "If you're so in love with him, then why are your arms wrapped around me begging for more?"

Before she can answer or I make matters worse, I leave, ignoring her stricken expression.

Lucrezia

So Dom is ignoring me at work. Since our little blowout a little over an hour ago, he's been burying himself in restoring some car. I didn't even get a chance to explain myself, or the fact that we were talking about two completely different things in Lucas' office.

Yes, his arrogance that he knew what I felt pissed me off. But in the end, I was only trying to communicate how I felt about him. I never imagined Dom had such strong feelings about my so-called lusting over Lucas, and that blindsided me.

So in retrospect, I can't blame him for how he acted, but—

What the hell is that noise?

Shouts emerge from the garage, and not the funny kind. When the second wave sounds, I run over in time to see Dom hit Lucas, then get punched in return. As if the first hits were some kind of catalyst, they go at it with a brutality that leaves me gaping.

Tristan and Finn are on the sidelines, arms crossed over their chests like they couldn't care less. I know my rash judgment is useless considering the reality they live, but it doesn't make me rethink my next actions, either.

"Stop!" The scream escapes me with enough intensity to make the duo on the sidelines turn to me, but it doesn't have the tiniest effect on Lucas and Dom.

I move to get closer, getting as far as passing by Tristan, but Finn wraps his arm around my middle and brings me to a full stop.

"Stay out of this, Luz," he mutters. "This is wolf business."

So they know I know.

I guess word must travel fast in such a small pack—which again begs the question of what the hell I got myself into. Yet my eyes are drawn to the fighters, helpless in Finn's arms as Lucas hits Dom again.

His glare, and the promise from earlier, echo in my mind. I notice the brutality of his punches, the clenched jaw, and wonder how in hell I could have ever felt anything for him. And why did I get so annoyed at Dom when he tried to tell me otherwise?

I groan in Finn's arms, and he must interpret it as a sound of pain. "Dom will be fine, Luz, at least once he submits to Lucas. He crossed paths one too many times, and if he doesn't submit, Lucas has no choice but to kick him out. A beta is no good to a leader unless he listens."

I remember all the times Dom pissed Lucas off on my behalf, for my stupid crush. Tears spring to my eyes, but I refuse to be the weak party in this trio.

A gasp escapes me again when another punch drops Dom to the ground. He's panting, taking in deep breaths. His eyes scan the surroundings, and he notices me in the crowd. Something passes over his expression, and it's enough to make Finn's grip loosen.

I don't waste time trying to understand things out of my control. Instead, I wiggle out of his remaining grip and jump between Lucas and Dom, arms spread on either side to keep them apart.

"Stop!"

Lucas freezes, his fist raised high, and I feel Dom's panting breath on my neck.

"This is stupid, even for you two! You're acting like mutts having a pissing contest, not adults."

Apparently my little speech has its effect, because next thing I know, Lucas moves away. There's a restless energy to him, and on a subconscious level I know I just interrupted something that should have finished.

Yet all I care about is Dom being all right. I turn my gaze to him, but his expression is not welcoming in the least.

"You should have stayed out of it."

"Dom, no, you—"

He shakes his head, pushing past me. "I wouldn't have harmed your pretty boy's face—much."

I don't even get a chance to tell him it was him that had me worried, not Lucas.

CHAPTER TEN

∞ Rebeliune ∞

"Those who excel in virtue have the best right of all to <u>rebel</u>, but then they are of all men the least inclined to do so."

-Aristotle-

Lucrezia

I'm staring, baffled, after Dom, aware but not quite of having eyes on me. By the time I snap out of it, I realize Lucas never left and Finn and Tristan are still here.

So I'm alone. With three werewolves of different abilities, according to Dom.

Rather than cower, I toss my hair back and put my hands on my hips. "Is anyone going to explain what just happened?

Because I'd prefer to understand more before I go hunt down my boyfriend and smack some sense into him."

Not that I'm sure we're still in a relationship at this point... But Lucas doesn't need to see that.

Finn and Tristan share an amused glance, but it's Lucas who holds out his hand towards me in invitation. "Walk with me."

To my surprise, Tristan's face hardens, and he moves towards us. "Talk to her here, with us."

I don't understand why he intervened, but Lucas narrows his gaze. "I'm your alpha. You don't trust her with me, amico?"

Finn, ever the peacemaker, steps in between them. "I think what Tristan is trying to say, albeit failing, is that it might be safer in here. You heard Dom's recounting—"

"—before it broke in a fight..." Tristan's interjection seems to irritate Lucas further, as his jaw clenches. Finn throws him a dark look, then shakes his head.

"Either way, boss, let's take the safe road until we know more."

"Fine." I'm taken aback by Lucas relenting—I thought alphas never back down. Or so my books say.

As if hearing my thoughts, Lucas smirks. "A good leader knows when to listen to his subjects." I try not to show my surprise. *He probably just reads people well.*

Unfortunately for him, his comment gives me ideas. "Great. So am I one of your subjects?"

Lucas tilts his head to the side, eyes darting to the other two. He has no idea where I'm going with this. "Sì... You are under my protection, as is everyone in the pack."

"And by your previous reasoning, you take your subjects' advice into reasoning, right?"

He squints at me, no longer amused yet unable to retract what he'd said. I catch Tristan snickering, but don't get distracted. "Well?" When he nods, I cross my arms over my chest. "Perfect. In that case, I suggest you stop fighting with Dom. I may be new to this, and not grasp all the intricacies of your little wolf pack, but I know this. Nothing good can come from you two fighting, especially when there are creatures and other neo-Nazi wolf packs that lurk around."

I can safely conclude three things, based on his expression. One, Lucas never expected me to talk this much. And two, he never guessed the attitude that hid underneath my overall calm exterior. And three, my words piss him off because I'm right.

Guess he's not the only one who can read expressions.

"Well, Dom sure picked well." The praise comes from Finn, who then walks over to Lucas and smacks him on the shoulder. "Nothing I wouldn't have said myself, boss."

"Nor I."

I glance at Tristan, catching his nod of acknowledgement towards me, and warmth spreads in my chest. For over a year, these guys have not only tolerated my presence here, but made me feel safe. When Tommy reappeared and turned my life upside down, they rallied together and protected me.

Maybe I *am* crazy. But nothing about them scares me. Rather, for the first time in my life, I feel like I belong, like I'm valued and don't have to hide who I really am as a person.

"You may be right." I focus my gaze on Lucas, who widens his stance. "But perhaps your efforts would be better suited convincing your boyfriend to stop ignoring my orders. If he does not obey me, make no mistake. I *will* throw him out of this pack. And a lone wolf is no good—for you, or for this town."

The implication is clear enough – if Dom gets expelled, so to speak, he'd have to leave town. Considering I don't plan to let that happen, I vow to try and change his mind.

"Fine, I will. But can we talk about the elephant in the room? Your guys' abilities?"

"I thought Dom already told you most of it."

I turn to Finn, shaking my head. "He explained he's a vârcolac, and you each have your different abilities. That Lucas' bite can turn me, and Jared's or Aiden's, but we never got much deeper in it."

The guys glance at each other, and I huff. "I know I'm human, and practically useless in your minds in fights. But I took self-defense classes and was more than able to take on Tommy by myself. I also helped Dom during the attack in the woods. So, not completely useless, here." I meet each of their gazes in return. "Please. Tell me."

Lucas retreats at my words, walking into a corner and leaning against a pole. He's watching me with hooded eyes, though I can't read his expression. Some kind of signal must have passed from him to the guys, because they start talking. But the entire time, Lucas is silent and sullen.

Finn gestures to a small stool near one of the cars. "All right, love. Take a seat, this might be a while." Once I do, he begins. "First, you need to understand not all packs are like ours. Mostly, they're larger—twice the size at least—and with only two strong-headed leaders. The alpha and beta. In our case, we're blessed with four heads."

"We all come from different spots of the world," Tristan continues. "Maybe one day we'll tell you our stories, but for now the gist is this. Finn and I each used to belong to a pack, before we left and sought freedom. Dom was a loner from the beginning and ended up here way before us. When me and Finn arrived in Rockland Creek within a few weeks of each other, we were one too many wolves to roam freely."

"So Lucas gave us a choice." I glance to the leader, but he's still resolutely silent, leaving me no choice but to give all my attention to Finn. "Join him in a pack, for a test drive at least.

After six months, if we were fine with how things were going, we would swear allegiance to him."

I had to interrupt at that point. "Is this how it's usually done? Not that I have anything to compare it to except books and mythology, but..."

"You're right, of course." Finn flashes a smile, throwing a look to Tristan who rolls his eyes. "We're a special case."

"He means we're *idiotas*—rejects." I snort at the term Tristan uses. "I'm serious. Lucas took in a bunch of broken kids and gave us a purpose."

I realize then the extent of the bond that links them all. It's more than just the pack, or a hierarchy that ties them. Underneath Lucas' tough exterior, and each guy's secret, there's a deep-seated friendship and trust between them. I'd wager nothing could break it, not even Dom's inability to obey orders.

"So you formed the pack." I try to get them back on track if only because thinking of Dom has my stomach in knots. I don't think the sensation will disappear until I get to talk to him and wipe the slate clean.

"Yeah, and after the six months were up—last summer—we pledged allegiance to Lucas."

I remember what Dom told me, about the pheromones in Lucas being triggered by his new alpha status. My crush on him started in the summer, which means... He was right all along.

Damn. Now I really owe him an apology.

I focus back on Finn, who's now talking about the rules of the pack. "It's simple. We don't show off to humans, stick to ourselves, and try to avoid a turf war with the Reapers."

"And obey the leader."

I ignore Tristan's input, focusing instead on Finn's last words. "The Reapers?"

"That's what we call Jared and his group. How much did Dom tell you about them?"

"Only that they hate humans, and to stay away. I got the impression they're very, um, racist."

Tristan snorts. "You could say that, beleza. Sadly, they're not the only ones. I've traveled enough in the military to have seen worse scums." He shakes his head as if to clear it of a bad memory. "Human hunters wiped out Jared's entire family back in the day. He moved here, but he was broken even as a child. The result is the Reapers."

Despite the easy explanation, I have a feeling there's more to them than that. Plus, I have a hard time grasping their role in all this. "So... What, they wreak havoc on the town?"

Finn glances at Lucas as if wondering how much to tell me. When he nods, Finn faces me again. "They stay away from most humans—unless they have the temerity to land on their land. Then it's open season on humans."

Got it. Stay away from the bad people. "What about the creature?"

The minute the words leave my mouth, I know I might have put my foot on a landmine. Tristan and Finn share shocked glances, and even Lucas straightens up.

"You saw it?"

I nod at Tristan, biting my lip. "It showed up when Aiden's group attacked us. There were... a lot of wolves, and I think even Dom was getting overwhelmed. Then this hellish, deformed wolf stepped out with yellow eyes...." Their gazes widen, and I trail off. "Surely Dom told you."

"No. He didn't." This comes from Lucas, who's now stalking towards me until he towers over me. "What happened with it?"

I bite my lip, unsure how much more to say. Lucas makes it easy when he grasps my forearm, tugging on me. "Lucrezia, *rispondimi!*"

Unfortunately for Lucas, his order to answer him only makes my stubborn side stand out. I jerk out of his grip, scowling. "Ask Dom."

His eyes glitter, but before he can do anything Finn intervenes. "Back off, Lucas. Dom didn't get a chance to tell us anything before you jumped him to assert your alpha."

Whatever Lucas communicates to him via his glare, it's done in silent language and it's enough to aggravate Finn. He clenches his jaw, angling his body so he's partly between me and Lucas. "Dom made it clear Luz is his, and if you harm her, you'll have to pay. You know the rules."

"Does *she*?" Lucas' growl takes me by surprise, but I don't back down. When his dark glare settles on me, he sneers. "Do you even know who you're shacking up with?"

The sting in my palm is the only indication of what I did. I stare down at the redness of it, then into Lucas' face. My imprint is visible on the side of his face, and a muscle ticks in his jaw.

I gulp, realizing I may have pissed off the alpha to the point of no return.

Lucas glares at Finn next, then stomps off. Tristan watches him leave, muscles corded and just as tense. "You alright?"

When he turns his gaze on me, I nod. "Yeah. No harm done."

"Forgive Lucas. He's under a lot of pressure and Dom isn't helping things out."

"Err... I just slapped your alpha. I'm pretty sure he has to forgive *me*, not the other way around."

Tristan snorts at that. "In all honesty, he deserves it when's acting like a *babaca*."

I'm pretty sure he means Lucas is asking like a bastard, but when I glance to Finn for confirmation, he only rolls his eyes and looks at the ceiling. After a beat, I get us back on track.

"What's going on? Besides Dom and Jared's pack? Does it have to do with this creature?"

Finn inclines his head, rubbing the back of his neck. "Yeah. A few weeks ago, bodies of animals showed up, eviscerated. At first we thought it was a human psycho, but all clues seem to point to this monster being the culprit."

"And it skulks around your place, or so Dom told us." Tristan's admission increases my heartbeat. The idea of that monstrosity anywhere near where I sleep is enough to raise the hairs on the back of my neck.

"Why is it... killing like that?"

"We don't know." Finn's admission doesn't make me feel any better. "We've been trying to track it down, but so far only Dom succeeded. Twice, it seems."

I wonder if I should tell them what else I'd seen, as we ran off to the car. When Tristan and Finn level their gazes on me, I sigh. *Might as well.* "You guys will want to up your game...because that creature's not alone."

There's a stunned beat of silence, then Finn steps closer. "What are you going on about, Red?"

"I mean..." I gulp past my nervousness. "When we were fighting the wolves, the only reason we escaped is because of the creature that showed up—along with its buddies. It let us go... That's why Dom and I were able to return here unharmed."

A string of curses escapes Finn, but in contrast Tristan is almost eerily calm. He follows his pacing friend, stepping to him and clasping his shoulder. "Go tell Lucas and find Dom. I'll bring Luz back home and wait until she's safe."

With one last glance at me, Finn takes off. And I'm left wondering if I made a mistake telling them this at all.

"Venha comigo," Tristan says, grabbing his car keys and a light jacket. "Let me tell you some more stories while I take you home... Give you some food for thought."

Dominic

After fighting Lucas, I took off on a run and didn't stop until I was back in the forest where I got attacked. Only four bodies litter the ground—all Reapers, Aiden's guys. Their guts are hanging out, much like the previously attacked animals.

Despite my need to retch and the stench driving me off, I push closer. I might as well try to figure out what's going on here. Maybe it will get Lucas off my back for good.

Why I didn't tell him about the creature letting us go, I don't know. If I had to guess, I would say it has to do with my own theories about what, exactly, it is. I'd seen the way it attacked the Reapers, and I recognized something of myself in it.

So yeah, deep down, I'm just being a coward because I'm afraid Lucas and the guys will turn on me if they figure out Tristan was right and this thing really is a vrykolakas.

Or they'll think I'm contaminated.

Who even knows? Either way, I kept my silence, and now I'm nose-deep in disgusting shit. But as I inspect the carcass of the wolf, I notice something. There's a deeper hole running through its chest, towards...

Ah, hell no.

I rip into the rest of the body with my claws, hoping I'm wrong. But, nope. After a few minutes that leave me bloody, I'm staring at an empty cavity where the heart should be.

And by the way the stomach is gutted open, I realize the one thing we've been missing. These killings are happening while the hosts are still alive. All to take out their beating hearts... and consume them.

I back away, having now received the answers we need. On my way out, I catch a fresh scent and follow it in the woods. My paws are silent on the ground, a shadow in the darkness. Night camouflages me and there's no moon out there to brighten the landscape.

After what feels like an hour, the scent stops. I've reached a frozen river, but a patch of ice is broken through—almost purposefully. I don't even hesitate before jumping in and swimming across. Once on the other side, I take measured steps, not sure if this is a trap or a lair.

The answer comes soon enough when I part through some bushes, keeping low to the ground. I'm on top of some hill, and about twenty feet down and across is the entrance to a cave. It's dug deep in the mountain, pitch black.

I'm not stupid enough to go there without backup, especially since I catch their scents from here. But who are they?

You know the answer to that question.

I jump up, looking around for the voice. Nothing jumps out of the shadows.

We are kindred, you and I.

My eyes keep scanning the surroundings, and they land back down. In the darkness of the cave, I see two yellow eyes staring straight at me. It's only then I realize the wind must have carried my scent down to the creature... And its companions, if I'm to guess by the amount of yellow eyes joining the first speaker.

Shit. I better get out of here.

As I crouch backwards, I hear a tinkling laugh. I run from the monsters as far as my feet will carry me, but out of the corner of my eyes I could have sworn seeing some kind of nymph hop through the trees. Running out of time, and not wanting to get caught, I let it go.

Instead, I push my feet towards The Cave. I know Lucas, at least, will be there tonight as he is every Saturday night.

∞ ♦ ∞

Lucas is playing pool with two human women and Finn. He's fooling around, acting all nonchalant but I see the tension in his back muscles, and in the way he hits the balls too hard.

I clear my throat when I'm behind him. He freezes, as does everyone else around him.

"Leave us." His tone is curt to the girls, who scurry away like scared rabbits. Finn meets my gaze, almost trying to warn me.

Before I can figure out what he means, Lucas whirls around, his fist catching me under the solar plexus with enough force to hurt. I grimace, but don't back away, instead tensing my abs. His next right hook hits me under the jaw, and I stagger backwards.

Still, my eyes don't waver from his face—and that's how I see the hurt and anger in his gaze.

"You not only disobey your leader, but lie to him!" Lucas growls, hitting me again—this time in the ribs. He's switching up his punches on purpose so I can't predict them, and while I could fight back, I choose not to.

I know the deal by now – you do something stupid, there are consequences. This is what I have to suffer through for Lucas to come out winner on the other end.

Finn steps between us when it looks like Lucas won't stop. "We're drawing attention. Let's at least take this outside."

Lucas glances at the bar where people have taken to staring our way. He nods and Finn ushers me outside, Lucas following our trail. My Irish buddy takes advantage of the slight reprieve and whispers, "Luz told me and Tristan about the creature. She didn't tell Lucas, stood up to him."

I glance back, noticing a slight reddening to Lucas' cheek. "Looks like she did more than stand up to him."

"Aye, he might have made a smart comment or two." Finn's mutter has my blood boil, but I know fighting my alpha now would be suicide.

So I push the urge back down instead. We emerge from the back of the bar into the alley they dump garbage in, and I turn to face Lucas. His right hook catches me again in the face, and I step out of his reach.

"Will you hear me out, at least?"

His glare is more telling than his words. "You not only lie to your alpha, but you get your girlfriend to keep secrets. Don't forget she's only protected by this pack at my edict, something I can easily rearrange."

And just like that, my control snaps. I snarl at Lucas, moving closer. "Don't you dare put her in danger to get back at me!"

He searches my expression, his hard as granite. "Tell me what you've been hiding. *Everything.* And then I'll consider it."

Through gritted teeth, I reveal all I know. Aiden's attack in the woods, the creature allowing our escape, and how there's more than one. I even mention finding their lair and their comments to me. At Finn's encouraging nod, I also give Lucas a play-by-play of our interrogation of Tiny, and what he revealed about the Reapers being victims.

When I'm done, I widen my stance, centering myself in case Lucas plans to take another swing at me. Luckily, he's too busy reflecting on the information to say anything, at least for a few moments.

I take advantage of it and turn to Finn. "Where's Luz?"

"Tristan took her home and said he'll make sure she's safe."

"Good." I address my next comment to Lucas. "The creature was around Luz's place because of me. Though I don't understand what this means, or how they're 'kindred' to me, I'm more than happy to play bait."

"No." Lucas' tone catches me by surprise.

"What?"

"You heard me. Remove yourself from this and let me, Tristan and Finn figure out what's going on."

"Don't do this, Lucas, not when you need another person to patrol!"

He steps closer, so we're nose to nose. "I said *no*. Capisci?"

My nostrils are flaring, but by some last shred of control I inhale deeply and not strike back. "Fine."

I turn to leave, but he's not done yet. "And you're also to keep away from Lucrezia."

"Excuse me?"

"Do I need to repeat myself?" He crosses his arms over his chest, raising an eyebrow. "Stay. Away. Do not claim her. I forbid it."

"That's *bullshit*!" I look to Finn for backup, but he only shakes his head in response. "You can't do this!"

Lucas stalks to me and raises his hand to my throat. I grab it midway, not about to submit. We crush each other's grips, snarling. "I am your alpha, and you *will* obey me. I forbid you to claim Lucrezia."

"Fuck you!" I let go of him and storm off, a need raging within me. My wolf is just as agitated, pushing to gain control and fight Lucas for alpha.

I know he's doing it to punish me. Beating me up is not enough, Lucas wants me to submit completely, to drop all my ideas of rebellion and *obey*. The word alone makes my mouth taste metallic, and I realize I'm gritting my teeth so hard I've manage to bite into my lip.

A few deep breaths do nothing to calm me down, so I turn to the closest thing I can—which happens to be the bumper of a car— and slam my fist into it. The bite of pain doesn't even register, and I stomp away.

If Lucas thinks this'll be enough to make me listen, he's sorely mistaken. Nothing and *no one* will keep me away from Luz, not now that she knows what I am, and accepts me.

My feet bring me closer to Luz's place with each angry stomp. I climb up the fire escape, and tap on the window. She appears clad in sweatpants and a shirt and lets me in. Relief is on her face when she hugs me.

"Dom, I was scared! I'm sorry about what I said, you were right about Lucas—"

I stop her with my index on her lips. His name is the last thing I want to hear pouring from her. Then my nostrils flare, smelling...

"Is that my shirt?"

She chuckles, glancing down at the oversized clothing I must have left here last time. "Yeah."

Whatever restraint I have evaporates at the realization my scent is on her. I pull her close, my mouth claiming hers with a fervor I barely recognize. Her lips open under mine, pure heaven. My hands move to her ass, lifting her so her legs wrap around me.

I move us to the dresser, lowering her so she's comfortable. My hands move up to her nipples, grasping them through the shirt and rolling them between my fingers.

Luz moans, and it's music to my ears.

"Dom..." There's an awed quality to her voice, like she's amazed at the sensations running through her, but I'm not about to stop.

"Shh... I may not be able to claim you, but I can give you this."

Lucrezia

His words make no sense, all I'm aware of is the need in my blood.

When Dom showed up, looking an avenging angel in need of consolation, I thought he'd missed me. When his lips made contact with mine, I felt his need, his hunger, and it awakened something inside me.

Now, with his body hovering over mine, his lips on my neck, I feel the ceiling swirl just like everything inside me. There's a tornado trying to take hold of me, something I can't control, something I can't stop...

"Dom..."

His fingers move between my thighs, touching me over my clothing. "Do you want me to stop?"

I manage to open my eyes halfway, enough to read his expression, see the need in his face. That same yearning is unraveling within me, and leaving me panting. One word alone escapes my lips. "No."

Dom takes my mouth again, at the same time his hand pushes aside my panties. His fingers trace me, then move within me, and I am gone. A puddle of nerves, emotions, sensations....

And then all I see is stars.

As my panting subsides, Dom lowers his forehead to mine, hovering just above my lips. When the kiss comes, it's tender and loving, but unforgiving. He takes everything in that embrace, and pulls back without saying a word.

In the darkness, his expression is haunted, his eyes unreadable. I know he wants me, the evidence is there.

Yet in the blink of an eye, he's gone in the night like the most forbidden of dreams.

∞ ∞ ∞

CHAPTER ELEVEN

∞ Schimbare ∞

"The secret of <u>change</u> is to focus all of your energy not on fighting the old, but on building the new."

-Socrates-

Lucrezia

I spend most of Sunday wallowing and waiting for Monday. Dom doesn't call, doesn't come by, and something tells me to give him space. So I do, despite wanting to see him, to figure out what, exactly, happened that Saturday night.

Deep down, I also just want to get it over with and tell him my feelings already. Keeping them locked up makes me go almost crazy, especially when I think of the misunderstanding between us.

In the evening, I see Tristan jogging around my place, and I figure he's probably checking out the area. I'm grateful to them for worrying about me, but I'd rather not be a nuisance or a weak link.

So I spend the remainder of the night working out on self-defense moves, then fall into a fitful sleep. I don't know what to expect the next day when I start work.

After the way we left things, you'd think Dom would at least talk to me, but he won't even look at me. When he shows up at the office, he only nods my way, then heads straight to the garage. Finn and Tristan follow close on his heels, and I'm not about to start a scene with the guys there.

It's not that I'm hurt, per se. I mean he offered me a very wonderful experience, dropped some cryptic words about claiming, then took off. If anything, after my last chat with Lucas, a weird heavy weight seems to have settled in my stomach.

So I bide my time until lunch.

Lucas' glares and sullen attitude are not much better for my nerves, though it doesn't bother me as much as Dom's silence. That, more than anything, confirms what I've already figured out – it's Dom I care about, not Lucas.

Funnily enough, it's only Finn and Tristan that act normal towards me, maybe too much so.

During one of their breaks, Finn comes by to bring me a coffee. He did a run for everyone earlier. It used to fall in my tasks, but by some unspoken agreement it seems to have now gone to someone who can turn into a wolf at a moment's notice.

I'm not sure if this is yet another way to protect me from hidden dangers like the Reapers and those creatures, but I try to see it as protectiveness rather than limitation. I realize they mean well, but there's a limit. Still, I take the coffee from Finn with a smile, and sip it. The warm liquid cascades down my throat, and I grin wider at the hint of hazelnut.

"How did you guess?"

He glances to the garage, catching Dom's eye before he turns away. "A little birdie told me."

I follow his gaze, then sigh. "Why is he keeping a distance, Finn? Last night..."

When I trail off, blushing, he smacks his forehead with a hiss. "Please tell me nothing happened between you two."

Flushing crimson, I avoid his knowing gaze. "Define nothing."

"Christ." He's looking in Dom's direction again. "He must have a death wish."

"What do you mean?"

Finn searches my expression, and I can see the conflict warring in his face. He mutters under his breath and drags me away to the kitchen. "They never said I couldn't tell you. Listen, Lucas ordered Dom to stay away from you."

"But... why?" And why would Dom listen?

As though hearing both my questions, Finn purses his lips. "You have to understand the pack bond, Luz. This has nothing to do with the strength of Dom's feelings for you, but rather with his wolf."

Something in my face must have given me away, because he lets go of my shoulders and moves away, running a hand through his hair. "All right, let's try it this way. A dog loves you unconditionally, yeah?"

I nod, unsure where he's going with the explanation.

"Right, hear me out. So if you had a dog that loves you so, and let's say you own this dog together with Dom. And one day Dom leaves, but orders the dog to stay behind. Then the dog has to listen, despite his unconditional love for you or Dom.... I'm not explaining this very well, am I?"

I chuckle despite my frayed nerves, trying to understand what he's getting at. "No, but I think I get what you're saying. Obeying Lucas is like a compulsion, because Dom is in his pack, right?"

Finn's eyes light up at my simplistic summary. "Right! So, really, it's not his choice. He has to stay away from you if he wants to stay in the pack. And with the way things are now, if Lucas gets cross one more time..."

"Then Lucas and I need to talk." I try to push past Finn, but he grabs me again, immobilizing me.

"You can't!"

"Finn, this is my life. My personal life he's interfering with! And he has no right." Finn grimaces in a way that makes me think I've just put my foot in my mouth. "What?"

"Well, while you're under his protection and the pack's, it means you owe him your obedience too. So, really, he does have the right."

There's a sound pounding in my ears—I can't make out if it's the blood rushing to my temples or just my head exploding. But all that comes out is a low hiss. "*What*? I never agreed to that, nor do I want it!"

"Be that as it may..."

I stomp my foot, huffing. "Fine! Tell me how to un-protect myself or whatever." At his quizzical expression, I elaborate, "How do I make it clear to Lucas that I don't need his pack's protection?"

"You won't like the answer."

I bet I won't.

At my insistent gaze, he relents. "You have to either get under another pack's protection, or mate with an alpha."

"You've got to be kidding me! There's no way to just leave?"

"Not in Lucas' world. He cares too much about each of us to let any harm come to us. And you, well, you're human." He shrugs as if that explains everything, placing one hand on my shoulder. "You'd be free game for any wolf in the region if you weren't with us. And the fact you have our scent on you—"

"Your *what*!?"

Finn holds up his free hand, shushing me. "I mean our wolf scent is around you. Other wolves would think you're open to interacting with them or..."

"Being turned."

I jump at his voice, turning to see Dom enter the kitchen. His glare falls on Finn's touch on my shoulder, which he drops as if I'm scorching him and takes a step back.

"What's going on here?"

My voice comes out biting. "So now you care?" Yes, I wanted his attention, but not in this way, as if he's marking his territory. What I want is to talk, but my desires seem to be a moot point right about now.

Dom clenches his jaw, glancing at Finn. He makes a move to leave, but I hold onto his sleeve. "I'm not done asking you questions!"

The thought crosses my mind that I'm putting Finn in an uncomfortable position, but he's a well of knowledge and I need any information I can get out of him to navigate these waters. Then perhaps I can figure out a way to get Dom out of his compulsion, and back in my arms.

Which reminds me, we never talked about our relationship. I turn to where Dom was, but find only an empty spot. "Dammit!"

"He'll come around." Finn's pitiful reassurance does nothing to boost my mood.

"Yeah. As soon as Lucas gets off his high horse and allows us to be together. This is such *bullshit*. Is there no way around this, Finn?"

I don't know if it's the tears brimming in my eyes or my pleading tone, but Finn sighs. Something in the way his shoulders droop and he leans against the wall, staring at the ceiling, brings me hope.

"There may be something. But this is just a theory, and I have no way of proving it."

"Please, tell me."

He takes a deep breath, then nods. "All right."

Dominic

Staying away from Luz is enough to drive my already tense body into turmoil. Especially after last night. But Lucas' orders are clear in my head.

I could have challenged him for alpha, but I would have been wrong. With all his faults, he's a good leader—if pigheaded when it comes to me and Luz. But despite my fury, and my wolf's resentment, I cannot deny a simple fact. This pack protects Luz. And that, if nothing else, is the cold shower I needed all along.

I'm not staying away for the sake of obeying. I've never been the puppy Lucas tries to make me. But I also don't want to get kicked out of the pack that is protecting Luz. On my own, I have nothing to offer her. Here, she remains safe.

And I intend to keep her so.

I need a few days to figure out how to smooth things over with Lucas, then I'm sure I can change his mind. He may not let me mate with Luz, but he should allow me to get closer—to date her.

For most of the morning, I'm busy tearing apart the engine of an old Challenger. Its owner inherited it from his grandfather and wants to add a new engine, new wheels, and fine tune it. It's a complicated enough job and it keeps my mind from wandering.

Finn with Luz was an image I didn't need in my already thick head. For all I know, Lucas is trying to set her up with Finn to get back at me.

Not even your alpha would play such games.

I try to listen to the voice of reason—really, I do. But it's hard. Then Finn walks back in the garage and heads for Lucas and Tristan who are working on a pickup.

"I need to take off for a few days, a week at most."

My wolf points its head, none too happy. I keep working on the engine, but slow my movements so I can listen in to the conversation.

"Why?" Lucas asks.

Finn glances at me and I pretend not to notice it. "Luz wants to go out of town. With Tommy incarcerated, she thinks she may have access to things from her old place, stuff she had to leave behind in a hurry."

Sensing their eyes on me, I stop working and drop my tools, facing them. "What?"

Lucas arches an eyebrow. "You got a problem with Finn's suggestion?"

I have a problem with you playing fucking mind games, Lucas. Instead of voicing that out loud, I shake my head. "Nope."

"Really?"

Yes, I have a fucking problem with another wolf near my girl. Even more so at the thought of him in the same car, protecting her. Taking the spot I should be in. But I'm not planning to admit this to you.

With a careless shrug, I go back to tinkering with the car. Tristan tells Lucas to drop it, and I see him nod to Finn. *Great. The fucker got permission. So much for buddy loyalty.*

To top it off, he has the nerve to come near me. Out of earshot from Lucas and Tristan, I keep my voice low—too low for even their wolf ears to pick it up. But I know about Finn's particular affinity.

"I'd watch your step if you get closer, mate."

Finn hesitates, but I hear his whisper. "We're doing this for you. I swear."

I glance up then, meeting his earnest gaze. "Who's we? You and Luz?"

At his nod, I sigh and release all the tension in my body. "What do you want from me, my permission?"

A hesitant grin, then, "Your car keys. There's no way mine can make the trip we need."

I scowl at him for a long moment, then dig into the pocket of my jeans and toss them. Finn catches them midway, and I see Lucas turn our way in surprise.

Yeah, I'm letting him borrow my girl and *my car. Go fuck yourself, Lucas.*

Finn smirks as if hearing my thoughts. "I'll bring them *both* back unscratched."

"You better, mate. Else it's your ass on the line."

Finn nods and takes off. Through the glass between the garage and the reception, I see Luz grab her jacket and they leave together.

Fuck me.

Lucrezia

Finn lied to them. He had to because it was not likely Lucas would agree to our little quest, at least not freely. In truth, I'm not sure even Dom would agree, since it's all tied in to his lineage and identity. And the answer to that might solve all our problems... *If* Finn is right.

So we take the long drive to New York City, where we can access internet, historical records, genealogy and everything that money can buy. Finn drives the entire ten hours, not even complaining about it, while I nap on and off.

When I wake up for the last time, it's to a gray sky and huge buildings. Cement and glass everywhere, and people. So. Many. *People.* I've heard NYC is the city that never sleeps, but jeez... On a Tuesday early morning, it's packed.

We park the car in an underground parking lot, then head out on foot.

"Where to first?" Finn asks.

I think about what little Dom told me. He said it had been an American couple that adopted him from the orphanage in Romania, and as far as he knew the adoption was finalized in the New York state. Which leaves us with one possibility where to start.

"The city hall."

∞ ♦ ∞

A week of searching later and countless nights spent awake pouring over records amount to snippets of information, but nothing concrete other than Dominic's true last name is not Kosta. And then there are the circles of bureaucracy we've fallen into...

One day, when I'm close to give up, I stumble upon something at the library.

"Finn, over here!"

We've been spending half days in the largest library we could find, both researching history and archives. At my not-so-whispered shout, Finn rushes from the latest bookshelf he's been perusing. I point at the screen of the computer I'm using, trying to contain my excitement.

"I found it! His birth name was Dominic Konstantin."

He gapes at the entry, then snaps out of it. "Konstantin... That rings a bell. Hang on. Hey buddy, can I borrow your computer?"

The nerdy kid who's busy playing some war game on the computer next to mine snorts and mumbles something, not even acknowledging Finn. So my companion does what he's been doing best all week, and loses his cool. For some reason, it seems people in NYC respond to authority—more or less.

Either way, Finn yanks the kid out of the seat, ignoring his complaints. "Sorry, emergency." Then his fingers are flying across the keyboard until he pulls up a different website.

Familii de Regi Române.

"What does that say? You can read Romanian?"

Finn shakes his head at my questions and hits the English button, translating the page instantly for both of us.

Families of Romanian Kings.

"What!?"

My outburst a few people in the vicinity, and I'm shushed into silence. Finn throws me a look to quiet me down. "Konstantin is an old Romanian name, as old as some lineages of kings. But this isn't what I'm searching for..."

He hunts for another five minutes that feel like an eternity, and lands on a few other pages before stopping on a particular one. I see depictions of werewolves, and something darker. A gasp escapes me when I recognize the creature from the forest.

"That's it!"

Finn stares at the picture. "That's what attacked you?"

"Yes!"

He nods, scanning the page for the text, but I'm too impatient to stay quiet. "What language is that?"

"Some mix of Latin... I can understand parts of it. It says here the vârcolaci split into five families, but they were all strigoi."

"What's a strigoi?"

"Vampires... Very undead." His voice is flat, and shivers run up my spine. "There's an entire history. And we were right, Luz. Dom's lineage goes way back."

We print the entire thing and hop back into the truck. This time, I spend the entire ten hours reading every bit of the history, and my heart lightens with every passage.

An exhausted half a day later, Finn drops me off in front of Claws Auto Shop, where I wait for Dom to get out. I step out of the shadows when I see him lock up.

"Dom."

Dominic

"Luz?"

She looks tired, and the jeans seem baggier on her than before. A week is a long time for me to go through every worst scenario in my head. But seeing her here, a mere few feet away from me, is almost enough to stop my heart.

I scan the surroundings, realize she must have waited here alone, and snap. "What are you thinking? There are dangers out at night. Where the hell is Finn?"

She rolls her eyes, unimpressed. "You won't even acknowledge me, but you lecture me about safety? And Finn dropped me off only two minutes ago. Trust me, I'm safe."

A growl surrounds us, and I realize it's coming from me. I stop, then take a deep breath. "What is it?"

She lifts a stack of pages, waving them in my face. "I have to show you something." There's a spark to her gaze, a tone in her voice that makes me jealous this discovery happened with Finn around.

"Not a good time."

Jealous *and* petty, apparently. But Luz is not one to give up. "Too bad. Cause you're walking me home. Unless you want me to walk alone. In the dark."

I scowl and grab her hand.

"I knew you'd see it my way!" She laughs.

Damn this woman!

We walk to her apartment, and I relish the touch of her hand in mine. Lucas has been off my back since Finn and Luz left. Maybe he saw my acceptance of this as a gesture of good will, who knows? I can't pretend to know his mind.

But two nights ago, he even let me join in a patrol around the area. Not that we found anything, and he refuses to go to the lair. He reasons there are too many creatures around and we don't understand what their purpose here is.

Since they've been staying away, we do the same while we gather information. Know thy enemy and all. I don't agree with the softball approach, but I've learned to take it low. Plus, the fact we're not really exploring my familial connection to these monsters eases my mind. Maybe I was wrong, after all.

I glance down at Luz, noticing her furrowed brow. Again, my gaze drops to the stack of papers in her hands. "So where did you and Finn go?"

Though I try to keep the jealousy out of my voice, it's a failed attempt. She smiles, looking up at me. "Jealous?"

I tug her towards me, pressing her against the wall in one movement. She gasps, grasping onto the front of my shirt. "You know I am." My admission is a low rumble, but she seems to like it as she licks her lips.

"Kiss me, Dom. Please?"

How can I resist such temptation? My mouth drops to hers, taking and devouring, leaving no prisoners. Luz hangs on, only able to moan and melt closer.

When I pull back enough to catch my breath, she's left panting. "What about Lucas' orders?"

"Fuck his orders."

And I mean it. No agony is worthy being separated from her, and no heaven compares to how complete she makes me feel. Lucas will have to get on board, one way or another.

Our lips melt together again, and this time I'm coaxing her, plundering, until the torture is more than either of us can stand.

There's a burning need inside me to claim her, to make her mine once and for all. My wolf growls, wanting the same. As if sensing my thoughts, Luz pushes me away, and I tense.

"What is it?"

There's no distress in her expression, only hesitation. "I need to tell you something."

∞ ∞ ∞

∞ Greşeli ∞

"There are only two <u>mistakes</u> one can make along the road to truth; not going all the way, and not starting."

-Buddha-

Dominic

Every scenario runs through my head, but my treacherous mind zeroes in on the worst. "Did something happen with Finn?"

Luz's eyes widen. "What?" Then she gets angry, flushing a nice shade of pink. "Seriously, Dom?"

I cup her cheeks between my hands, trying to backtrack. "Sorry." My lips press against her and I'm kissing her again, apologizing all over. "My head's messed up. I missed you so damn much."

My admission seems to pacify her, at least enough that she tugs on my shirt to get my attention. "No, nothing happened with Finn. We were working day and night trying to uncover this for you. It was his idea, you know."

Now I'm confused. "What was?"

Luz glances around, and I realize we're still out in the open. "Let's get to my place, then I'll tell you."

I follow her home, racking my brain to figure out her cryptic words. Finn had hinted at much the same, saying, *We're doing this for you*. But what?

Once we're inside Luz's place, she takes off her jacket and gestures to the sofa. I refuse her silent request to sit. "Can we get this over with? I hate waiting."

She bites her lip, and I realize my tone was a tad harsh. I try to soften it, stepping closer and tucking a wayward strand behind her ear, enjoying her slight shiver. "There are many other ways I'd prefer to have this reunion and none involve going over the papers in your hands. Let's get it over with."

Luz nods, then pecks me before rifling through the stack. "I guess I should explain where the idea came from. I was mad over you ignoring me, listening to Lucas—"

"He's my alpha, *draga mea*. I can't disobey him." My words have less conviction than before, seeing as I'm doing exactly that by being around her.

She waves off my interruption, and paces away. Her hair bounces with every movement, and in the dim light it looks almost like living fire. "I know that. Or, well, Finn explained it. Sort of." She grimaces, as if recalling something. "He made a terrible analogy about dogs and their masters."

I'm going to kill him.

Then Luz shakes her head and lifts the paper my way. "Anyway, this is research. About you and your lineage. See, when I vented to Finn about alpha rules and crap, and pushed him about another way to break the compulsion to your leader, he admitted a theory he had."

"Theory about what?"

She smiles at my grumble, though I find nothing funny in the situation. "About why you're so thick-headed and clash with Lucas, despite being his beta."

"But you just said it – I'm thick-headed. We've always had our issues, this didn't start with you."

"Perhaps you're right." Luz lifts a paper. "But there's a reason for it."

Too impatient to wait, I snatch them out of her hands and pour over the words. It's Romanian pages translated to English, riddled with mistakes from whatever translator they used. Despite the jumble of words, I realize I'm staring at a history of Romanian Kings.

I glance back up and Luz, who's biting her thumb nail while waiting. "What is this?"

She blows an exasperated breath at my confused expression and grabs the papers back. "If you'd had half the patience until I finish.... Yeesh." She plops down on the floor, spreading the papers everywhere. "All right, here's the gist of it. Finn and I were in New York City, hunting through adoption records. *Your* adoption records. And we discovered your last name isn't Kosta, like your adopted parents let you believe. It's Konstantin. They must have thought it was too long or something."

I frown at the piece of information, trying out the new name. "Dominic Konstantin... Has a nice ring to it, I guess. So what?"

Luz shifts in place, then says, "Your parents had you while still young, and they were good people. Both were teachers at a local elementary school, until a house fire in the middle of winter killed them." Her eyes search mine, filled with tears. "You had a dog as a small child, and he woke you up in time to save you. But your parents... They died of smoke inhalation." A pause, then, "I'm so sorry, Dom."

Maybe it's because I'm no longer an orphan, but an adult who found his other half...Or maybe because I have my pack? Either way, the revelation doesn't feel earth shattering, but rather like closure. When I speak, I'm surprised to find my voice even-toned. "Don't be. On some level, I think I expected something terrible had to take them away from me.

It's funny… Even though I can't remember their faces, their love is something that I can't forget."

Luz moves closer, then gently pulls me into a hug. I breathe in her scent, and it calms my longing for a family, at least for the moment. Then I make the mistake of glancing at the paper closest to her knee, which looks suspiciously like a family tree.

I pull away from her, lifting up the paper so I can get a better read. "This isn't an adoption record."

It's a diagram, of houses. In Romania, Wallachia back then, the land was divided amongst houses. Akin to nobles, they were the aristocracy of the time. There's a particular house that's circled in red, and my heart nearly stops. *Drăculești—House of Basarab.*

"I…I know that name." My eyes meet hers, and this time the words choke in my throat. *If this is true, if I'm related to that house…* The image of the monsters from the forest flashes in my mind. There's no doubt then as to how they're my brethren.

Luz tilts her head at my expression, a slight frown creasing her forehead. Then she peaks over my shoulder to see what has me so stunned. "Oh, that. You're looking at the wrong thing, silly." She crawls in my lap to reach the paper, pointing just under the rectangle I'd been staring at. "There."

My eyes catch what I missed the first time around. *Vlad III.*

Cue my jaw dropping, and Luz laughing as if it's the funniest thing in the world. "That's..."

"Vlad the Impaler, I know! Isn't it amazing?"

I don't think amazing is the word I'd use, considering my *gifts*. "We're talking about the source of all Dracula legends."

"Mhmm." Her sparkling green eyes tell me there's more to the story, but I'm too hung up on this to push forward.

"Luz... This can't be."

"There's more!"

I get up from the ground, pacing a few feet, then turning back to her. My hands are shaky when I run them through my hair, still trying to wrap my mind around this. "This is impossible. I can't be related to Vlad freaking the Impaler."

Luz rolls her eyes, hunting for another paper. "You are, and you can get over it now. It's something to proud of, not something to fear."

"Lucrezia." This is the first time in close to a year I've called her by her full name, and it's enough to get her attention. "You don't understand. If this is true, then those creatures in the forest—"

"We'll get to that."

Say what? When I voice something a little more intelligible than that out loud, Luz waves me off. "It's not as big of a deal as you're making it."

I gape at her, unable to rein in my shock. "I'm a *werewolf*! And you're telling me I'm related to a *vampire*?"

"Vârcolac and strigoi."

Her words freeze me in my steps. "What...?"

Luz doesn't glance up from the papers, talking out of the corner of her mouth. "The correct terms are vârcolac and strigoi, if you go by Romanian folklore. Though, technically, Finn says Tristan calls the bad vârcolaci by their Greek name, vrykolakas, but we'll get to those later."

I grab her shoulders and force her to stay still. "How do you *know* all this?"

"Your buddies talk. A lot."

I scowl. "And you've had time to talk to them?"

"Yup." She notices my bemused expression and quickly brushes her lips against mine, as if consoling a sulking child. Her kiss distracts me, as does her contaminating joy.

"All right, hit me with the rest of it."

She pulls back on her heels and reaches behind me to pull the paper she wanted. "There's another thing about Vlad, other than all the stories of vampires and impaling people. Read this."

I squint where she points, making out one word. "Voivode. What's that?"

"See, we took a while to figure it out. But it means prince. He was prince of Wallachia."

"How is it you know so much more about my country's history than I do?"

Luz laughs at my annoyed tone. "Because I haven't been busy running around chasing rabbits. And there's a thing called a library, and internet."

My scowl doesn't improve with her explanation, but she ignores me. "There's more. As prince of Wallachia, Vlad's line was assured by his own offspring. Cue a few centuries down, and your great-great-great-grandfather emerged from the lineage. Born out of wedlock, a bastard to one of Vlad's offspring, he was a piece of work, but still technically had heregie—heredity, blue blood." I know she means the last part for my benefit. And despite it, I find this history interesting.

Who would have thought it explained my issues with authority? Still, something doesn't make sense. "Luz, but we're still talking about Dracula here. His genes would carry vampire traits, not werewolf."

"Yeah, that's what Finn thought, too. Until I found this." She reveals yet another piece of paper, this one a study published by an old Romanian hermit. "Vlad was a carrier of both genes. That's why he was able to change shapes. Remember stories of him turning into a bat, or a wolf? He was a shifter who lived off blood."

I motion for her to continue, curious to see what else Luz unearthed.

"This is where the story kind of breaks apart, until Finn found a link back to it. So this old relative of yours, after a few crimes and such, was excommunicated from his community by a Romanian priest. Some said at the time it was a political move, destined to kill the last of the line of Vlad the Impaler."

Her blue eyes settle on me, but I can only shake my head. "I had no idea about any of this."

"I know." Her tone is soft, and she rests her forehead against mine. "Should I keep going?"

I won't lie, I hesitate. There is that old saying about leaving dead ghosts to lie in the past... But I was always a stubborn bastard, and today no more so.

"Go on."

Luz nods, then picks up another paper. "While Finn was digging this up, I researched werewolves. And there's a lot of your species, I mean... It's kind of mind-boggling, what different abilities they have. There's even some that are more like shifters and can turn into birds!"

I tap her nose to get her attention, much as I enjoy her excited tone. Luz blinks, then focuses back on the paper. "Right. Anyway, so this excommunicated relative. In the legends, they always say that if a poor soul dies excommunicated, then he returns to life as a vârcolac. Of course, they forget to explain you need to have the gene carried through the family."

"Which was the case for my great-great-whatever, because he was a descendant of Vlad."

"Exactly. So after he died, rather than move on, his soul was tortured and wouldn't let go of the body. He was resurrected as the undead and haunted his entire community. This led to the priest himself being excommunicated, and the town by comparison. The then-king dispatched a group of soldiers to kill everyone and cleanse the area, but it was already too late. They had died at the hands of your relative and returned as vârcolaci. This was the first full tribe of them in that area, and they roamed the land recruiting many more with them."

Images of blood-thirsty monsters, what we called vrykolakas, fill my head. As if catching onto my thoughts, Luz says, "Vrykolakas. I should really be using Tristan's term for them, it seems much more appropriate."

"So they're also descendants from Vlad's lineage, like me?"

Luz meets my gaze, and for a moment I fear she might not have connected the dots yet. That I could have become like that. But she nods, biting her lip. "Yeah. They're the rotten apples, so to speak."

My relief at her taking all this in stride is short-lived as I recall there's a pack of them living not too far from us, and my arms wrap around Luz's waist. She leans into me, lost in the story.

"Somewhere down this whole line of carnal consumption, more vrykolakas appearing and more death, the Church accepted one of them back into the fold. There are two records of the story, one saying that a priest exorcized him, and the other that the vrykolakas found his own salvation through some mysterious benefactor." She looks at me again. "No one really knows what happened. But the bottom line is, he was cured."

"And he lived happily ever after?"

"Not quite..." Luz bites her lip, then says, "He became a missionary for peace. His life's work was to cure vrykolakas of their evil and turn them onto the right path. The studies I read, I mean, they say these monsters can actually be turned back to regular vârcolaci, through exorcism and a baptism from the Church. Your relative, he helped a lot of them... And some not."

"Okay... So what's the direct link to me?"

"That guy was your great-grandfather."

The words pass my ears, but I take a moment to assimilate them, let alone understand what Luz is saying. "He cured people?"

"Mhmm."

"So that's why I'm... not a monster?"

Her eyes soften, and she melts into me further. "You'd never be a monster to me, Dom. But yes, his salvation ensured every child born with his blood was safe."

"So there's more of my family out there?"

Luz taps her chin at that, hesitating. "The little we could find was an uncle and cousin, but they're... vrykolakas. They sinned and in their life of crime were killed. Only, instead of dying, they rose as undead."

"That's what happens to my kind?"

Luz nods, her gaze unwavering from mine. "Finn says that's what Tristan saw, in the wars he fought. It was why he guessed what you were way before you said anything."

Fuck.

I move Luz off me and get to my feet again. There's restlessness inside me, but I refuse to let it be. "Is there more?"

"Yes... But don't you see it, yet?"

"See what?"

"Dom... This is why you weren't backing down from the fight with Lucas!" Luz gets to her feet, her eyes shining again. "Your lineage descends from a prince of Wallachia. *The Impaler.* Your relatives have all been heads of packs, leaders in some way or another. Dom... Being a subordinate is impossible for you."

"Stop."

I know what she's getting at, yet I fear hearing it. But Luz is too far gone, the excitement almost vibrating in her voice. "You could be alpha of your own pack!"

I stare at her, my mind going haywire again. "Wow. You must really want an alpha for a mate, huh?"

She freezes at the tone of my voice, and I can tell she's taking a mental step back, analyzing my body language.

"That's not it at all," Luz stutters, but I'm shaking my head and walking towards the door. I need to be away from her, to think about this. "Dom, wait!"

My hand is on the door knob, but I take a deep breath. "This arrangement isn't working anymore."

"No, it isn't."

Luz's words surprise me enough to turn around, and I see the relief in her expression. She steps nearer, closing the distance between us one inch at a time. "I don't want to pretend to be with you anymore."

Did she... My wolf pokes his head, but I'm zeroing in on Luz's movements like my breathing depends on it.

"I want to be with you, period."

My hand drops from the knob, and I'm already taking a step towards her. "What did you just say?"

"You were right about Lucas, but not about why I stepped between you in that fight. You didn't let me explain that day, but it was because of you. I couldn't stand to see you hurt. Dom, I want you, only you and—"

I move before she can react, my hand wrapping around her neck and pulling her close. Then my lips are cutting off her air supply, and I don't plan to let her up for a long, long time.

Lucrezia

After a make-out session that leaves my toes curling and every nerve in my body going haywire, Dom says I seem tired and we should rest. While I crawl into bed, he hops atop the blankets, crossing his arms under his head.

A heartbeat later, I move closer, resting my head on his chest and listening to the rise and fall of his breathing. "I missed you too, you know."

One hand drops around my waist, pulling me tighter. "Good. Because I wanted to rip Finn's head for taking off with you."

I can't help my chuckle against him, though a peek up to his expression shows me he's not amused. My body stretches until I can brush my lips against his, then meet his blue eyes full on. "This coming from the player of Rockland Creek?"

He rolls his eyes, scoffing. "You give me far too much credit. People talk a lot, Luz. Doesn't mean they always tell the truth."

I hesitate to ask my next question, but I do anyway. "So you haven't been as...prolific as they make you be?"

His expression softens at that and he kisses my forehead. "Nope." He waits a beat, then arches an eyebrow. "This is serious territory we're getting into. So you meant it when you said you're done pretending?"

I nod, wrapping my arm around him as far as I can reach and burrowing my head in his chest. "I think I've always known deep down that it was only lust I felt for Lucas. But it was easier to accept that than the fact I might be falling in love with you. That meant I had to share myself with you, and all my vulnerabilities."

Though I do my best to avoid his gaze, Dom lifts my chin with his index. "You know you can always trust me."

"I do. But it wasn't easy. Now that we're here though, I mean to be in it completely, whatever that entails." I search his gaze, biting my lip. "What *does* that entail, exactly?"

Dom drops my chin, throwing his head back and looking up at the ceiling. "Lucas' approval."

I raise myself to my elbows. "Even with everything I told you?"

"Sort of. Here's the thing, Luz. A lone wolf is dangerous, reckless. I've been there, and something settled in me when I became part of this pack. Though I'm not a fan of obedience, I've been able to make do. Lucas' little games where we're concerned will have to stop, make no mistake about that. But

I also want to stay... I like it here. I like being where I am, with you."

I nod, understanding on some level. "But what I told you..."

"It helps fight the compulsion, meaning I don't intend to let you go anymore. And we will be upfront with Lucas and let him do whatever."

"What about claiming me?" He lifts his head, looking down at me in surprise. "That's what you said the night when we... When you..." A blush creeps on my cheeks and I trail off.

"Do you understand what you're asking me?"

Something in his tone has me fight my embarrassment and meet Dom's expression. There's an intensity in his gaze, same as what I saw there that night, and my breath stops for a second. The thing is, I know what it means—I can guess. And I want it so much it scares me.

Dom must read conflict on my expression because he cups one cheek and runs his thumb over it. "Don't worry, *iubirea mea*. When you're ready, and only then, we'll talk about claiming."

I gulp, nodding my head in assent. Dom's eyes flash in response, and I can feel his wolf held at bay. Then he smiles, and it warms my insides, making me melt against him again.

"What does that mean, *iubirea mea*?"

"My love."

I grin against his chest, then the rise and fall lulls me to sleep.

∞ ◆ ∞

The next morning, the smell of bacon and eggs wakes me up. After a shower and a change of clothes, I tiptoe into the kitchen. Dom's seated at my tiny dining table, flicking through his phone without much purpose.

He looks up even though I make no noise and grins as his eyes take me in—yoga pants, t-shirt and sneakers. "Breakfast?"

I glance at the table full of enough food for five people and laugh. "Are you trying to fatten me up?"

"Maybe."

A chuckle escapes me as I walk over and kiss him, then take a seat at the table and fill up a plate with goodies. "So I take it this is my reward for all the info I dumped on you last night?"

Dom chokes on a bite of bacon, then laughs, low and rumbling. "You could say that."

I grin into my plate, unable to hold it back. With everything out between us, it feels good to be...free. Normal. Vulnerable.

We're silent as we eat, but halfway through I point to Dom's phone. "Anything from Lucas?"

"Nah, just Finn asking if it's safe to come in to work today."
He grins, eyes glittering. "I told him you assured me nothing
happened and I won't bite his head off."

I roll my eyes, then another thing pops in my head. "Dom,
those creatures that attacked us in the forest, you're also
pretty convinced they're like the vrykolakas from my
research, right?" When he nods, I add, "Did you tell Lucas?"

He drops his fork down, grimacing. "He knows enough, but
not everything. I found their lair in a cave nearby here, but
Lucas doesn't want to attack, he wants to get more
information. If I was to guess, I'd say it'll be part of the
blowout today."

Nervousness cuts my appetite and I stop eating, munching
on my biting lip instead at the thought of what would greet
us today at the shop. Dom points to my plate. "Done?"

I nod and help him clean up, packing the rest of the food in
the fridge. Before we leave, Dom tugs on my hand and pulls
me in his arms. He lowers his mouth to mine, savoring my
lips like the tastiest of wine, before letting me go.

And somehow, facing Lucas doesn't seem so bad anymore.

∞ ∞ ∞

∞ Timpul ∞

"<u>Time</u> flows away like the water in the river."

-Confucius-

Lucrezia

It doesn't take long for Lucas to snap after we walk into the shop. Only, rather than go for Dom, he surprises me by asking to speak to me privately.

With Dom in the garage with the guys, I step into Lucas' office. He's sitting behind his desk, a glare settled on me. "Are you decided to disobey my orders, too?"

Something in his tone sparks the wrong reaction in me. Rather than take on a more submissive attitude, I cock my hip and raise my chin towards him. "What orders? As far as

I was aware, you told me to print your new reports, which is what I was doing before you interrupted me."

He scowls at my words, leaning over his desk. "That's not what I'm talking about, cara. You do not understand what you've gotten involved in with Dominic, Lucrezia."

"Actually, I do. We had a very lengthy conversation about it last night after my return. And this is happening—us together—whether or not you like it."

"Bene. You want to play it that way, we will." He stands up and takes a few steps towards me. Despite the darkness in his expression, I don't move. "You think you know how this works, but you don't. Dom cannot be going around ignoring my orders—not even for his mate."

I scowl at that, crossing my arms over my chest. "So what do you expect me to do?"

"Rein him in." Lucas steps closer, towering over me. "As his mate, you can influence him."

"You forget he can't claim me thanks to your stupid rules."

Lucas' eyes narrow on me and he mimics my stance. "Somehow, I don't remember you being this stubborn."

"Funny, I don't recall you being such an ass either."

We glare at each other for a moment, then a corner of his mouth twitches in a half-grin. A few weeks ago, it would have made my heart flutter, but all it does now is annoy me. Scoffing, I spin on my heels and walk off.

"One more thing."

His words make me pause, but only barely as I wait for the rest, not turning to face him.

"I expect you to stay away and safe while we investigate these animal killings and figure out what the creatures are up to."

"Bite me." The words leave my lips as I storm out of the office, half-hoping he didn't catch it. But Lucas' loud guffaw behind me tells me he heard.

Damn wolf hearing.

I'm shaking my head at the so-called pack leader, when I turn a corner and run smack into Dom.

Dominic

I glance from Luz to Lucas in his office, a half-smile playing on his lips and amusement in his dark eyes. It's obvious he's trying to play me, yet I can't help rising to the challenge—especially after what she told me about my background.

So I do what a wolf in my position does best, and stake my claim. With one finger, I tilt Luz's chin up and drop my mouth to hers, savoring her lips.

Enough!

Lucas' order is loud and clear, but I ignore him. Instead, I take my sweet time wrapping up the kiss. By the time I pull back, I sense his energy like a dark cloud. But all I care about is Luz's dazed expression staring up at me, lips still red from our kiss.

"You good?"

She nods, taking my hand in hers. "Nothing I can't handle."

We're about to head back to the reception area when Lucas shows up around the corner. "Dominic."

He rarely, if ever, calls me by my full name, so it gets my attention. He jerks his head towards his office, a silent command to join him. Luz tugs on my hand instead, but I kiss her forehead and follow him. "I'll be back in a second."

In Lucas' office, he closes the door and faces me with an ever-growing scowl. "I ordered you not to claim her."

"And I haven't—yet."

A muscle ticks in his jaw, and he steps closer. "My orders still stand. And you are aware what the punishment will be."

"You do whatever you want, Lucas. I want to be in this pack, and continue being your beta, not that you make it easy. But I love this girl and I am not about to let her go. So either you get with the program or kick me out, your choice."

I move past him to the door, but can't resist tossing one last thing over my shoulder. "Before you decide, you should know those creatures and I *are* related, and I may be your best bet at catching them. Maybe it's time you stop keeping me away and use me instead in this, *boss*."

When I walk away, a huge weight has vanished off my shoulders. Luz's expression when I get to her tells me all I need to know, and this day can't get any better.

∞ ♦ ∞

It's the middle of the night, and Luz is sleeping sprawled over me, her red hair a flaming curtain over her face. No damn birds have disturbed my sleep, yet my eyes snapped open for some reason or other.

I turn my nose up, sniffing. There's an odd scent in the air, something sweet and... *Cinnamon?*

With careful movements, I shift Luz off me and slide out of bed. I'm still wearing only my sleeping sweatpants, so I walk barefoot towards her living room.

When I turn the corner, I stop dead in my tracks, unsure if I'm hallucinating or dreaming.

There's a woman in Luz's living room, but she's not in solid form. She has a glow around her and her entire being seems to be... fluid, like water. She has long, wavy brown hair with eyes the color of the sun. A robe of flowers wraps her body, and she faces me with the smile of an angel.

I gape, recognizing her from legends of long ago. "You can't be real."

She laughs, a sound like running water, and floats closer. When she speaks, a faint Eastern European accent lines her voice. "Why not? *You* are, and you are a wolf. More the stuff of dreams and myths, not reality, no?"

I can't seem to pick up my jaw off the floor while I try to wrap my head around this latest development. "You're Ileana Cosânzeana, but what are you doing here?"

She tilts her head, and her hair flows around her shoulder. Her appearance distracts me, though she's even more ethereal than the stories picture her. Shit, I can't even believe I'm standing in front of her.

Back home, she's the embodiment of the ultimate heroine, the savior of women, the perfect goddess. As a demi-goddess, she's linked to many stories of white magic, but I never imagined...

Ileana smiles, and it's like a thousand suns. "You found your other half, wolf. Now it's time to get your strength. Come with me..."

I glance towards the bedroom, then follow her. After all, what else are you supposed to do when a thousand-year-old immortal shows up on your doorstep?

Lucrezia

"Have either of you guys seen Dom?"

I've been as patient as I could be after waking up alone this morning and no word of where he'd gone. But now it's almost lunch, and he hasn't shown up to work, nor called, yet the guys are acting as if it's normal.

So, at the risk of sounding like a clingy girlfriend, I stepped on my pride and walked into the garage when Lucas was not around.

Tristan ignores my question, bending over the car he's tinkering with, but Finn glances up and shakes his head. "Sorry, love. Not since last night."

I bite on my lower lip, hesitating to push. I can tell they're busy, what with Dom not around and Lucas off who knows where. But I can't shake the feeling something is wrong. The connection between the creature and Dom keeps going on a loop in my mind, and I shuffle my feet.

"Will you spit it out already?"

Tristan's growl makes me jump, but he's not even looking at me, focused on polishing the emerald green Porsche now. *He must have had another bad night, judging by the circles under his eyes.* I swallow past the lump in my throat, glancing at Finn. "How much did you tell him, of what we found out?"

Finn drops his tool at that, straightening up from under the car. It's odd to have his green eyes focused on me alone, but his gaze is gentle enough. "Was waiting on Dom to bring it up."

Tristan stops his movements at that and his chocolate eyes dart between us. "Bring what up?"

As Finn brings him up to speed, I wander back and forth in the garage, too restless to sit still. When they fall silent, I move closer once more. Tristan is pacing in agitation now, and something about it doesn't sit well with me.

"What is it?"

Finn lifts a hand up to silence me, his gaze unwavering from his buddy. "Tristan, talk to us."

He's shaking his head, his movements growing more agitated, and mumbling under his breath. My gaze lowers to his fists, which are clenching and unclenching, and his breathing that has grown erratic.

"It's a fit, it'll pass," Finn tries to reassure me.

But I ignore him, moving closer to Tristan. I can recognize the signs only too well. After Tommy attacked me, I had panic attacks almost every day, to the point I was incapable to function. They always came when I was alone, and it took a while to learn to control them.

"Tristan."

His eyes dart towards me, his pupils dilated and unfocused, then he goes back to pacing. I realize it's critical we find out what triggered this, but first he has to calm down.

I make the mistake of touching his shoulder too fast. Tristan whirls around, whipping his fist in blind reaction. It's only my quick reflexes that have me duck in time, avoiding a black eye. He takes a swing again, and Finn snaps out of his stupor, moving towards us.

"Tristan, it's me!" I push against his chest with all my force—he doesn't move. But the contact is enough to make him blink and scan his surroundings.

His breathing is still erratic, but he seems to be holding himself in check. "Tristan?"

He looks at me, noticing my palms held up—in case he'd planned to strike again—followed by his clenched fists. Horror falls on his expression, and a glance to Finn confirms it.

Finn nods his head, and Tristan jerks away from us, swearing under his breath. Then he turns around, rubbing the back of his neck. "Merda! I'm so sorry, beleza. I didn't... If I'd hit you..."

"It's okay—"

"No, it *isn't*!" I flinch at his booming voice, and Tristan lowers his voice. "It's never all right for a guy to raise his hand to a woman."

I step closer to him, touching his shoulder. "In normal circumstances, I would agree. But I understand what you were feeling, Tristan. I've been there. The numbing panic, the room closing in, shortness of breath..."

He clenches his jaw, turning his head away. "I don't need a shrink."

My hand drops and I bite my lip. "I never said you do. But if you ever need to talk, I'm here."

Tristan meets my gaze, nodding. Finn breaks the moment with a reality check. "Which part of what I told you triggered it?"

"The vrykolakas. You said Dom's from a line of descendants of Dracula—"

"Vlad Țepeș," I correct. "The man, not the legend."

Tristan rolls his eyes, but something tugs at the corners of his lips. "Claro. Anyway, the pack I ran into, the ones who killed an entire village, they boasted the same... Before I killed some."

Finn narrows his eyes. "You're saying they're related, more than by their abilities? Legit blood relatives? And it's the same one that's here now?"

"It would make sense why they let Dom and Luz leave, without harming them." There's a moment of tense silence as we absorb these implications, then Tristan inhales sharply. "There would be one way to know for sure. The monstro I saw during the war, the leader, has a stripe of white under his chest. The rest of his body is dark black, with eyes as yellow as a snake's."

They both turn to see if the description rings a bell. My expression must be a dead giveaway because it sets them in a string of curses.

"Guys... *Guys*!" They stop, giving me their full attention. "We have to find Dom. Now."

Tristan glances at Finn, his expression grim. "Vá, find Dom. I'll watch over Luz."

Dominic

I'm sitting on the couch, watching Ileana move about my house, when the doorbell rings. I can smell Finn at the door and get up with a sigh.

He pushes past me with an annoyed growl, but stops dead in his tracks when his eyes fall on Ileana. When he faces me, I'm surprised to see the anger in his expression. "You bloody wanker! We've been worried sick thinking your bloody relatives kidnapped you, and you're here shacking up with another girl!?"

"Oy!" I hold my fist back, but only because of who's in the room. Ileana's eyes are on us, head tilted. I can see how this may look bad, but Finn has no right jumping to conclusions.

"Luz is worried about you!" Finn shoves me, and I clench my jaw. "Are you going to defend yourself, or what?"

"Stay out of things you don't understand, man. Let it go. And what's this about relatives?"

He scowls at me, appearing ready to throw a punch. "You're a real arse, you know that?"

"Mă prezinți, dragul meu?" Ileana's voice snaps me out of my angry haze, and I sigh. She wants me to introduce her.

"Finn." I unclench my teeth and point to the immortal. "Meet Ileana Cosânzeana—my godmother."

His jaw drops and his eyes dart between us twice before settling on me. "Your... what?"

"Godmother." The answer comes from Ileana, who steps closer to Finn. "And like all good ones, I'm here to offer guidance at a time he needs it most."

"I would have thought a pack's for that." He shoots another glare my way, but I only roll my eyes and drop back on the couch.

"A pack can be many things," Ileana says, "but what my godson needs is a firm hand and some knowledge that eludes him."

"Like the fact he's related to these nutters going around the city killing people?"

I straighten up at that, meeting Ileana's own startled gaze. "How do you know that?"

Finn seems to realize it's not news for me, as he settles into the couch opposite me. "The same way you do, apparently. I have my sources." Another glance at Ileana, then me. "So, what's the plan?"

"There is no plan. Lucas won't go near the vrykolakas until he has more information."

"Like why they're here."

Ileana nods at my questioning gaze, permitting me to share what she told me. "They're killing their victims alive, tearing their hearts out while still beating to consume them."

Finn's features contort in horror and disgust. "Why?"

"Because the hearts keep them alive, feeding their hunger and thirst for blood alike."

Ileana moves closer, her sad eyes on Finn. "But also, because a live beating heart still contains a shred of a person's soul. And with each one they consume, the vrykolakas get stronger."

Finn grits his teeth, moving his jaw and finally unclenching it. His expression is as unreadable as I've ever seen it. "Convenient you know all this, no?"

"Finn—" My warning falls on deaf ears, as he stands up until he's towering over Ileana.

"Come on, you expect me to believe this is all a coincidence, you showing up here just as we learn of Dom's lineage?" His hand rises to touch her shoulder, but before it makes contact, Finn ends up blasted backwards into my wall.

With his bulk, he actually leaves a dent in the paint, before falling to the ground with a groan of pain. I bite back my frustrated growl and walk over, helping him to his feet.

"You might've warned me your new godmother's a witch."

His fiery green eyes turn to Ileana, a scowl darkening his expression at her obvious amusement. "This isn't funny."

"I never said otherwise," Ileana smiles, gesturing to the sofa. "My apologies for that, but white magic tends to be unruly at times."

Somehow, I highly doubt it acted without her nudge, but I keep my thoughts to myself. No sense in stirring a pot that's already close to boiling.

"As for your accusation, you are correct, it is not a coincidence. But I am not a *new* godmother to Dominic, I am the only one he ever had." Her expression softens when it meets mine, then Ileana says, "I've kept an eye on him through the years, despite the distance. And I followed the vrykolakas here when they moved across the ocean."

When she trails off, it catches my attention. "You knew where they were headed?"

"Not at first, no." Something about the way she answers makes me think there's more to it. "But when I realized what was happening, I knew I had to come to you."

"What's your connection to those monsters?" The blunt question comes from Finn, surprising me again with his perceptive skills. "There's obviously one."

Ileana's gaze darts between us, then she inclines her head softly. "It was I who saved your great-grandfather, Dominic.

And, unfortunately, created this division between your species."

The answer itself doesn't stun me considering everything Luz told me, but Ileana's obvious regret does. "Do you feel guilty for giving them a second chance?"

"No, but I regret not being able to save them all. That's why I came to you, hoping in the end, you'd be able to make a difference."

"I'm just a beta to another pack, Ileana." My tone lacks conviction, enough so that Finn picks up on it.

"We all know that's not true." With a shake of his head, he stands to his feet, making sure to keep a distance from Ileana. "And you don't think knowing this would decide Lucas, one way or another?"

I shrug. "Be my guest to tell him, it's not like he listens to his beta nowadays."

"Fine. I will." Another pause, then his attention shifts to Ileana. "So you're... what? A fairy?"

She laughs, and the room seems brighter for it. "I am an immortal. In Romanian lore, I've become their favorite heroine, the epitome of the perfect woman. But I only showed up at a few rightly placed moments... And found my Prince Charming."

Finn stares at me as if asking, *Is she serious?*

I shrug again, at a loss for words. It's why I left Luz this morning and spent hours with my godmother, trying to read through her riddles.

"What about Luz?"

"Keep her safe. Ileana wants to show me something today. After, I'll go back to Luz. Watch over her though, I don't want her in danger."

Finn nods and gets up to leave. "Be careful."

∞ ♦ ∞

We wait until dusk, then Ileana faces me. "It is time." Her eyes search mine, her tone soft. "Are you ready for this?"

"I can't really answer that now, can I? Considering you haven't explained what we're doing."

She smiles, inclining her head like a mother indulging a child. "All in due time. For now, follow my scent."

So I morph into wolf form, and trail her across land, city and forest, until we end up near the cave again. I recognize the putrid scent and turn to her shimmering form. *Why bring me here?*

I'm not sure if she'll be able to hear me, but she seems to just fine. "Because the darkest part of your family is in there. And if you succeed here, you can save your hide, and theirs."

What exactly am I supposed to do?

"Inside that cave, the entire vrykolakas pack awaits. Their leader, Radu, is your first cousin. His father died years ago, and he has only become darker. He is the alpha of these damned souls. The only way you will get them to stop impeding on your territory is to order them off. And the only way to do that..."

Is to become their alpha. Shit. My gaze turns to the cave, assessing it. Going in there without backup is a suicide mission. Yet if I was to bring my pack, and they see me submitted to another alpha, the fight would be lost before it could start.

Ileana... I look around, but she's gone. *Wonderful.*

I crouch lower, trying to decide. On some level, her suggestion makes sense. But can I do it?

Before I can decide, I catch another's scent. I whirl around in time to see a wolf lunge at me and roll out of the way. By the time I'm back on my feet, I'm facing Aiden.

You owe me a life for all those I lost in the last fight.

That was your own fault, man. I had nothing to do with it.

Liar! He snarls, moving closer. My eyes dart over his shoulder, wary we might attract the vrykolakas' attention.

Aiden, cut it out. You don't get what's going on here.

He jumps at me, and I avoid him again. *You're colluding with these monsters.*

I am not! I'm trying to get them the fuck off our territory.

Aiden shakes his head. *You're trying to distract me.*

I'm not! But despite my vehement denial, he doesn't back down. He attacks me again, and this time I lift a paw and smack him to the side. He hits a tree, falling down with a thud.

Stay down, man. For your own good.

A groan is my only answer, and I walk away. I can't do what Ileana wants me to, at least not tonight. *And not without talking to my alpha first.*

There's a yelp behind me, and I whirl around to a horrific sight. One of those creatures is on top of Aiden, its muzzle dug deep into his chest. Aiden's shrieks die down at the same time there's a gut-wrenching ripping sound.

The creature moves away, turning to face me. He gulps down the heart, licking his bloody muzzle.

I suppose it's about time we were introduced. I'm Radu—your cousin.

CHAPTER FOURTEEN

∞ Exil ∞

"An <u>exile</u>'s life is no life."

-Leonidas of Tarentum-

Lucrezia

Finn enters the shop, and I curse the fact I'm busy explaining an invoice to a customer. An agonizing thirty minutes later, the client leaves satisfied and I barge into the garage. All the guys, including Lucas, are there in what appears to be a meeting.

Lucas' eyes narrow on me and he doesn't seem pleased, but that's not much different from the last days. "You shouldn't be here, you don't have the proper safety equipment on."

I scowl, pointing to his jeans and sneakers. "Seriously?"

He shrugs, and I dismiss him by focusing on Finn. "What happened? Where's Dom?"

Finn glances between me and Lucas, then says, "Dom's all right and should be back by tonight. In the meantime, Tristan's to keep an eye on you."

"Great. But *where* is he? Is his disappearance related to the creatures?"

"Not....quite." His eyes dart to Lucas again, and he clenches his jaw. I'm guessing Lucas is ordering him to shut up. "He's fine."

My gaze shifts between them while I tap my foot. "One of you better tell me what's going on, otherwise I'll go find out on my own."

"And how do you plan to do that, beleza?" Tristan crosses his arms over his chest, smirking. "By playing bait?"

"Precisely." I might have spoken in anger, but I enjoy his startled expression all the same.

"*Basta!* Enough, all of you." Lucas moves off the hood of the car he was leaning against, stepping closer. "Your precious Dom is with an immortal. She's taking good care of him."

Something about his tone irks me, then I realize he means the words to rile me up. So I don't give him the satisfaction, instead choosing to walk away.

"I'll figure it out myself," I throw over my shoulder.

Dominic

It's night time when I slink back into the shop and morph human, pulling on a pair of jeans and whatever shirt I get my hands on. The light is still on in Lucas' office, but no one else is around.

Lucas is sitting in his chair, nursing a glass of whiskey. The half-emptied bottle is next to him, and I don't take it as a good sign. For someone who loathes losing control, this is not normal.

"Lucas."

He glances up when I enter, then downs down the rest of the amber liquid. "The prodigal beta returns."

I frown at his tone. "Listen, this is a really bad time for you to be getting drunk. I need your help."

"Really?" He stares at his glass, unseeing. "Funny. See, that's something I would expect to hear from a friend. But then again, that ship sailed a long time ago with us, huh?"

"What are you going on about?" I stalk to the desk, leaning over it. "Lucas, Aiden attacked me without provocation. The Reapers aren't following protocol any longer! And he's *dead*."

That seems to jostle him some, and he meets my gaze. "You killed him?"

I stagger back, recalling Radu's bloody jaws. "No. My..." I gulp, feeling sick to my stomach. "My cousin did."

Lucas snorts and grabs the bottle of whiskey, drinking straight from it. When he places it back down, I try again. "Please, Lucas, I need your help."

He toys with the glass in his hand, then in an access of rage throws it at the wall. It shatters in pieces, and I'm too stunned to react when Lucas moves.

Then he's in my face, hand on my throat, pushing me back against the wall. His grip is strong, and I could probably break it. But there's a pain in his glare that gets me, and my will to fight drops.

"You lied to me, *amico*! Your lineage. Your bloodline. You're as much an alpha as I am, Dom. So is that what friendship means to you? Lies? Secrets? Betrayal?"

The words escape me in a hoarse whisper. "I never betrayed you."

He's searching my gaze, then he drops his hand and I fall to my knees. I get back up, palms outstretched in a peaceful gesture, not wanting to trigger him again. "Lucas, they'll come after me. The Reapers. They'll think it was I who killed Aiden, and the rest of their pack that was caught in the crossfire."

"So maybe you did."

"What?"

He turns to face me, his features hard. "Non piu. I am done with you, Dominic. I will not offer you protection any further."

I stagger back at his words, formal and cold. "You're not doing this..."

A dull ache spreads through me, like something is being ripped away. Lucas meets my gaze full on, and with each word out of his mouth the agony increases. "Dominic Konstantin, as alpha of your pack, I dismiss your allegiance, and your service. You have until dawn to leave this town, *my* territory, on pain of death."

When he's done, there's a hollow feeling inside me. The connection I once had to him, to Finn, Tristan—it's gone. It used to be part of my subconscious, as reassuring as a blanket or a comfortable sweater.

Now, there's nothing there, like there had been nothing a year ago. "You can't..."

Lucas bares his teeth, turning his back on me. "I have nothing left to say to you."

The words get stuck in my throat—anger at his dismissal, fury at the way he's acting. But I bite them down, my pride concealing them. "Fine. But I hope Finn told you everything, so you understand what you're dealing with. The vrykolakas won't back off, especially with me out of the picture."

When I walk out of his office, there's no victorious feel. Only defeat – and the sensation I'm leaving a piece of me behind.

I squint at Luz's window for long moments, debating if this is smart, before giving in and climbing the fire escape. The minute I knock on the door, she's there to open it, and tugs me inside.

"Dom!" She's burying her head in my chest, hugging me as hard as she can. "I was so worried." She pulls back, looking at me. "Why didn't you say where you were going?"

As she searches my expression, some of my agony must show because she drops her arms, frowning. "What's going on? Has there been another attack on animals?"

I shake my head, dropping my forehead to hers. Closing my eyes, I inhale her scent like it's the last time I'll ever breathe it—and it very well might be.

"Dom, you're scaring me."

My mouth drops to hers, tasting her lips, taking my time even though it's counted. I feel her tears on my cheeks and pull back.

"I need to leave."

Her eyes widen but she remains unmoving, stunned by my flat declaration. After a long beat, she says, "What... why?"

"Lucas kicked me out of the pack."

"He did *what*!?"

I tuck a strand of hair behind her ear, and cup her cheek. "Listen to me. He had his reasons, not that I agree with them. But this whole thing with the vrykolakas, I have to fix it."

"Why does it have to be you?" Her fingers cling to my shirt as if to keep me here. "If Lucas kicked you out, why can't we just leave?"

I'm shaking my head before she's even done talking. "This morning, when I disappeared, I was with my godmother, Ileana. I... If I ever get another chance, I'll tell you about her. But she confirmed as much as Finn did that these vrykolakas are my relatives. And tonight, I met my cousin, who's leading them. I can't let them hurt anyone else, Luz. If I do, it'll be on my shoulders, and a regret I'll have to live with forever."

Fresh tears spring to her eyes, and she grabs my hand as if to keep me here. "Dom, please don't do this alone. It's suicide! Lucas will get over his anger, and once he does you can fight these monsters together! He's just pissed that there's another alpha in town."

If it was only that. "He's hurt, Luz. I kept too much from him, and now he's lashing out. Whatever you do, don't piss him off." She opens her mouth at that, but I place my index on her lips. "I need you to promise me you'll stay with them, with the pack. You need their protection."

"But I want to be with *you*."

My heart clenches, my wolf rebelling against what I'm doing. "I know, because I do as well. But they can offer you protection like a lone wolf can't. Please, Luz. *Please*."

Her green eyes meet mine and she nods, though I can tell it's tearing her up. "Fine. I promise."

I kiss her one last time, then I wrench myself from her grip and leave before I do something that will make me stay forever.

Lucrezia

The next day, I don't see Dom. Or the next. There's a tension around the shop, but no one is saying anything. By the third day, I barge into Lucas' office.

"You're a real ass, you know that?"

His eyes don't move from his papers. "Not the first time you said that."

"Where's Dom?"

"Beats me."

His coolness is infuriating, considering I'm standing there panting and my hair is flying all over. I move closer and push all the papers off his desk—my job be damned. If he wants to fire me, let him.

Lucas looks at me then, awareness creeping in his eyes. "I guess I never really saw it, but I do now, cara. You love me."

I snort at the statement. "Because I barge in here making demands? Boy, you really are full of yourself, aren't you?"

He leans back into his chair, assurance oozing from his pores. "It's been known to happen."

My teeth hurt from gritting them. "I don't love you, I never did. Your damn pheromones messed with my mind. What I felt was lust, nothing more. I do, however, love Dominic."

I've half a mind to hit Lucas, but he gets up, eyes glinting and jaw clenched with purpose. Slowly, he moves around the desk, but I refuse to back away. He stares at me for the longest moment, and I don't see it coming.

Before I know it, he's kissing me. One hand wraps around my nape, holding me still, the other reaching for my hip. And if I wasn't already convinced of my feelings for Dom, the kiss would have done the job.

It's nothing like having Dom's lips on mine, nor does it spark anything in me in the two-point-five seconds it takes my brain to register my surprise and act. I shove Lucas away, throwing in a resounding slap for good measure.

Lucas stares at me, his eyes glittering with unreadable emotion. "I guess I missed my chance there."

"Go to hell, Lucas." I stalk away, but stop before exiting, turning to see him staring at the carpet. "Dom knew nothing about his lineage until me and Finn dug it up. He didn't even realize the vrykolakas were linked to him. You need to stomp over that pride of yours before it ruins you and everyone around you."

I take off before I say something that'll get me into more trouble, and barge instead into the garage where Finn and Tristan are working. "Did you two know Lucas exiled Dom?"

They glance at me, then each other. Tristan drops his wrench to the ground where it clatters. "That *idiota*!" He moves as if to go after Lucas, but Finn steps in his way.

"Dom pushed too many limits, it was bound to happen."

Tristan releases a string of curses in Portuguese, and I swear his glare could melt an iceberg. "And you knew he did this?"

Finn lets him go, stepping away with a peculiar expression on his face. "I felt something a few nights ago. When we didn't hear from Dom, I just assumed." He glances at me. "Where is he?"

"Gone." I hate that my voice shakes and tears spring to my eyes. But I miss Dom. His smile, his presence, his touch – it's all I can think about.

"He wouldn't leave you." I look up at Tristan, feeling his certainty. "I don't care what Lucas threatened him with, I know Dominic and he would not leave you behind."

"He said you'd all protect me."

"It's not about protection, love." Finn places a hand on my shoulder, squeezing once before letting go. "His wolf won't allow him to be far from you. He's still around, trust us, but he must be in hiding."

Hope blooms in my chest at his words, and it doesn't take me long to decide my next course of action. "Then I'll find him."

"I'll help." Tristan turns his glare to the door. "But first I need to have a chat with our fearless leader."

He's off before Finn can intervene this time, and he shakes his head. "I better go after him, before he does something he'll regret. Wait for us here, and we'll all go find Dominic."

"Sure." Once he's gone around the corner, I grab his car keys off the tool table, as well as a jacket and baseball cap.

I'll be damned if I waste time waiting while you three have your pissing contest.

In retrospect, taking off on my own while my boyfriend is MIA, and the pack is busy not falling apart, was not my best decision. But love will have you doing crazy things, right?

Or so I tell myself when night catches me way too far off from Claws Auto Shop, and with a car that runs out of gas. Because of course Finn didn't foresee I would take it for a joyride around town and waste all the gas for hours on end.

Shit.

So I'm staring around and realizing I have little choice except to get out and walk somewhere to get help. My phone is dead too. At first I turned the sound off, but by the time I was willing to return the guys' missed calls, the battery had died because of the cold.

I pull the jacket tighter around me, lower the baseball cap on my head and try to knot my hair under the collar. Maybe if people think I'm a man, they'll pay less attention to me. Just in case, I grab a screwdriver from the side door and pocket it. It may not be much in terms of weapon, but at least it's something.

It seems a good idea until a few blocks down the road I hear growls. Three wolves emerge out of an alleyway, their yellow eyes glinting in the darkness. For a second, I wonder if I might be lucky enough and these are regular wolves.

That idea is shot to hell when I notice the way the smaller ones stare at the leader and the intelligence gleaming in his eyes. I don't have to speak wolf to understand what's going on in their heads. *Fresh meat.*

I glance around, but sure enough there's no one. At the end of the street I can see cars at an intersection, but that's blocks away. No way can I outrun these wolves... So I do the next best thing and reach for the screwdriver.

The leader's eyes go to it, then dart towards me as if he can't believe I plan to fight them. I shrug. "I'm stubborn food. Trust me, you won't enjoy me."

The wolf scoffs, jerking his head to the others. They leave the cover of the alleyway and fan out, surrounding me in all corners. I shift my feet, centering myself for better movement. When the first one jumps at me, I elbow him in the chest and push him off.

The second grabs for my leg. Fearing his bite might be one of those that could turn me, I jerk out of the way but end up hitting my knee on the cement. I clench the screwdriver, biting back a groan of pain, and drive it into the approaching wolf's side. He jumps back, whining.

The leader is last to face me, eyes slanted now as if recognizing an adversary. I stagger to my feet, grimacing at the jolt of pain in my knee. There's little doubt in my mind I won't be able to hold all of them off if they attack together. *But I plan to damn well try.*

The wolf hunches over, looking ready to pounce—then he stills. I feel it too, right before a stranger's voice washes over me. "Leave her."

I whirl around, dropping my guard with the wolf and ready to jab the newcomer with a screwdriver. But he stops my hit with one hand, gripping my wrist in his larger—*much* larger—hand that engulfs mine.

A stormy gaze stares into mine for a beat, silver irises searching mine. A lock of dark hair falls over his forehead, and his lips move in a half-smirk. He's not a pretty boy—but dark and scruffy with a day's worth of beard. Yet the faded jeans and shirt are clean, and his presence is overwhelming.

I gulp as at his insistent gaze, almost numb when he removes the screwdriver and throws it away. Still holding my wrist, he tugs me to his side and levels a hardened expression on the wolves. They've now grouped around their leader.

"You're still here?"

The head one takes a step closer, but the stranger snarls. I glance at him, seeing his upper lip curled over bared teeth, and shiver. *Who is this guy? Another wolf?*

With a whine, my attackers leave us alone, disappearing around a corner. The stranger releases my wrist at that point, tilting his head as he looks me up and down.

"Do you make a habit of facing off wolves armed with only a screwdriver?"

I gulp past the fear lodged in my throat. "Not really. My car ran out of gas, and my cell ran out of battery. I was trying to find help."

"And what were you doing in this part of town to begin with?"

My eyes narrow at his patronizing tone. "I was looking for my boyfriend."

His nostrils flare as if taking in my scent. "Ah. I see. He's missing?"

"You know, I think I'm done answering your questions. Thank you for your help, but I'll be fine from here." Despite me walking away, he matches my pace until we're side by side. "I meant it."

"Yes, you did." He sounds amused, and a quick glance confirms his gray eyes are now sparkling merrily. "But I wouldn't be a gentleman if I let a lonely, unprotected woman walk by herself in these dangerous parts."

"You keep talking, but I'm neither lonely nor unprotected."

He ignores my mutter, stepping ahead of me and blocking my path. I glare up at him, having to throw my head back to see him. "You're annoying."

"And *you* are refreshing, Red. What's your name?"

My eyes narrow, but the fierce expression I'm trying to portray doesn't seem to faze him. "I'll scream for help."

"Much as I would enjoy that, I propose something different. My car is parked over there." He points to the busy intersection where a dark Hummer is pulled over to the side. "I will take you wherever you want."

"What's the catch?"

He grins. "Tell me your name."

Only my desperation to find Dom makes me give in. The quicker I can get to Claws Auto Shop, the sooner I'll be back out searching for him—this time, with backup.

With a sigh, I move past him. "Lucrezia San Marco."

∞ ◆ ∞

A few minutes later, we pull in front of the shop. My mysterious benefactor didn't say a word during the entire ride—other than ask for the address—and was a perfect gentleman.

Now that we're here, and I'm still alive, I unbuckle my seat belt and face him. "Thank you. And...I'm sorry for my rudeness."

He grins, waving off my apology. "The pleasure was all mine, Lucrezia."

My hand automatically moves to the door to open it, but I hesitate, realizing I never even asked his name. "What's your name? So I can thank you properly, at least."

His eyes roam over my features as if trying to figure out if I'm worthy of the information. After another beat, he says, "Tytus. But friends call me Ty."

"Well, thank you, Ty." His eyes seem brighter in the car, or maybe it's the light. I gulp past that odd unease in my throat and step out.

Tristan storms out of the shop, followed by Finn. "Merda, Lucrezia! Where the hell have you been? And who's that guy?"

I glance where Tristan is scowling, noticing Ty has now exited the car and is standing off to the side, his nostrils flaring. "*That guy* is the man who brought back what you obviously lost. Perhaps a change of tone would be appropriate."

Something in his voice makes me shiver, but I don't move. Finn steps closer, nose turned up in the air. "What are you? Your smell..."

I gape at them. "He's not human?"

"Não, not even close." Tristan's tone is none too pleased.

Ty either wants to piss them off, or he's not great with people. Either way, he doesn't answer them and instead catches my gaze. "By the way, I know where your boyfriend is, if you'd like to find him tonight."

"Where?" I ignore the guys' shouts of protest, already stepping closer to the car.

"Where all lost souls go."

I bite my lip, glancing back at the guys. They've been nothing but supportive, and I know the tight spot I'm putting them in by doing what I plan to. But I've come too far, and there's no way I intend to be away from Dom a minute longer.

"Sorry, guys, but I need to find Dom. And Ty's my best chance at that."

With one last glance at their stunned expressions, I hop back into the Hummer and Ty takes off in a screech of tires.

∞ ♦ ∞

Barely twenty minutes later, we park in the middle of nowhere, on the outskirts of town. A small building with a neon sign announces it's a bar, open twenty-four-seven, but the light is partly shut off and the place doesn't inspire confidence.

Ty gets out of the car and I follow him, wringing my hands together. Despite my uneasiness, if Dom is in there, I need to woman up and get him. So I straighten my back and stomp over, my boots crunching over the hardened snow.

When we enter the bar, the smell of beer, cheap cologne and smoke assails me, so potent it makes me cough. Ty's there to tap my back gently, then points to a corner.

Past the run-down bar and stools, across the laminated floor, my eyes fall on Dom—and the girl on his lap. She's barely wearing anything and he's not touching her, despite her efforts to the contrary.

Dom's expression, when I zero in on it, makes my heart squeeze. His gaze is lost in the beyond, and there's an empty bottle of liquor at his feet. The girl shifts in his lap, but it doesn't draw a single reaction out of him.

"How did you know he was here?" My words are a murmur, but my companion seems to hear them easily enough.

"Caught his scent on you."

I glance up at Ty, surprised he so easily confirmed what the guys said. "So you're really not human."

A flash of teeth in the dark, then he backs away. "Like your friend said, I'm as far from it as they come. I'll be at the bar if you run into any trouble. Take care, Lucrezia."

I recognize the goodbye, and after he disappears in the crowd, I stomp over to my boyfriend, my blood boiling. I tap the woman's shoulder, setting my face in my most angry scowl. "Move off my man."

"Excuse me?" She's slurring, drunk out of her mind.

"You heard me. Move off him. *Now.*"

The girl doesn't budge, so I yank her off Dom. She stumbles away muttering about rude bitches, but I tune her out. My entire focus is on Dom, and the glaze in his eyes.

Those blue eyes that I love stare unseeing at me, and when he speaks it's rough and toneless. "What are you doing here?"

Instead of answering, I grab his hand in mine and try to pull him to his feet. "Come with me."

"No."

Dom pulls his hand out mine and goes to take a swing of his drink, but realizes it's empty. He throws it back to the ground, putting up a hand to cover his eyes. "Leave."

I do the opposite. If there's no way he'll answer rationally, then perhaps I can entice his wolf enough to follow me. So I sit on his lap, ignoring the hoots and whistles around us, and kiss him with everything I have.

At first, his lips remain motionless against mine, making me growl in frustration. *Dammit, Dom.* I tug on his lower lip with my teeth, and when he still doesn't react, I bite down on it. A hiss of pain escapes him and he tries to move away, but I don't let go, kissing him harder instead.

There's a shift of energy, and a groan escapes him. A heartbeat later, Dom's hand goes to my lower back, pulling me closer into him. Then his other catches my loose hair and grips it for leverage, before angling my mouth to take control of the kiss.

The hollers increase around us, but the only thing I care about is the man finally responding to my touch. When his hand at my back moves lower, gripping my ass, I shift in his lap and pull back from the kiss.

"Come with me."

Dom stares at me for a long beat, still holding onto my hair. My scalp tingles from the tight grip, but I don't look away from him, afraid of losing him. Then he shudders out a breath, and lets go of me as if all fight left him.

I get off him, my cheeks flushed at the whistles still going on. When I hold out my hand this time, Dom grasps it. Then he gets up and follows me out, stumbling with every step.

CHAPTER FIFTEEN

∞ Dragoste ∞

"The madness of <u>love</u> is the greatest of heaven's blessings."

-Plato-

Lucrezia

It's easy enough to find Dom's pickup truck parked in the filthy parking lot. Harder, however, to find the keys while trying to keep him standing up. "How much alcohol did you consume, anyway?"

Considering the past times I saw him drink, it must have been a lot to incapacitate him so. And let me tell you, trying to get him in the car while drunk is a workout in itself.

After a few attempts, I buckle Dom in the passenger seat, and hop behind the wheel. The entire drive, I feel his stare is on me, as vivid as his touch, yet he doesn't say anything.

It's with a sigh of relief that I park in front of my building and turn off the engine. I rest my head against the wheel for a second, running through the night's events in my head.

"Dom..." I glance up, so many things on the tip of tongue, but choke on them when I see his expression.

In the semi-darkness, his features are taut, his gaze intense with a hunger that pulls at me—because it's also within me, and it's clouding my judgment.

Without a word, Dom unbuckles both our seatbelts and pulls me into his lap. This close, I notice his clear eyes, no longer glazed by the drink. My frown must show my surprise, as he shrugs.

"Werewolf perks." His voice is not what I'm used to, like he's trying to rein himself in. Then his nostrils flare, and his entire body underneath mine grows taut with tension. "Lucas' scent is on you—"

I kiss him before he can finish, putting everything I can in that. His hand at my neck draws me closer, and he takes over the kiss. I'm so out of my depth in this, but his every touch feels right, and I want him.

Panting, I pull back and rest my forehead against his. "Lucas was trying to salvage his ego. I was clear about whom I love.

Dom... You're my first choice, always. Alpha or no alpha, I couldn't care less. I love you."

He runs his knuckles down my cheek, then pulls my mouth to his. "Good. Because I've loved you since I laid eyes on you that first day... And tonight, I want to show you in every possible way. It will also mean I'm claiming you as my mate. So if you have any objections, now's the time, draga mea."

I look him in the eyes, shaking my head. "No objections. I'm yours."

He growls and takes my mouth with his. For long, epic moments, his lips are the only anchor in the ocean of sensations I'm drowning in. Then I feel cold air on me and realize somehow Dom opened the car door and has extracted both of us, kicking it closed behind us.

I wrap my legs around him, allowing him to carry me upstairs. "Dom, the car—"

His kiss stops me, but he shifts around until two beeps break the silence of the night. I relax back in his embrace, but his chuckles distract me.

"What?"

He moves quickly, because within seconds we're at the top of the stairs. I'm pinned between him and the wall, two steps away from my apartment, and he's busy laughing in the crook of my shoulder. "I can't believe you interrupted this to make sure my car doesn't get stolen."

"Oh." My cheeks warm up and he lifts his head to kiss the tip of my nose.

Then his mouth moves back to mine, and I hear a click behind us. Dom kicks open the door to the apartment and moves us in.

Dominic

If heaven exists, it must start with what I'm feeling because I could die a happy man. If Luz thinks I'm about to speed things up, she's dead wrong. I've waited a year to touch her like this, and there's no way tonight will go any other way than slow—torturously slow, for both of us.

I take my time kissing her by the entrance, her cute butt perched atop the coffee table near the door. My hands roam down her sides, taking off her jacket and sweater until she's only got on her tank top and jeans.

Satisfied with her level of undress, I settle back to enjoy her lips. But it's not long before both my wolf and Luz demand more—much more.

Her deft arms grab unto my belt, trying to unbuckle it. When that doesn't work, she runs her hands under my shirt, trying to peel it off me. I pull back with a chuckle, meeting her darkened emerald gaze.

"In a hurry?"

"Yes!" The answer is more of a growl, and her brow furrows as she focuses on getting me naked.

I help by taking my shirt off, and her hands roam everywhere—my chest, my abs, then move to my back, raking her nails. I hiss, and Luz draws back with wide eyes. "Did I hurt you?"

"Hell, no." I claim her mouth again, picking her up in my arms without releasing her lips. We head towards the bedroom this time, dismissing the comfortable-looking couch.

Luz clings to my shoulders, peppering every inch of skin she can get to with light kisses, and I groan. Dropping her to the bed gently is a feat, especially when my wolf pushes for a more direct approach. But I push back, unwavering in my resolution to take my time.

I move us both in a position where Luz is straddling me, which means I have access to everything. My lips move from her lips down her neck, before I drop lower and kiss along her collarbone, venturing as far as the top of her breasts.

Luz moans against me, pressing her hips down into mine with enough urgency to make me catch fire. It's a good thing I'm fireproof—I think.

My hands slip under her thin top, taking it off and the bra that goes with it. Then she's there in all her glorious semi-naked beauty and I can't help but slow down my pace again. I kiss every inch of skin I can get my mouth on, ignoring her mewls of protest at my pace.

When I latch onto a nipple, Luz gives the most delighted gasp—so I do it again, and again, until she's writhing and moaning and begging me for things she doesn't understand.

I move us so her back lands on the bed. Never interrupting contact with her skin, I trail lower, taking my time with her waist and belly button as I undo her jeans. I peel them off along with her panties, taking a deep breath of her arousal.

"Dom... Please..."

I know what she's asking, but it's too early. "Not yet, iubirea mea. Not quite yet." She hits the covers in frustration, and I chuckle as I kiss my way up from one ankle to her thigh, and do the same thing with the other leg.

Once I reach the apex of her thighs, Luz is sobbing with need. I part her folds with my fingers first, then my tongue, and heavens she tastes like the sweetest of nectars. But what's even sweeter is the glorious sounds she makes, and the way she lets go, trusting me implicitly.

Only when I've brought her to the stars and back more than once, do I give in and pull a condom from my jeans pocket, the slide it on. Luz parts her legs, biting her lip as she meets my gaze. "Please."

I nudge her slightly, pushing in one inch at a time. With it being her first time, the last thing I want is to hurt her—though I know it's impossible not to. When I reach the last of her barriers, I stop and hoist myself on my elbows.

"We can stop if you want to, you've only to say the word."

Luz bites harder on her lip, shaking her head. Before I can do anything, she arches her back and pushes her hips towards me—and cries out. I'm buried to the hilt, deep enough I can feel her every tremor.

I don't move, watching her face for the tell-tale sign to go ahead. At first, she's still biting her lip hard enough to draw blood, and I stop her with a kiss. My mouth nibbles and sucks on hers, teasing her, until she sighs in my mouth.

My hands focus on her breasts, massaging them and trailing light kisses on her nipples. Luz's sighs become moans, and soon enough she's moving against me of her own volition.

When I pull back from the kiss this time, she's smiling, nodding her head. "*Please.* Keep going."

I pull back, gritting my teeth and cording my muscles, feeling like I'm about to snap. She's so tight against me, it's all I can do to take things slow, but she deserves every moment of torture it costs me—and then some.

When her nails rake my back again, tugging on me, and begging me to go faster, only then do I let myself increase my pace and plunge deeper, until we both break on the cliffs of ecstasy.

Lucrezia

I can't sleep, my mind going haywire over what we shared. Dom's drawing lazy circles on my back, causing delicious shivers to run up and down my spine. Low in my belly, desire stirs anew and I shift.

Dom stops his ministrations, chuckling. "Ready for more already?"

I peek at him, nibbling on my lip. "Maybe."

His eyes flare dark and one hand rises to cup my cheek. "Much as I want to take you up on that—and trust me, I do—it might be a good idea to let your body rest."

I know I'm pouting by the way he laughs, his entire chest rumbling with it. It's such a change from the man I dragged out of the bar and it fills me with female power.

Dom shifts so I'm sprawled even more over him, and plays with my hair. "What's going on in that pretty head of yours?"

"Many things. But mainly, I have this weird urge to be honest with you."

When I meet his gaze, it's not surprised. "I claimed you, Luz. And since wolves mate for life, that's the purest form of commitment you can get into, stronger than any bonds of human marriage. There's no glowing light or singing angels, but I think it's normal a part of you feels the purity of what we just shared, hence the honesty."

It makes sense, on a bizarre level. "Well then, to answer your question, my head was recalling the bar, and picking you up from there. And I was thinking how much of a difference there's in you now."

I search his gaze, sensing his body tense underneath mine. "What happened, Dom? Why were you there?"

He sighs, running his free hand—the one not on my back—over his face. "When Lucas kicked me out of the pack, it broke the connection I had with them. You have to understand that being part of something like that, it's... It's big. Especially for someone like me, who lost his link to wolves when I was so young."

My heart clenches for him, but I don't want to interrupt. So instead I wrap my arm around his waist and set my chin on his chest, giving him my full undivided attention.

"At first, I wanted to go after the creatures, or find something to sink my teeth into—a fight, preferably. But then my feet carried me there, and I didn't move. It's the type of place that lets you fall into oblivion."

"I noticed." My tone was meant to be neutral, Dom picks up something in it and his gaze returns to my face.

"Luz, I touched no one there, you have to believe me. Hell if I know how that girl got near me."

I wave my hand, dismissing the thought of her. "Don't worry, I get it."

Dom seems relieved, but a slight frown creases his brow. "How did you find me, anyway? The guys couldn't have known where I was, disconnected as we were."

"Yeah, about that..." I shift, biting my lip. Before I have time to finish, my buzzer rings—repeatedly.

Dom scowls at the door. "Expecting someone?"

"Not really…" But I slide out of bed anyway and pull on my robe. His eyes follow my every movement, his heated gaze making me blush.

Then the buzzer breaks the moment and I huff. "Something better be on fire, somewhere." Dom's laugh follows me into the hallway and back to my front door. To my annoyance, the buzzer stops ringing as I near it.

I'm about to return to the bedroom when loud, insistent banging starts on my front door. I tiptoe to it, peek through the peephole, and sigh.

"Seriously?" I open the door, having a faint idea what this is about. Tristan and Finn are gracing my doorstep, both appearing flustered—and relieved at finding me.

Their eyes grow wide as saucers when they notice what I'm wearing. I feel the tell-tale sign of a flush on my cheeks, but refuse to back down. "What's so damn urgent?"

They share a look, and Finn says, "We wanted to make sure you were all right. After the way you left…"

"And the guy you left *with*!" I scowl at Tristan's interruption, but heat behind me interrupts the verbal lashing I was about to give him.

"What guy?"

Dom opens the door wider, at the same time throwing an arm around my waist and pulling me to his side. I warn Tristan to behave with a glare—which he ignores.

"Hummer guy."

I roll my eyes at Tristan. "His name is Tytus, and he was more help than you two."

"You took off before we returned!"

"You were about to get in a pissing match with Lucas. Do you honestly think I wanted to waste time waiting when I could be out there, finding Dom?"

Tristan falls silent at that, and I realize Dom has been just as quiet, listening to the entire exchange. Recalling his mention of honesty from earlier, I glance up at him.

"When I went looking for you, Finn's car ran out of gas. I was in the middle of nowhere with no cellphone battery, so I got out and walked to the closest intersection. A small cluster of wolves tried to start something, and I fought them off. This guy Tytus showed up and called them off."

Dom's expression is unreadable, but at least he's not throwing a tantrum like Tristan. "Called them off? How?"

I shrug. "Beats me. He told them to leave, and they did."

"Then he's a wolf." He glances to Tristan and Finn for confirmation, but they shake their heads.

"He's not, amigo. Finn won't say what he is, and I can't place the smell, but he's neither human nor wolf."

"I see..." Dom's gaze darts between them. "Well, I'm assuming you both came here to see if Luz is alright?" When they nod, he says, "As you can see, she's fine. And we have some catching up to do."

Finn coughs into his palm to hide a smile, but Tristan's nowhere near that subtle. "About damn time!"

Dom shakes his head, moving me back inside. He's closing the door when Tristan puts a hand on it. "Hold up. What Lucas did... You need to know, we didn't vote on it. He didn't run it by us."

Finn nods. "And we don't support it, and have told him as much."

"Thank you." Dom pats them on the back one at a time. "I'll let you know if I get anything useful on those creatures. And... You can tell Lucas I'm still in town. I don't need you lying to your alpha for me."

With that, he shuts the door all the way and faces me. Something in his expression shifts, and his hands come to rest on my hips. "This guy Tytus. Did he try anything?"

"Nope, he was a perfect gentleman. Almost old-school." I hesitate for a second, then shrug. "He's the one that showed me where you were."

"And how did he know it was me?"

"Said he caught your scent on me."

Dom's nostrils flare, then he pulls me closer. His mouth moves to my cheek, my ear, kissing all the way down to my shoulder. "If you see him again..."

I gasp when he nibbles on the sensitive skin, my body arching towards his. There's an aching need inside me, and I can no longer control it. "I'll tell you. I promise."

His mouth cuts off any further comments, and talk of Tytus is forgotten.

Dominic

I wake up with a start, breathing heavily. Next to me, Luz mutters and shifts on the bed, draping her body over mine.

My eyes move to the hallway where a faint light shines. I recognize the glow enough to call out. "Ileana?"

Luz stirs against me, blinking. When she lifts her head and her gaze lands on my godmother in our bedroom, her jaw goes slack.

"Lucrezia, meet my godmother, Ileana."

The immortal waves from afar, a soft smile on her lips. "It is a pleasure."

Luz pulls the blanket to her chin, blushing three shades of crimson. "The pleasure is all mine." She glances at me, her expression questioning.

"Remember when you told me my great-grandfather was forgiven by the Church?" When she nods, I jerk my head towards Ileana. "She made it happen with her white magic. And she's been a benefactor for my family ever since."

Luz sits up straighter, making sure the blanket still covers her. "So you were around during Dom's childhood?"

Ileana inclines her head, stepping closer to the bed. "I was, though he could not see me. When his parents died in that horrible house fire, I made sure he was placed with a good family. Knowing he was safe and hidden from his vrykolakas relatives, I focused my energy on keeping an eye on them, and lost track of him."

Before Luz can follow the same train of thought Finn did, I intervene. "Ileana followed Radu, my cousin, across the ocean, and that's how she ended up back here. She feels guilty over not being able to save all their souls, and hopes I might be able to change that."

"By taking over as their alpha?"

Surprise must show on my face at her question, as Luz chuckles softly. "You forget I went all the way to New York to get this information. I can draw my own conclusions."

Humbled by all she's done for me, I kiss her forehead and squeeze her against my chest. Everything else I want to say will have to wait until later, because there's no way in hell my godmother is here just for kicks.

So I turn to Ileana, frowning. "What is it?"

"Your cousin grows restless. They need more kills to feed the habit, Dominic. If you ever plan to take my advice, now is the time. Not later."

"I'll do it. I have no alpha to answer to, so nothing stands in my way now."

Ileana glances between me and Luz. "You should take your mate with you."

"Absolutely not."

"Hey!"

Luz shifts again, and I can sense her agitation. But I tighten my arm around her waist instead, immobilizing her. "I don't want her in danger."

Ileana moves closer to the bed, her eyes saddened. "Her love grounds you. When you meet your brethren, they will want to turn you. Tonight is a full moon, and you will be at your most vulnerable. Heed my words, godson."

With the cryptic words, she disappears before we can ask anything else. Luz breaks out of my hold and gets to a kneeling position on the bed, wrapping the covers around her.

"What did Ileana mean, about a full moon making you vulnerable?"

I sigh, rubbing the back of my neck. "Remember that old legend I told you about how the vârcolaci eat the moon and that's why it's bloody?"

"Yeah... You also mentioned something about how a full moon makes you faster." Her green eyes shine with confusion, trying to see where I'm going with my evasive answer.

"True, I can run at three times my regular speed. But it also makes my concentration less than optimal, and my ability to heal is impaired. Most importantly, it emphasizes the primal part of me, making it easier for my wolf to rule me."

Luz completely ignores that last part, focusing instead on the hurting part. "So a regular morphing back to human won't fix you, if you get bad wounds?"

I shake my head, watching her closely. "Not until the full moon is completely gone." Which, we both know, could take a few days.

Luz is silent as she absorbs the knowledge, but what she ends up saying is nowhere close to what I'm expecting. "I want to come with you."

"You don't even know what this is about."

Her emerald eyes sparkle, and not with amusement. I know she wants to help, but if anything happens to her...

As if reading my thoughts, Luz's expression softens. "I'll be careful and listen to what you tell me, I promise. But please let me come."

In a weak moment, I nod, praying to all the gods I don't live to regret it.

The forest is quiet, except for their constant howls. Me and Luz move as a unit, silent, and I keep my human form for ease of communication. Her hand is warm in mine, and despite my worry over her well-being, something in me says this was the right decision.

When we pass through the area we were last attacked in, she wrinkles her nose at the dead bodies. Their rotting scent fills the air and we quicken our pace through it, on the way to the cave.

"It's weird, but I feel bad for them."

Her whisper reaches me and I nod in agreement. "They didn't deserve the atrocious ending. Which is why I was afraid to bring you."

My grip tightens on her as we cross the river, keeping to the unbroken ice this time. Luz squeezes my hand in reassurance once we're over.

"I'll be fine." She flashes me the army knife I gave her in the car. "Armed and ready."

I snort at her poor attempt of a joke. We bend under the last of the branches and emerge in the area Aiden was killed. Radu must have dragged his body elsewhere, a small blessing that keeps the air only semi-clear. The cave is below us, and I point it to Luz.

"That's where I need to go."

She nods, biting her lip. I had intended to scope out the territory, but a voice at the back of my head tells me that won't be possible.

"Welcome back, cousin. Returned to join us so soon?"

I whirl around, as does Luz at my abrupt movement. Our eyes fall on Radu, only a few feet away. And this time, he's not alone.

CHAPTER SIXTEEN

∞ Luptă ∞

"It is better to stand and <u>fight.</u> If you run, you'll only die tired."

-A Viking Saying-

Dominic

This is the first time I see my cousin in human form. He's blonde like me, but with lifeless brown eyes and a mean sneer. His body is built, but jagged scars cross his naked chest. He's wearing a pair of jeans, faded and ripped like they've seen better days, and he's barefoot.

"Who's your pretty lady?"

I shift to cover Luz halfway with my body. His smirk at my knee-jerk reaction tells me that's exactly what he wanted. But rather than get distracted by it, I notice his yellowed teeth and hollow cheeks.

His hair in shoulder-length, dirty and covered with leaves. And there's a scent off him...

"Picked up a habit, cousin?" My retort seems to hit a nerve as one hand clenches in a fist. But he releases it, sneering instead.

"And if I did?"

His chaotic attitude is not reassuring and I'm regretting bringing Luz here. "What does a wolf get out of drugs, anyway?"

"Why don't you see for yourself?" He jerks his head towards me, and I tense, expecting the creatures behind me to move.

Instead, I hear Lucrezia yelp and whirl around. One wolf morphed to human and has her in his grip. *Damned freaking concentration and impaired abilities. And damn this full moon.* I'm about to lunge at him, but he pushes her neck to the side and bares his long canines.

My feet are rooted to the ground, unsure what I'm witnessing until my cousin moves in my periphery. "Easy, Vlad. Human necks are so very fragile. Let's not upset our visitors just yet." To me, he says, "I bet you thought our eating of hearts was only for show, didn't you?"

"No." My eyes are on Luz the entire time, willing her to be strong, and I read only determination in her expression and trust that I'll get her out of this. *Brave girl.* I try to be worthy of her faith, keeping my voice strong and holding my fury at bay. "I thought you were a bunch of psychos in it for the thrill."

Radu growls, and Vlad's grip tightens on Luz. "Watch yourself, cousin. Unless you want your human to suffer."

I glare at him for a moment, before turning back to Luz. "She's my mate, you stupid bastard. Can't you smell it on her? You're harming my *claimed* mate. You know what the punishment is for that, in any pack."

Radu laughs, and it's long, hard and brittle. It stops in a coughing fit, then he straightens. "None of those rules apply to us. We are superior in every way, cousin. The hearts ensure this by increasing our natural abilities, including strength. They also affect the venom in our canines, turning it into an acid. That's how it was so easy to dispose of those wolves that attacked you."

"Why did you let me go, in that case?"

Radu snorts. "It wasn't because I was sentimental, believe me. I thought if I showed you some good faith, your curiosity would get the best of you and you would return to the fold." His glare settles on Luz. "Evidently, I was wrong and your loyalty is elsewhere. So before anything else, we must remedy that."

Vlad moves his mouth closer to Luz's neck, and every muscle in my body is ready to snap. "Enough! Leave her be. What do you want, Radu?" I turn to face him, forcing my fists to unclench.

He recognizes the effort and a swift, victorious gleam passes through his gaze before he nods to another wolf. It skulks near me and drops a pouch at my feet. I bend over and pick it up, hesitating to open it. I can feel what's it in it, but don't understand the purpose.

"You want me to shoot myself up with drugs?" Sure enough, when I tear open the pouch a clean syringe falls out, along with a vial of an amber liquid.

Radu grins at my confusion. "Yes."

"Will you at least tell me why?"

"See, that's your problem. You think there's a reason to this whole thing, a plan. But there's none, cousin. I want you to shoot yourself up with drugs because I want to see you lose control. It pleases me to wreak havoc on someone's life."

He smirks, darting a glance to Luz. "And once you're high enough, maybe you'll consent to sharing."

My wolf has had enough, and it tears through my consciousness before I can decide it. I shift mid-way a lunge, and it's my claws that land on Radu's chest, digging in and drawing blood. We grapple, rolling on the ground until someone hurtles into me and sends me flying.

I shake off the hit and turn to face them, not noticing the wolf in human form creeping up behind me.

"Dominic!"

Luz's scream has me turn, in time to see the needle jab into me. It drops to the ground, empty. I shake my head, but my vision narrows, going blurry and out of focus.

"We could have done this the easy way." Radu is kneeling next to me now, and I must be on the ground but don't know how I got like that.

My breathing is shaky, and every movement of my chest feels like lifting weights. Yet euphoria is spreading through my veins, a sense of invincibility... A desire to ravage. I move my head, my eyes zeroing in on Luz—and the precious organ hidden deep within her chest.

I can hear her heartbeat, loud and clear. Its power calls to me, my mouth salivating for it. Radu bends over me, his putrid scent overpowering my senses.

"You want her heart. Take it. Take it and join us, embrace your full nature, holding nothing back. There is more power here than you can guess, cousin."

I want to shake my head, I want to say no. But for once, I am not in control, the full moon contributing to the fog in my head. And I know now why Radu wanted me high for this—my senses are dulled, and the darkness of the vrykolakas is calling out like a siren.

The problem is, I'm not sure I can resist it.

Lucrezia

I don't know how it all went wrong, but we miscalculated at some point. Held tightly by a naked, smelly human-wolf who's about to dig his teeth into me is not my idea of fun, and I want to escape him and help Dom.

They shot him up with something, some kind of drug, and now he's lying down and looking at me. But what scares me is his eyes are no longer blue like they were, but the yellow is gaining on it. And for a second, I almost think I see a flash of red through them.

We need the pack to help get us out of this mess... We need someone.

Guys! I don't know if it'll work, I'm no wolf. But I try to think of Tristan, Finn and Lucas, closing my eyes and picturing their faces in my head. *We need help. Please!*

A slap on my cheek has me blink, startled. Radu is now standing before me, glaring at me and baring his teeth. "What the hell are you doing?"

I might miss what he's talking about, but damn my cheek stings! I raise my hand to cradle it, and taste blood on my lip. It's then I realize the guy holding me has now backed away, and I'm free.

"Answer my question, human."

Radu's eyes are cold when I raise my gaze to his, trying not to gag at his scent. "I have no idea what you're talking about."

Unfortunately, my attitude seems to piss him off more. He grabs me by the shoulders, shaking me hard enough to make my teeth rattle. "Who were you calling out to?"

Calling out? My eyes widen, but I mask my surprise at my success. If he heard me, then maybe the guys did, too. *If so, we need time...* I glance at Dom, who's now struggling to get to his feet.

Radu lets go of me with a disgusted snort, and turns to Dom. "She's all yours, cousin. I like breaking my women in, but this one's too much trouble."

I glare at his back, picturing running my fist through his thick skull. A growl draws my attention back to Dom. He's standing up now, albeit on staggering paws. And he's taking a few steps towards me. But his eyes...

Dom, what did they do to you?

There's no blue left. They're full yellow, with a rim of red, much like the rest of the creatures. Even his claws seem to have elongated, as did his canines. And he's walking towards me like I'm his next meal.

Shit.

I glance around, searching for something I might use as a weapon, if only until I can break through to him. But the vrykolakas have closed in, and Radu is watching with a satisfied smirk.

Despite the change in my boyfriend, I refuse to fear him. I remember Ileana's words, how she'd been so sure I could bring him back from the brink of darkness. I glance up at the moon, full and shining on us.

Really wish this relationship came with an instruction manual.

Dom is almost upon me now, and judging by the way his muscles tense, he's getting ready to pounce. Then clouds shift over the moon, covering it. Radu raises an annoyed glance up to the sky, the only indication that it's something significant.

I focus back on Dom, and he's faltering in his step. He blinks, and the blue returns to his gaze. Then his explanation rings in my ears, making me gasp. *The moon!* It must be screwing with his head, encouraging the primal part of him, and the drugs aren't helping.

"Dom?" My whisper makes him tilt his head, and I try to rein in my excitement. "Dom, you have to fight this, please!"

A gust of wind picks up and everything is brighter again, the moon no longer covered. The yellow returns to his eyes, and I know I lost my one chance to get through to him.

In the next breath, Dom pounces towards me. I have a moment of clarity and shift my stance, grabbing his head mid-way and using his momentum to flip him. He lands on his back with a thud, and I throw all my weight on him.

In this form, flattened on his back, Dom is as long as he is in human form. He jerks against me, struggling, but the drugs in his system make him weaker, dimming his strength and capacity to fight.

I thank my lucky stars for that small blessing. "Dominic, please!" My whispers are urgent in his ear. "You need to snap out of this."

Dominic

It's like I'm in a badly lighted alleyway, with a light flickering on and off. On, and all I want to do is rip my mate's heart out of her chest and consume it. Off, and I see her face, hear her pleas, and want to struggle against this impulse with all my might.

The drug in my system is wearing off, not that I'm sure it's a good thing. This time, when I come to, Lucrezia's on top of me, her scent filling my nostrils.

Flashes of what we shared mere hours earlier run through my head, warming my heart and dispelling the fog that seems to have consumed me.

But before I can intervene, Radu yanks her off me. He throws her in the arms of one of his acolytes, jabbing a finger towards her and yelling. I can't make out his words at first, but catch the end.

"If you fuck this up for me, you'll regret it, bitch!"

A snarl erupts from my throat, my wolf protesting his mistreatment of our girl.

"I'll kill him before I let you corrupt him!" Luz spits in his face, and Radu loses it.

He swings his hand back to hit her, and I see red. Despite the dizziness and the ground moving under my paws unsteadily, I lunge towards him, hitting his back and sprawling atop it. My claws dig in it, drawing blood. Out of the corner of my eye, I catch Luz elbowing the guy holding her and releasing herself.

I step off Radu, joining her side and morphing back into human form. I pull her in my arms, inhaling her scent. "Lucrezia..."

She shivers in my arms, and at first I think it's because she wants me off her. But then her hands wrap around my neck, pulling me closer and burying her head in my neck. "I thought I'd lost you!"

My grip tightens on her. "Never."

"How touching. But I'm not done with you yet, cousin."

I pull back enough to look at Radu, not dropping my hand off Luz. "Leave these parts while you still can, cousin. You cannot win this fight."

He sneers and is about to say something when growls surround us. I scan the surroundings as the creatures move closer to their leader, not noticing anything at first. Glowing eyes pop out of the shadows, and I recognize the large wolf at their head.

"Jared."

It's pretty evident what he's here for, judging by the number of wolves with him. It's the entire pack, clustered together in pairs. Luz's grip tightens on my hand, and I squeeze back.

Yeah, I know. This keeps getting better by the second.

I pull her to my chest in a one-armed hug, using the opportunity to whisper in her ear. "I have to morph again. Do you still have your knife?" She nods against me. "Good. Try to get the hell out of here at the earliest opportunity."

"I'm not leaving you!"

"Luz..." Her gaze is stubborn when it meets mine, and I sigh, knowing I can't deter her. "Try to play them off against each other. Jab the knife in the eyes or near the ears, they're more sensitive there."

Her swift agreement makes my heart swell with pride. Though I blame myself for getting her in this situation, I know I never would have been able to return without her presence to ground me. Ileana was right all along.

I let her go and take my wolf form, placing myself in front of her. *What are you doing here, Jared?*

What's it look like? Vengeance. Your fuckers killed a third of my men, Aiden included.

You've got half of that right. I jerk my head towards the creatures watching us with interest—and hunger. I bet our hearts would make great candidates for snacks. *They killed your wolves, all right. But they're not mine.*

Jared snorts, not believing me. *What does it matter? You'll all die tonight, your redhead included.*

Without bothering with more threats, Jared throws his head back and howls. It must be the signal the pack is waiting on, because they lunge forward with ferocious snarls, two against each creature.

Jared moves towards me and Radu, the intent to kill shining in his eyes. Movement on the periphery grabs my attention, and I catch Luz stabbing the hand of one wolf in human form that tried to grab her. The guy pulls back with a hissed curse, and she follows up the attack with a kick to the groin that leaves him crawling away on the ground.

Then she turns, scanning her surroundings for the next threat. My wolf roars his approval, loud enough to make her smile.

Using my distraction to his advantage, Jared slams into my side, and we roll on the ground. He comes up on top, snarling. *Your death will be sweet.*

I was not involved, you fool!

Too bad. I see his jaws move towards my neck and cord my feet, pushing against his belly. He's in a position to dominate, but I'm stronger. I throw him off me and before he can attack again, another wolf jumps between us.

I recognize Tristan's colors, and his voice comes in my head. *You okay, meu amigo?*

Yes. I glance around, not noticing Finn or Lucas. *How did you know?*

We all heard Luz's call. Finn and Lucas are just slower.

Her what?

Tristan throws me a look. *Lucrezia was able to tap into our pack link. Must be due to her connection with you, or whatever. Does it matter? She called, we came. And we don't have time for this, Dom. Go after your cousin, I'll handle the rest.*

It's only then I notice Radu took off, and it seems half of his creatures followed him. I hesitate to leave Luz alone, especially after what she just survived. As if sensing it, she glances up from the last wolf she wrestled to the ground. "GO! I'll be fine."

I take a hesitant step towards her, but she shakes her head and points to the path Radu disappeared on. It's then I know exactly why Ileana wanted me to have Luz with me. To bring me back from the edge, but also to push me forward to finish this.

With one jump, I move past Tristan. *Watch over her.*

Go do what you have to do. I got your back, and hers.

Lucrezia

I could have cried in relief when Tristan showed up. At first I thought he was another wolf, but then he turns and I recognized the soft chocolate eyes. When he joined Dom's side, I knew he was an ally.

It's about time! Between Jared and his wolves, and Radu and his crazies, the clearing we're in is filling up.

Dom listens to us and goes chasing after Radu. There is no way he can get them all to leave unless he takes the alpha position away from Radu. I shiver, hoping this doesn't mean he must turn vrykolakas to be worthy.

As the thought strikes me, I pause. Ileana said he needed me... I bite my lip, glancing around for Tristan. He's fighting two wolves, and with little thought for my safety I jump in the fray, knife in hand.

Tristan nudges me with his muzzle, presumably to push me away, but I don't listen and instead kick the wolf to his right to get his attention. There's a manic gleam in his eyes when he whirls to face me, jaws wide open for a bite, and jumps.

I duck under, jabbing the knife upwards. A spurt of blood shoots out and catches me in the face. I grimace, wiping my face on the sleeve of my jacket. The wolf is crawling away to a bush, disappearing within.

Tristan smacks the wolf closest to him about, then turns back to me. He meets my gaze and looks behind me. A quick glance over my shoulder confirms he's pointing to the path Dom disappeared through.

"You think I should follow him?"

He nods, but I hesitate. Sure, Tristan is strong and a wolf, and yes, the vrykolakas are mostly engaged in fights with Jared's wolves. But I don't like leaving him alone without backup.

Tristan decides for me, pushing me towards the path again. "All right, I'm going! But howl if you need help."

He rolls his eyes and turns his back to me, leaving me standing at the edge of the clearing. With one last glance around, I turn tail and head down, hoping I can find Dom.

Though I'm no wolf, I try to keep my footsteps as silent as possible. There's no telling what else is hiding in these woods, and I'd rather not find out. The fresh coat of snow makes it easy to follow Dom's tracks, overlapping Radu's.

At one particular crossing, I stop and frown. There are a lot of tracks, and my worry for Dom increases. Can he really win against Radu, especially if he doesn't fight fair? And what if he shoots him up with some other drugs?

I quicken my step, not watching where I'm going. I pass through some bushes, grappling for support and my foot slips on something. Next thing I know, I'm sliding down, down, and *down*. My butt hits a root poking out of the snow, and it breaks my fall but also makes me sprawl everywhere.

By the time I get back up, wiping at my face to dust the snow, my clothes are wet and my jeans are clinging to my feet. Shivers run down my spine, but that's not what worries me. My knife, my only real weapon in this fight, is gone.

Too late to go back.

Determined, I dust myself up and move around another bend. This time, I can see a cave—and a dark wolf heading towards it. I recognize the white stripe on his back.

Dom stops before the cave, tilting his head as if listening to something. Then he enters it, disappearing from my view. I strain my ears, trying to hear what's going on. The uneasy silence has me edgy, twitching on my feet.

The rational part of my brain tries to tell me I'm human, with many weaknesses. But my heart, tangled with Dom's, is only worried at losing him. So when I hear snarls within, I straighten my stance and take a few steps closer. Those self-defense lessons should come in handy right about now.

"Not so fast, human."

∞ Lege ∞

"At his best, man is the nobles of all animals; separated from <u>law</u> and justice he is the worst."

-Aristotle-

Lucrezia

I whirl around, unable to believe my bad luck. Jared's teeth flash in the moonlight, and behind him are four other wolves. Oh yeah, and he's completely naked.

I avert my gaze, and his laugh raises shivers up my spine—and not the good kind. "Come now, I can't be that bad."

He must have escaped from Tristan's vigilance, leaving him and the Reapers to deal with the creatures. I clench my empty fist, wishing I still had my knife. This is not a fight I want to start defenseless.

Jared takes another step forward, and the wolves behind him fan out. If they surround me, I'm royally screwed.

"I'm taken," I force through gritted teeth while meeting his gaze. "And under the protection of a pack. You can't touch me."

"Are you, now? Funny. I don't see Lucas anywhere. And last we heard, he ousted your boy toy. Which means you're free game."

Shivers run through me, both from my wet clothes as from the implication of his words. *This is what Dom warned me against, if he was to leave the pack...* One look at Jared's face, and the glint in his eyes confirms he doesn't plan to kill me quickly. No, Jared wants to play.

"I thought touching humans is beneath you."

Apparently, that's the worst thing I could say as Jared moves even closer. "For you, I'll make an exception, human."

I can't overpower him alone. It's one thing to fight three small wolves in a dark alley somewhere, but Jared is strong and twice my size and weight. My odds aren't looking good, and my muscles are clenching because of the cold.

Fear must flash on my face—or maybe he hears my heartbeat increasing—because his smile grows wider. "Run while you can, darling. 'Cause when I catch you, it'll be that much sweeter."

I take one step to the side, intending to do just that. Then I see the excitement flare in his eyes—and other places—and freeze. *Hell, no.*

I fought Tommy on my own and survived, and he had a gun. There's no way I'm going to let this macho racist asshole get the better of me. A deep breath later, my panicked heartbeat slows down. I scan the area, trying to pretend like I'm searching for someone to help.

The ruse works and my eyes catch sight of a branch to my left, only a foot away. If I can get to it, it'll give me some leverage. In some corner of my mind, I realize fighting these Reapers alone is suicide. But if I call out to Tristan or Dom, I risk distracting them and endangering them.

Whether I like it or not, I'm on my own. *And I'm no one's damn prey.*

Instead of running, I face Jared, straightening my back. "Sorry, I don't do role-playing. If you want me, you'll have to get me the old-fashioned way."

His lip curls over his teeth, and a low snarl starts in his chest.

Dominic

The cave is dark, but my eyesight is no longer blurry and I see perfectly where I'm stepping. More vrykolakas line the walls, and I lose count after the first dozens. There must be at least fifty of them in here, if not more. Yet they let me walk amid them, giving no sign of noticing me other than a flash of yellow eyes and growls to my sides.

I get to the center of the cave. Of all the people in the world, it had to be my crack-addicted cousin who leads this band of idiots. He's in wolf form, shaking his head and pacing in agitation.

My flank is bleeding as is my neck, but they're flesh wounds. If I morph, they won't be too bad and can heal over the next few days, despite the full moon. Still, I know full well I need to watch for other strikes, otherwise one of them could be my last.

And I can't let that happen. I need to get out here for Luz, so we can finally enjoy quality time without this crap hanging over our heads. At thoughts of her, something nags at me. It's like I feel her panic, followed by some kind of resolution.

She should be with Tristan, but the disconnection I catch predicts nothing good. I've got half a mind to turn back and check on her, but Radu stops in his movements and faces me.

Well, well. Look who wandered back to the den.

My jaw opens and I bare my teeth. *You and I have unfinished business.*

Not really, cousin. You refused to join us. Our business is as finished as it comes. He glances at a wolf to my side, nodding his permission. *He's all yours.*

I kick myself for not attacking first and asking questions later, but it's too late. The cluster of wolves moves towards me, caging me in. One daring vrykolakas snaps his jaw near me, but I smack him over the muzzle, moving out of his reach.

Another one jumps on my back, his claws tearing into my back. I howl at the pain, but it gets cut off when a third wolf claws at my face. They're attacking from all sides, and there's no way I can face off against their testosterone and drug-enhanced bodies.

Yet I try. I fight each of them as they come, landing hits, biting, ripping into their flesh. Though they manage to scratch me, I don't let them get close enough to bite into me, recalling what their venom does to others.

There's no escape from their midst, not if I continue like this. So I curl into myself, letting them all pile on top of one another, trying to get me. At the last moment, I gather all my strength and jump from their midst, landing to face Radu. I'm panting, and blood is dripping off me to the floor.

Enough.

Radu tilts his head as if surprised by my demand. *I am the alpha here, cousin. You may have the white stripe of our royal bloodline, but you do not call things off.*

The...what? Looks like I still have things to learn.

My cousin snorts, rolling his eyes. *You've never wondered why you have a white line on your back? Didn't you notice I have one on my chest?* He puffs said part of his body to better showcase it. *It's the imprint of our royal bloodline.* His gaze lingers on me, then he scoffs. *Too bad you're unworthy of it.*

I beg to differ. On the contrary, I think I deserve anything that comes with that lineage more than you do. Taking a step closer, but keeping out of reach, I straighten up. *Which is why I'm challenging you for alpha.*

Radu's eyes flash complete red as he throws his head back and laughs. *You? You want to challenge me for alpha?*

There's an eerie silence around us now, as the other vrykolakas have stopped fighting. Their stench is overpowering, but I'm almost used to it by now. *Yes.*

Radu shakes his head, dismissing the idea as ludicrous. *You're a fool, Dominic Konstantin. And I will enjoy ripping you to shreds. When I'm done with you, I'll take my time with your precious mate.*

I refuse to rise to the bait, instead shaking my fur and testing my muscles. Radu watches me like a cat would a bird it's about to eat, then inclines his head. *Very well. I will humor you, though you will end up paying with your life.*

We'll see. I feint to the right, but change mid-move and lunge at him. He thinks I'm going for his neck, so he moves to protect it. But instead my razor-sharp canines dig into his flank, long and deep enough to draw blood.

At his howl, I pull back and Radu smacks empty air. The other vrykolakas have now gathered around, circling us. We have a few feet only to move, but I know they won't intervene. Creatures of the night or not, an alpha contention is the same across any wolf pack, between the current leader and the contender. *No one may stop it.*

Not that cheating isn't allowed. I focus my attention back on my cousin, wary of his next move. And still I sense Luz's agitation, and pray she's alright.

Keep her safe, Tristan. You made me a promise.

Lucrezia

I guess Jared doesn't expect me to face him because his expression when I step closer rather than run is priceless.

"I won't give you the satisfaction. You want me? Come and get me. But at least be a man and fight me in human form, don't be a pussy." Not that I want to see more of his naked body, but I definitely don't want those wolfish canines anywhere near my flesh.

Jared flushes, but takes a few steps forward with clenched fists. I put up my palm, grimacing. "Would it kill you to put on a pair of pants?"

He scowls, his eyes flashing. "You're annoying me, human." He takes a swing at me, and I pretend to duck, but do so clumsily. When Jared moves, I allow him to put me in a chokehold.

His breath is on my neck, and every part of his body presses against me. *Yuck.*

Still, I keep my eyes on the prize, glued to the branch that's so close by. Reaching for it with all their eyes on me would be suicide. But if I use a ruse, it'll at least give me the advantage of surprise.

So when Jared puts his mouth to my ear, whispering how he'll enjoy this, I ignore him and clench my teeth, closing my eyes. "What's the matter, human? Cat got your tongue?"

I wait until his lips opens on my neck as if to bite down, trying to hold back my shivers of disgust and fear. Dom was clear about Jared's bite being enough to turn a human into a wolf. Since I have no intention of becoming a furry creature, I bide my time.

When Jared stops to inhale, savoring the moment, I jerk my head back with all my might and hear the crack of bone. Ignoring his swearing, I then stomp on his bare foot, putting my entire weight on it. My boots, if nothing else, have a hard sole, and Jared loosens his hold on me enough for part two.

I grab the arm wrapped around my neck and drop to my knees, flipping him over my head. Then I let the momentum carry me too, and land a few feet away. Buried in the snow, I pretend to moan in pain, taking my time to stand back up.

By the time I'm facing the wolves again, I have one hand behind me, gripping the branch and hiding it behind my legs. *Gotcha.*

Jared's back on his feet as well, scowling and bleeding from the nose. I doubt I actually broke anything, but I must have pushed his buttons because he switches to wolf form without warning. I hold the branch tighter in my hand, ready for him.

When he lunges, I swing it like a baseball bat and get him in the chest. With an oomph of distress, he falls to the ground, rolling away. I'm panting, biting back my scream of victory as he staggers back to his feet, shaking his head.

Jared's goons snarl, moving in closer. But he rights himself and jerks towards them, plainly ordering them to stay away. Then he side-steps, circling me.

I'm forced to move with him, while still keeping my back clear of the other wolves. Jared's eyes drop to the branch in my hand, narrowing. Somehow, I doubt I've endeared myself to him.

Snarls grab my attention, but this time they're faint. I glance towards the cave, biting my lip. *Dom...*

Jared uses my moment of inattention and jumps again. I turn back in time to duck his attack, but his claws grab hold of my calf, tearing through jeans and ripping into my ankle. I scream, loud and long, and smack his muzzle with the branch.

He lets go, crawling away, and I drag my foot away. Trying to stand up is a fail, and I fall back. Blood seeps from the wound, painting the snow burgundy, and I feel the color leave my cheeks.

I never liked blood, least of all my own. And seeing the gaping flesh around my wound now, the snow getting wetter with the red liquid, is making my breath hitch.

Movement grabs my attention, and I scan my surroundings. *Now's not the time to lose focus.* Jared is getting to his feet, and his wolves are moving in closer to him. This time, he doesn't push them away. He towers over them, alpha in his own right, and whatever he tells them causes ripples of amusement to run through them.

Then Jared advances towards me, his muscles shifting with every movement. His wolves follow from behind, and I don't have to hear their voices to know what he's trying to tell me.

You're mine now.

The gleam in his eyes passes the message clear as crystal, and I gulp, gripping the branch tighter.

Dominic

Radu's still circling me when I hear a scream from outside the cave—a human scream. I step towards it, recognizing Luz's voice, but the vrykolakas to the side gather closer, blocking my path.

Their beady eyes tell me everything I want to ignore. Now that the challenge has been called out, I cannot back down. Not if I want to keep my life.

Taking advantage of my distraction, Radu jumps on me. We roll on the floor, snarling and fighting like animals, but my heart's not in it. If Luz gets hurt because of me, none of this will mean anything. None.

I smack Radu off me, and get up at the same time he does. *You should have stayed off this territory.*

He laughs, finding my words amusing. *You still don't see it, do you?*

I pause in my movements, though my eyes never leave his form, watching for any sudden movements. *See what?*

We were invited, cousin. Do you honestly think I would have traveled such a long way, and risk fighting various packs, for no reason? My expression must have shown confusion because his voice grows smugger. *I took a few vrykolakas and crossed the ocean months ago. Europe is growing restless, hunters appearing everywhere, and with my father dead I thought it was time to try out for new pastures.*

He moves again, pacing from side to side but staying out of my reach. *Luz...* My wolf is impatient, wanting to be by her side now, not ten minutes from now. Yet much as I want to finish this, I also think there's more to the story, something we've missed amid all the chaos.

While we were getting a supply of drugs, we ran into a wolf from this region. He saw the value in our gifts, and invited us over, thinking we could help with a change of leadership.

And you expect me to believe this bullshit?

Radu shrugs. *Why would I lie, cousin? What do I have to gain from it, when the wolf is already dead?*

Already.... I flash back to the last time I'd seen Radu, and his unfortunate victim. *Aiden? He's the one who invited you here?*

Radu nods, watching me. The rest of it dawns on me, and I shake my head. *Wow, cousin. You even had me fooled. You were never there to help me that day, were you? Aiden came to blackmail you or some other stupid idea of his. And you weren't about to let him leave alive.*

Well done. My cousin's yellow-reddish eyes gleam, and I think he would have clapped if in human form. *You're right, of course. Aiden thought the fact he let us into the Reapers' territory was enough to make us obey him. He found out how mistaken he was, albeit later on.*

But why? He had a secured position as beta of his pack. Yet according to you, he'd throw it away?

Aiden thought his alpha was weak, letting you four settle in and not doing anything against it. Then there's the story of the zmeu he struck a deal with.

My mind is whirling at the information, but I catch the Romanian word. *The what?*

Of course, I forget you were not bred in the lore as I was. He snorts, echoed by a few of the surrounding vrykolakas. *You would know him as a draco.*

A dragon? *You're telling me there's a dragon* here, *in Rockland Creek?*

Radu laughs, shifting his body to face me. *I think we've chatted enough. It's time to finish this, cousin.*

I prepare for his attack, crouching low and keeping my eyes on him. Luz needs my help, that certainty is almost clear in my head, echoed only by my wolf's whimpers of unease. The only way I can fix the situation, drive the vrykolakas away, is by showing them this territory is taken.

And they don't answer to outsiders, especially Lucas. So that leaves me with one option, and it's not one I can do half-assed. *You don't win alpha by letting the current leader walk off.*

Not in my world. And not in the world of the vrykolakas.

Looks like you were right, Ileana. Time to own up to who I am.

When Radu jumps, I move out of the way. His body flies over me, and I lunge at the right moment, my paw clawing his chest. Radu hits the wall of the cave and falls down with a thud.

I prowl towards him, taking my time. His heartbeat is going haywire, and I realize it's from the pain of the hit. My cousin may be strong, but he's not invincible.

He stumbles up, wobbling on four paws, no longer stable. This time, it's my turn to attack. I tackle him to the ground and we roll a few times. He ends up on top, but with a smack of my paw he flies on the ground again.

My wolf nudges my consciousness, demanding the kill, and I let him take over. We move as one, unhurried, unrestrained. Radu is on his back, panting. I place my paw on his chest, ensuring he doesn't move.

The other paw presses into his neck, baring it for my teeth. There's no forgiveness, no death bed demands, no last words. No barriers between us, only my canines digging into his flesh, ripping his throat—and the sweetness of his heartbeats stopping.

I pull back and spit a patch of fur. Blood is dripping from my muzzle, and my wounds. The vrykolakas watch my every move, and I know they're waiting for a sign of weakness. My thoughts are on Luz—I need to survive this and make sure she's all right.

So despite the agony of my own wounds, the pain trying to incapacitate me, I puff out my chest, head held high, and stand up to my full height. *You've all born witness to what has taken place here. Şeful vostru e mort.*

There is a ripple at my announcement of their leader being dead, but their yellow eyes remain on me, unwavering. *By wolf law, you all know what this means. If anyone wants to contest me, now is the time, or you may all forever hold your peace.*

I turn my gaze to each wolf, until one passes through the pack. He's bulky and young, enough so that he could probably take me if that's what he's after. To my surprise, rather than be aggressive, he bends his front paw to the ground.

His yellow eyes, previously meeting mine, are now downcast to the ground and he exposes his neck for my taking. *All hail the alpha!*

One by one, each vrykolakas bends their paw until I'm towering over them all. Cheers of *hail the alpha* surround me, and I know what they're all expecting.

I throw my head back, letting my wolf loose, and we howl in tandem. The noise is deafening, but it feels like home.

Lucrezia

Jared is only a foot away from me, his jaw open and ready to snap my neck. My knuckles are white from clenching the branch, and I know he's waiting for me to weaken enough so I don't fight back.

Just when I think I'm seeing two of him, another wolf hops over my head and lands between us. He's followed by another... and another.

I gape at the trio of reddish fur, snowy white and dark grey, knowing it can only be two others that have joined Tristan – Lucas and Finn.

The middle snowy white wolf turns his head towards me, nostrils flaring as he notices my ankle. He backs away from facing Jared and disappears into the woods. A minute later, it's Finn in human form who crosses through the snow, barefoot and in jeans, a shirt held ripped in his clenched fist.

"Finn..." My mouth is pasty, and I glance down to see the snow soaked with my blood.

"You're all right, love. Hang on." He kneels next to me, and the surrounding growls from Lucas and Tristan fade away, until all I can focus on is his touch on my ankle.

With careful movements, Finn picks up a fistful of clean snow and wipes my ankle. I hiss as the cold hits my overheated flesh, then numbness spreads through me.

Finn glances up, frowning. "Why didn't you call out to us? We were helping Tristan up the hill, unaware of what was going on here."

I have enough strength to shake my head though my words come out as a mumble. "I didn't want... to distract you guys. Thought I could...fight..."

Finn's lips press together, and I distinctly hear his teeth grinding. "You're part of our pack, Luz. That means we help you, distractions or not." Despite his firm tone, his touch is gentle as he wraps the ripped shirt around my ankle, tightening it to stop the blood flow.

When all the pieces are wrapped around the wound, he stands up and holds a hand for me to grasp, helping me to my feet. I wince at the pain in my ankle.

"Lean on me," Finn whispers, not once taking his eyes off Lucas and the face off. I grimace, but do as he says. Step by step, he brings us closer.

By their tense bodies, I can tell Lucas and Jared are arguing. Tristan is keeping watch over the other wolves, though he throws a look over his shoulder when Finn and I inch near.

Finn shakes his head at whatever he asks. "She'll be alright, don't worry."

I tug on his hand, trying to ask what's going on, but my mouth doesn't function. I think I'm leaning all my weight on him now, but Finn says nothing, instead firming his grip so I don't fall.

"Tristan's worried about you, and he feels guilty for letting you go off on your own."

I take forever to get out the words. "Not.... your... fault."

Tristan whines low, and somehow I don't think he believes me. Communication is limited by his wolf form, but I make a mental note to talk to him when he's back to human.

A hair-rising howl interrupts us, and we all turn to the cave—minus Lucas and Jared.

"Where's Dom?"

Finn squeezes my waist in reassurance though I see him share a look with Tristan and Lucas. "One thing at a time, love."

Whatever conversation is going on with them passes right over my head until Finn whispers. "We've got trouble."

I crane my neck to where he's pointing. Row after row of creatures emerges from the cave, paired or alone. They fan out until they surround us, and I recall everything me and Finn learned about their special abilities.

"I'm not leaving you two alone and neither will Luz."

I glance at Finn in surprise, then Lucas who moved by his side. He's still in wolf form, glaring at me with an almost annoyed look on his face. Tristan is keeping an eye on Jared, ensuring he's not leaving anywhere.

Finn's words now make sense, and I realize Lucas must have told him to take me away, leaving him and Tristan to face off against the creatures alone. "Finn's right. I'm not leaving any of you. If we fight, we all fight together."

Movement interrupts our conversation. The creatures closest to us part like water, and in their midst another wolf emerges. He's covered in blood, his fur matted and bleeding in parts. But I can see the white stripe on his back, and the blue of his eyes when they land on me.

"Dom!"

CHAPTER EIGHTEEN

∞ Curaj ∞

"Courage is knowing what not to fear."

-Plato-

Dominic

I walk past the vrykolakas—my pack—dragging my back leg, and emerge at their head. Their strength is like a second heart behind me, tangible and encouraging. Despite my beat-up state, their presence fills me with renewed energy.

Still in wolf form, I scan the area until I have a clearer picture of what's going on. I see Luz in Finn's arms, and Lucas facing off Jared, Tristan by his side.

My wolf growls at the sight of Luz in another man's arms, until my friend's narrowed gaze sinks in. I smell blood on her and notice her bandaged ankle.

Finn must have understood my question because he snaps his fingers to get my attention. "She's fine. Injured, but she'll be alright."

My eyes shift to Luz next, noticing her glazed look. She's leaning way too heavily on Finn, which makes me think she's in dire need of medical attention. A snarl takes my attention away, and I notice Lucas moving to stop Jared from advancing.

Wait here. The order is meant for my pack, and they take a step back and wait for my next command. I pass by Luz, sniffing at her ankle and giving it a soft lick. Her hand runs over my fur, and I nudge her.

I'll be back soon. Stay strong, draga mea.

I know she can't hear me, but her slight nod shows she understands. So I focus all my attention on Jared and his wolves. Joining Lucas, I stand straight—even if full of blood.

My thoughts focus on my former alpha, ensuring whatever I say will only be heard by him. *One of his pack called the vrykolakas here,* I inform Lucas.

He glances at me, noticing I'm step in step with him, not to the side like a beta does. For a moment, considering the way we ended things, I fear he might start something. Instead, he nods. *Do you know who?*

Yeah, not that it's much use. It was Aiden, and my cousin killed him.

Lucas narrows his eyes as if coming to a decision and steps to Jared. *This ends now. From alpha to alpha, you have transgressed our laws and tried to harm one of my own.*

She's a filthy human!

I snarl, stepping closer until I'm muzzle to muzzle with him. *Watch yourself, Jared. You're already on a thin leash.*

He glares at me. *Back off, beta. This is a conversation between alphas.*

And he is exactly where he's meant to be. I glance at Lucas, surprised by his support, but his attention doesn't waver from Jared. *You're speaking to the leader of the vrykolakas, so show some respect.*

Jared gapes at me, then laughs, a low rumble. *I knew it! I knew from the beginning you had a hand in bringing those creatures here!*

My wolf takes over and we move, growling low. *Second warning, Jared. Heed my tone. I'm no traitor to my pack—old or new. And I had nothing to do with them, other than being related to their previous leader. The same can't be said for the traitor in your midst.*

Jared stops talking, letting my words sink in. He looks to Lucas. *What's that?*

You have a traitor among you. It is he who let the vrykolakas into your territory, allowing them protection without your knowledge.

There's a rumble behind Jared from his wolves that have been following the exchange. I keep a close eye on them in case they attack. But they're mellow, expecting a signal from their leader.

Jared stares between me and Lucas, then shrugs. *And why do I care?*

Because you may be racist pricks, but you also value loyalty in your own.

Who is it, then?

Lucas snorts, his body shaking with silent laughter. *Not so fast. You agree to my terms, then we talk.* When Jared goes silent, he continues, *You leave our human alone—and I mean for good. Regardless of whether she stays with us or goes with Dominic, Lucrezia is untouchable. In exchange, I give you the name of your traitor.*

Your bitch humiliated me!

A quick glance over my shoulder confirms the discarded branch near Luz, and my tail wags. *That's my girl.* She notices it and smiles back.

My attention shifts to Jared and I step until I overshadow Lucas. *Disrespect my mate one more time, and you'll wish she's the one fighting you next time. Accept his terms, or else.*

She's human! How dare you corrupt your blood so? She's garbage to us, food, a—

Enough!

Too late. Lucas' growl might have echoed, but I'm already lunging at Jared. We grapple on the ground until I overpower him, jaw on his jugular, my teeth close to sinking in.

I could kill you right now, and your pack would be none the wiser. But I know what losing a leader does to idiots like yours. So I will spare you. But you owe me a life debt, Jared, don't you ever forget that.

Despite the pain from my wounds, I move off him without showing weakness and re-join Lucas. Jared jerks to his feet, evidently intending to fight. Snarls from both me and Lucas quickly change his mind, and his eyes dart to the two packs in the background. No matter how much he wants to fight, he realizes he's outnumbered and his ears flatten on his head. *Very well. I agree to your terms. Who is the traitor?*

Lucas looks back at me, and takes a step back, allowing me to speak. I incline my head in acknowledgement, before addressing Jared. *It was Aiden who betrayed you. He disliked your policies, thought them weak, especially when you struck the deal with the zmeu.*

I must have said something right, because Jared doesn't react, nor does he try to argue the point. Instead, he turns to his wolves. *We've suffered enough losses here. The redhead is off limits, you all bore witness to the pact. Now move.*

I wait until they're all gone, disappearing in the bushes, which is how I see Jared throw one last glare my way, then Luz's. I wouldn't trust the guy as far as I can throw him, and I intend to keep an eye on him.

Once they're gone, I turn back to Lucas. *You knew I won alpha?*

I know the sound of an alpha howl, brother. His jaw opens in a grin. *Congratulations are in order, I believe.*

Distracted, my gaze lingers on Luz, then the vrykolakas. The simple thing here would be to leave with them, to lead them somewhere else. Ileana said I could save them if I so choose… But Lucas, Tristan and Finn are my wolf family, not these creatures that are more beast than wolf.

And then there's Luz. I notice the blood again seeping from her wound. There is no way I can survive away from her, even for a short time.

She can leave with you, amico.

I meet Lucas' knowing gaze. He's been following my train of thought, but I'm not ready to decide yet. *What would happen to the vrykolakas?*

If they leave our territory, they can keep their lives. Otherwise, it's death.

I nod, aware this is not a decision I can make on my own. Yet if they see me with Luz, there is a strong chance I'll lose my one advantage over them.

Lucas settles the matter for me. *You wouldn't. They are bound to you, and your Luna. In fact, they're already protecting her. Look closer.*

I follow his advice and peer at the vrykolakas. While half of their attention is on me, the other half is focused on Luz, on her every breath. When Finn shifts and she gasps in pain, one daring vrykolakas moves closer.

Stand down. He hears me and steps back in line. I take that moment to morph and head to Luz, taking her in my arms. Despite being covered as I am with blood, grime and dust, she wraps her arms around my waist and buries her head in my chest.

Dimly, she notices my naked self and mutters, "Can you put some clothes on?"

I chuckle and glance over her head, where Lucas is stepping closer, also in human form. He's zipping his jeans on and throws me a faded pair. I let go of Luz to pull them on, but don't bother with dirtying a shirt.

When I wrap my arm around her again, her entire weight leans on me and I glance down with worry. "How are you holding up?"

She opens her mouth to answer me, but Finn beats her to it. He interrupts our little moment with a slap on my back—hard enough to jostle me forward.

"Your girl is something! She took on Jared all by herself. By the time we got here, he was shaking his head like he didn't know what hit him."

Pride swells within me, but Luz only flushes in embarrassment. I'm glad to see some color in her pale cheeks. Tristan joins us next, a half-smile on his smug face. "It was funny watching the *babaca* squirm."

I nudge Luz's neck with my nose, breathing in her scent. She shivers in my arms, and I fear she'll need solid medical attention after this. Unless my talk with Lucas goes well, that is.

"Can you wait a bit longer?"

She looks up at me, green eyes full of relief and love, searching my expression. "I'll be fine—whatever you decide, Dom. Go do what you have to."

I kiss her full-on, relishing the way she melts against me. It's short-lived before I release her back in Finn's arms. "Watch over her."

"With my life." I nod, satisfied he got my meaning, and follow Lucas to the edge of the clearing. I turn so I can keep an eye on Luz and my pack from afar.

"So." Lucas widens his stance, hands in his pockets, a relaxed pose.

I can't exactly mimic him with my wounds, which I'm still doing my best to ignore, but I cross my arms over my chest instead. "So."

"Mi dispiace... I'm sorry for what went down last time." Lucas rubs the back of his neck and straightens up. "Though you withheld things from me and acted like a righteous prick, I can't fault you for something you did not know of."

I nod, acknowledging his apology. "And I'm sorry for the way things ended. You have to believe me, I never meant to hurt you, Lucas. As my alpha, you were everything a wolf needs."

Despite my best intentions, hurt flashes in his eyes when I use the past tense, and his nod is terse this time around. "What will you do now, as alpha of the vrykolakas? Leave with them, and Luz?"

My gaze lingers on the creatures. Maybe it's because of my new status, but I feel a certain pity towards them, knowing they will never have the peace I do. Yet I can't judge, because they seem happy where they're at right now.

"I will make sure they stop ripping hearts out, for one. And they'll leave your territory, don't worry."

Lucas glances at them, then back at me. A muscle ticks in his jaw and his brow furrows as if trying to decide something pivotal. His nod is more to himself when he extends a hand towards me. "*Our* territory, if you so wish."

My jaw slackens as I stare at his offered hand for what feels like a long, long time. I get what he's asking, of course, but the intricacies of how that would work...

As if reading my mind, Lucas says, "I will not ask you to give up the alpha of the pack. But you can continue being my beta as long as you are on my territory. If ever you wish to leave, you are free to do so."

"So basically, nothing changes?"

Lucas nods, searching my gaze. "I want this to work, Dom. The four of us, we've been through a lot together."

I move my hand, about to shake his, but a thought stops me. "And Luz?"

"I will not stand between you, if that is your worry. Though for her protection, we should initiate her under our pack—but mated to you."

"So for all intents and purposes, she would be my Luna." Lucas nods at the term, reserved for the mate of the alpha. I grin, then shake his hand with a resounding smack. "We've got a deal."

Lucas turns back to the rest of our pack, grinning. "Bene. Though I have to say, I don't envy you her spirit, amico."

"That's because you're not wolf enough to handle it." Lucas' laugh echoes behind me as I stride over to my mate, my shoulders a million years lighter now.

Lucrezia

While Dom and Lucas are chatting, I'm doing my best to stay awake in Finn's arms. "About that hospital..."

His grip tightens on my waist, and I draw in a breath. "You may not need it, love."

I peer at the blood still oozing from my ankle, then up at him. The sky seems to move above me, and I hear Finn whispering my name urgently.

"I'm okay, I'm okay," I mutter, leaning even more against him. "But I don't agree, I think I lost a lot of blood."

Tristan moves closer, gripping my shoulder. "Beleza, stay with us. They're almost done." What the hell does Dom's conversation with Lucas have to do with the fact I'm bleeding my entire bloodstream here?

My blurry vision moves to Dom and Lucas shaking hands, then my boyfriend is moving closer. He pulls me from Finn's arms into his own, and his heat seeps through my wet clothes. I notice his body is unmarred by scratches or battle wounds, and somehow that eases the worry that had been plaguing me.

"I got you." Dom's whisper is close to my ear. "I know it's hard, draga mea, but I need you to hang on. You have to decide something... And if you say yes, you'll be better after, I promise."

I blink, forcing my eyes to meet his. "Say yes to what?"

Lucas inches nearer, his eyes on me. "I have a proposition... If you're all right to stay in the pack, that is."

"Stay in the pack?" I repeat, frowning. "Why wouldn't we? Lucas, if this is about me—"

He holds up his hand, smiling. It's such a change from the guy I last interacted with, that I know my confused expression shows on my face.

"I owe you an apology, cara, much like I did Dom. For the way I acted." His eyes dart between us, and a corner of his mouth pulls up into a half-smile. "Truth be told, what you two have is pure enough to make any wolf in this vicinity jealous."

I'm too far gone in my weakness to stop my snort, and Dom chuckles in response. His arm tightens around me, and it's all the heads up I get before Lucas' intense gaze drags mine.

"Until now, you have been under our wing. But I would like to offer you full initiation into our midst."

I lick my dry lips, managing one question. "Does this mean I have to learn how to turn furry?"

Lucas' burst of laughter is echoed by the guys, and I even catch a few snorts from the silent creatures behind us. Our fearless leader faces everyone, spreading his palms open.

"Let's give Luz the full protection of the pack, sì?"

"Hell yeah!" Finn hollers, ripping me from Dom's arms and swinging me around. I laugh, begging him to let me go until he relents—straight into Tristan's arms.

My eyes meet Tristan's chocolate ones. "I will agree, but on one condition."

"And what's that, beleza?"

"You don't feel guilty for what happened with Jared. I was the one who left, Tristan, and what happened after is on my shoulders alone."

He searches my expression and I try to appear as resolute as possible. Tristan ends up shaking his head, half-smirking. "You're serious, aren't you? You won't say yes unless I agree to this?"

"Agree and *mean it*."

Tristan nods, and I know his word is one thing he won't break. Before I can leave the circle of his arms, he pulls me into a hug. "I'll agree to that on another condition. That you learn to ask for help next time. Claro?"

I pull back, seeing the earnest look in his eyes. Knowing what I do of Tristan, how he lost his squadron in the last war he fought, how he suffers from nightmares... I nod, and I vow to myself that I'll stop playing hero. These guys deserve better than that.

Dom pulls me away, grasping my hand. "You already know my vote," he grins to Lucas.

The alpha clasps his hands and I sense the vrykolakas getting agitated behind me. I glance there, then back at Dom. "Should they be here for this?"

He squeezes my hand. "It's better if they are and understand your role in this pack."

"So you really did...?"

Dom nods, and I can't help the pride that swells within me. When he grins, his eyes crinkle at the corners. "Enough about me, gorgeous. It's your turn now."

We face Lucas, though I don't know what to expect. The mind-numbing cold has somehow left my body, perhaps due to the temperature rising. After all, it's almost sunrise.

Yet when Lucas kneels before me, all my senses focus on his movement. He pulls a knife from his jeans' pocket, and my eyes widen. Dom must have caught my panic because his hand squeezes mine.

"Breathe, draga mea. It'll only take a minute."

Lucas' features are all business and hard granite as he unwraps the bandages Finn placed around my ankle. When the last of the material is off, blood trickles down my foot, spilling into the snow below, and my head spins again.

"Hurry, mate, she's ready to lose consciousness."

Lucas nods, bringing the knife closer to the wound. He holds it close to the skin, glancing up at me. "Normally, we would cut on the wrist or finger, but seeing as you're already hurt, there's no point in marring your skin further."

He gets up, the knife now full of blood. The guys gather close and hold their hands out, including Dom. Lucas flicks the knife onto each of their extended palms, and drops of my blood fall in them.

I watch, fascinated, as Finn licks the drops first. Then Tristan does the same, his nostrils flaring. Dom laps his until his palm is clean.

Finally, it's Lucas' turn. He meets my gaze, again with that half-smile. "Once I taste your blood, and the sun rises over that horizon, the ritual will be complete. You'll have been initiated into this pack. This means we will sense where you are, and be able to speak to you whether in wolf form or human. It also means you will get a few perks—enhancements, if you will, because of your mating with Dom."

His face is getting blurry, and I wish he'd finish up already so I can go to a hospital. But still, I ask, "Such as?"

"Easier healing, better hearing and sight in the dark." Lucas peers at me, hesitating with his mouth above the knife. "Before I take this last step, I need to ask you something. Lucrezia San Marco, do you willfully enter this pack and promise me, your alpha, your loyalty and allegiance, above all others?"

I sigh, leaning against Dominic. "I do. But not above Dominic." It's hard to keep my eyes open, but it's worth it to observe Lucas' stunned expression. "Sorry, Lucas, but you'll always come second to my mate."

His rumble of laughter is the last I hear before Lucas licks the knife, silently accepting my condition. At the same moment, the sun rises above the mountain, hitting us all with its light. I lift my arm to shield my eyes, oddly sensitive to it.

Then the light dims, and I drop my hand. My head feels lighter, and when I blink and glance around, my vision seems sharper. The guys' faces are more focused, the colors around me a bit more vibrant.

Lucas is staring at me, the knife still in his hand. I notice the sun is not up yet, but rather poking over the horizon.

"That's weird, I thought the sun..."

"Not quite, iubirea mea." Dom's there, my rock in this new world. "The flash of light you saw was the magic of the ritual being complete. That's how it works with Lucas' genes, and it's a variation of the same across cultures."

"Hmm." My speculative gaze falls on our new alpha, and there's a few questions already forming on the tip of my tongue. Before I can form a full one, I realize something else. My ankle doesn't hurt anymore.

I guess the questions can wait.

Agape, I glance down, only to see the wound healed. I'm still bloody, but it's dried and crusted, no longer the flowing liquid it was mere seconds ago. When my stunned gaze meets Lucas', he grins.

"Told you so, cara."

"I... Thank you."

He inclines his head, a smile playing on his lips. "Il piacere è tutto mio."

Show-off. I guess my new alpha can't even say *my pleasure* without trying to turn heads. It's a good thing mine's already occupied with another, equally stubborn wolf.

I hear Finn and Tristan high-five over my head, murmuring to each other, and I feel a slow grin spread over my face. But it's not the end, as Dom proves merely a heartbeat later.

"Lucas, one more favor." He reaches for the knife, wordlessly asking for more.

Lucas seems to understand the unspoken demand as he flicks a few more drops of blood. Dom drops my hand and walks over to the vrykolakas gathered behind us.

His gaze oversees the mass of them—fifty or so wolves with glowing yellowish-red eyes and dark furs—and stops on one towards the back.

"Come here."

I shiver at his tone, firm and commanding, and turn to watch what's happening. Far at the back, a creature moves forward. He's older than most, with white fur under his chin and chest.

Yet when he reaches Dom, there is only submission in his posture as he kneels and bows his head. Dom holds out his palm, full of my blood, towards him.

"This is my Luna's scent. Taste it, remember it. If ever she calls upon you—*any* of you—it is your duty to come, no matter how far you find yourselves at that point. Do you understand and acknowledge my command?"

Heads nod all around, and a few gazes turn to me, taking me in. I must be quite the sight in my ripped jacket and jeans, bloody ankle and mess of a hair. Not that it seems to matter to the vrykolakas, several of whom bow their heads in deference.

Dom speaks again, drawing all their attention. My gaze roams over his broad back, his tight muscles and ripped abs, and something coils within me, a need deeper than before. I bite it down—at least for now.

"My Luna is my everything—my life, my breath. If your paths cross, your duty is to protect her against anything and everything, even if it is one of your own. Clear?" Again, Dom's new pack nods and the elder vrykolakas nuzzles Dom's hand. Then his pink tongue darts out, licking the blood off.

When Dom next speaks, his voice is softer, but still as firm. He places his hand atop the creature's head. "You will act as my proxy with the pack. I cannot travel with you as my place is here. But I cannot leave you without a leader, either. I took your alpha from you, and replaced him, and I intend to fulfill my duties to the best of my abilities."

His gaze roams over them, and he takes a deep breath. This time, all softness is gone from him, and his profile is hard, stony almost. His voice, when he speaks, is cutthroat and almost makes me drop to my knees.

"Your history with drugs, it is over. Your ripping of hearts, it ends now. Radu continued to lead you all into sin, further and further a path of darkness that I cannot follow. My goal is different. I want salvation for you, and it is salvation I will get. Live free, breathe free, but *do not* harm humans or wolves. Live free of sin, of further darkness... And stay off this territory that you are no longer invited on. Do this for me, your alpha, and one day our paths will cross again. And when they do, I promise I will take my place as your prince—for good."

The vrykolakas are silent when he stops, their rapt gazes unwavering from Dom's face. And in that moment, with the sun rising as it does, he looks evermore the vengeful voivode—the true heir to Vlad Țepeș.

One by one, the creatures throw their heads back and howl, long and heavy. And Dom watches over them, silent, brooding, strong. It lasts a few moments, long enough for the sun to peak off the horizon, and bathe us all in light.

The noise stops, and the creatures move away. Only the elderly one stands by Dom, communicating something to him. When my mate inclines his head, he leaves as well, disappearing into the bushes.

Dom remains standing for a long moment, then turns to us. His stride is different when he walks towards me, and his eyes shine with newfound hope when he grabs my hand in his. "Let's go home."

∞ Înțelepciune ∞

"<u>Wisdom</u> cannot be gained without learning."

-Democritus-

Lucrezia

We take Dom's pickup home, while the guys take off in Lucas' Hummer. I've never seen his car before, and it reminds me of Ty and his.

Dom squeezes my hand as if sensing my wayward thoughts. "What are you thinking about?"

"So many things..." I chuckle, recalling what happened only hours earlier—what I had agreed to. "But right then, I found it weird Lucas has the same car as Tytus. I never pictured him for a Hummer kind of guy, you know?"

Dom lifts one shoulder in a careless shrug though his brow draws together. "This Tytus... Did he ever mention what kind of creature he is?"

"No... But Finn might know. If there's one thing I can tell you after that trip to New York, is that he's got loads of mythological information in that head of his."

We fall silent, and it's only a few moments later I realize we're not heading to my place. We pull over next to a small bungalow, and Dom turns off the engine.

"This is me." His grin is contagious, and he steps out the car, then he's by my door before I can even move.

He pulls it open and picks me up in his arms, in such a way I have no choice but to wrap my legs around his waist. I try to squirm out of his grip, but Dom walks us over to his house.

We barely get in and he kicks the door shut with his foot, capturing my mouth with his, unforgiving and demanding. I surrender to his skillful tongue, and before long I'm pressing my body against his, demanding more.

The need, the hunger I felt back in the clearing is back full on, and I can't deny my body any longer. Either Dom's feeling the same, or he catches my impatience, because he makes our clothes practically disappear in his haste, ripping when fabrics won't move out of the way like he wants.

Then there's only me, and him, and bare skin as he slides inside me. One hand toys with my breast, his mouth on my neck kissing, biting, nibbling... I don't recognize the sounds coming out of me, but before long I'm scratching his back, begging for more.

And Dom, wonderful lover that he is, gives in to my demands. He goes deeper, picking my ass up with one hand to increase the angle. His kiss swallows my gasp of pleasure, moving down my neck again, his powerful body undulating against me.

I throw my head back, powerless to his skills, uncaring of who may hear me. All I feel is Dom, all I care about is him moving inside me, hitting that spot, and then I'm close to touching the stars. So, so close…

"Luz. Look at me. I want to see those beautiful eyes, draga mea."

With a huge effort, I raise my head, meeting his darkened gaze. His jaw clenches, his every muscle tense with restraint. I lift a boneless hand, cupping his cheek, and brushing my lips against his. "I won't break. Let go, Dom."

He bites his lip, his hesitation clear, and I shift my hips against his. Control shatters his expression and he drives deeper inside me, staking his claim in the most primal way there is.

And I love every second of it.

Dominic

Luz is shaking me awake, but I'm having a hard time stirring from sleep after the marathon we just ran together. "You're a demanding little minx."

Her laugh shakes the bed—where we ended up for round three, four and then I lost count—but the jostling doesn't stop. "Dom, wake up."

I blink, noticing it's still dark outside. But there's a light coming from my backyard, and that alone dissipates the remnants of sleep as I sit up in bed.

"Your backyard's glowing." Luz's laughing expression calms my pounding heart, but I'm still wary as I pull on a pair of sweatpants and head out.

Near my tool shed, Ileana is busy sauntering about, her head thrown back and staring at the moon. I groan, running a hand over my face. "Godmother, you have the worst timing."

Twinkling eyes turn to me, and she smiles. "Te felicit, dragul meu."

I lean against the house wall, crossing my arms over my chest. "And what exactly are you congratulating me for?"

"You took charge of the vrykolakas, and became their alpha. I could not be more proud."

"But I wasn't able to give them salvation. They are still walking about undead. I... maybe I should have gone with them."

Ileana's eyes shine brighter. "You did what you had to, and it was the right choice. But make no mistake, your time with the vrykolakas has not ended." She steps closer, her gaze falling on my bedroom window. "And to think, amid all that, you found your mate. If only the others would do the same..."

I frown, picking up on something in her tone. "Ileana... I don't think Lucas would welcome your interference."

She laughs, waving me off, and her expression grows serious. "There is more happening in this little town of yours, things you have not yet seen. I cannot in all due conscience leave you here alone, my godson."

"So you'll stay?"

Ileana nods, her hair bouncing about her shoulders. "For a time."

"What about Făt Frumos?" I doubt her husband—or consort, if you go by certain tales—would take kindly to being left alone. When I point out as much to my godmother, she has on a secret little smile.

"He has someone to watch over, and it is not as if we will not see each other." Another laugh, another twirl. "Fate has funny ways of bringing people together when you least expect it, don't you think?"

Before I can answer, she disappears, and I shuffle back inside the house. Luz is sprawled over the bed by the time I get in, but she scoots to make room for me. "Everything all right?"

I nod, kissing her bare shoulder and pulling her close. "It will be."

Lucrezia

The next day, after a quick breakfast, we head over to the shop. I see Lucas, Finn and Tristan already gathered in the garage, and head over to my usual spot. Dom tugs on my hand, shaking his head.

"You're with me, today." Bemused, I follow him in the garage where we greet everyone.

Once we're there, Lucas nods and shifts so he's facing us all. "Today, we're closing up shop. We need to go up in the woods and clean up after the fight." He meets my gaze, grimacing. "This'll be disgusting as hell, Lucrezia, I won't lie. But if we leave those bodies out there and humans fall upon them, there's no telling what will happen."

"You mean because of bacteria?"

Tristan laughs at what I deem a perfectly good question, and I glare at him until he shuts up. But it's Finn who explains further. "Partly, yes. But also because any hunter that falls on those wolves will realize they're not regular ones. It might start a witching expedition, and we try to avoid those at all costs."

Dom's hand tightens around mine, and I glance up at him. "Ileana told me last night there's more in this town we're not aware of."

"Then it's a good thing Luz is now been initiated into the pack. Whoever they are, they would have to be stupid to attempt anything—on any of us." Lucas seems sure of this, his gaze steady on Dom's.

His certainty is enough to calm my mate, at least until Tristan opens his big mouth. "What about the guy Luz was with?"

I scowl. "Tytus doesn't pose a threat, he's harmless."

All eyes turn to Finn for confirmation, and it's the first time I see him struggle with something. He won't quite meet Lucas' gaze, nor mine for that matter. After a long, tense moment, he nods. "I agree with Luz's assessment on this one."

"Yet you won't tell us what he is?"

Finn shrugs, moving to grab jugs of gas and flares. "I would if I knew it."

Something tells me Finn is not being a hundred percent truthful, but I bite my tongue. Lucas calls us back to order and instructs us how to proceed. It's a good thing it's supposed to snow again tonight, which will cover the currently bloody snow. As for the carcasses, well, Lucas' instructions are pretty clear.

I team up with Dom, Finn with Tristan, and we head out in three cars—Lucas takes his Hummer. By the time we get to the mountain, it's mid-morning and the air itself feels stifled with the stench of death.

Dom sees me wrinkle my nose and laughs. "Imagine what this feels like to us."

When you put it that way...

We put on rubber gloves and I push past my disgust, bending down and helping Dom with the carcasses. On Lucas' orders, we pile them up in front of the cave the vrykolakas were hiding in. He thinks because of the wind's direction, it'll be easier to have a bonfire of charred meat and not attract any of the locals.

Our paths intersect with Finn, Tristan and Lucas as we work, but for the most part it's done in silence. Once we've picked up the carcasses from up the hill, Dom and I leave the remaining ones to the guys and head into the cave.

I know Radu's body will be in there, but I don't expect seeing it quite like that. In wolf form, he has the same white stripe Dom has, but it's under his belly. It's now matted with dry blood, and he has cuts and lacerations everywhere on his body.

His jaw is hanging open, eyes staring lifeless ahead. But most telling of all is the jugular, ripped apart by powerful canines. I glance at Dom out of the corner of my eyes, knowing this was his work, and am surprised to see him staring at me rather than Radu.

"Scared yet?"

"Of you?" He nods, and there's a wariness in his eyes I don't like seeing. So I move closer until I can wrap my arms around his neck, tugging him closer. "I knew what I was getting into, Dom, and though this is the first I see of your handiwork, it won't be the last if we're being real." A muscle ticks in his jaw, and I move one hand to trace it. "Our worlds are different, but I understand what governs yours – survival of the fittest. So no, I'm not scared of you, or anything here. I love you, Dominic Konstantin, and will go wherever you go. The only thing I fear in this new world is losing you."

Dom buries his head in my neck, inhaling my scent and kissing my skin. Then he moves up to my mouth, drawing kiss after kiss from my lips for long moments, as if to put salve on his wounds.

When he lets me go, his blue eyes are shining. "I love you, Lucrezia San Marco. And I swear you will never lose me."

We turn to Radu and pick up his body, moving him out of the cave and throwing him on top of the others. Finn brings the jugs of gasoline nearby and pours them over the bodies while Tristan lights up two flares.

We move up the hill, far enough from the flames, and at Lucas' nod Tristan throws the flares on the bodies. Flames blaze from nothing, consuming rotting flesh and charring everything in their path. The wind, as Lucas predicted, carries the smell downhill, away from our town—and our already sensitive noses.

Dominic

Luz falls asleep in my arms after the bonfire, and I relax against the tree. Finn looks at us with a half-smile, but Tristan's gaze is lost in the flames. I know the recent fight spiked more of his nightmares, but how to help him evades me.

Lucas's thoughts seem to be running along the same path, as he's watching Tristan with a frown. After a beat, he speaks. "I think we're all on the same wavelength here, but just to make sure. If any of you see vrykolakas running free in town, going forward, you report it to Dom or me. They're Dom's pack, so it will be his decision how he deals with them. But we will have no vigilante murders, you hear me?"

Heads nod all around, and I shift so Luz leans easier on my chest. "We hear you. What about Jared? Finn, what was your take on it?"

With his uncanny way of catching feelings, he's always the first to give a report. This time, like many others, Finn doesn't disappoint. "There's a lot of resentment from Jared, more so than his usual racist shite. But I doubt we'll be getting trouble from him. He may be a wanker, but he's not a nutty one."

Lucas nods, rubbing the back of his neck. "Grazie, Finn. I thought as much. But his pack is a different story."

My hold on Luz tightens. "What, you think they'll try something?"

Lucas meets my gaze, shaking his head. "Not towards you or Luz. But there's a strong chance the Reapers will rebel against their leader. They saw him get his ass kicked by a human woman, and there's all the other stuff." Another frown. "Which reminds me. What was it you told Jared about a deal with a *zmeu*?"

Oh, that. With my free hand, I rub my chin, trying to figure out a way to explain it. After a few beats, I go with the truth. "When I was fighting Radu, he said Aiden wanted to undermine Jared because of his weakness towards us—letting us settle in—and the recent deal he made with a zmeu. In Romanian mythology, they're, umm..."

"Dragons." All eyes turn to Finn, but he keeps his gaze locked onto the flames. "I read about them when in New York, researching your past with Luz."

Tristan says nothing, only dropping his head in his hands. Despite his evident despair, it's Finn's reaction that raises the hair on the back of my neck. Face unreadable, he refuses to look up from the fire, yet his jaw is clenched, as are his fists.

Lucas notices it too, but shakes his head towards me to let it go. I ease back against the tree, tightening my hold on Luz. "Radu may have lied about it."

My pitiful attempt at reassurance doesn't fool anyone, so Lucas picks up the thread of the conversation. "Whether there is one or not, we can only wait and see. But as for the Reapers and their potential unfurling... If they *do* fall apart, the reality is we may have a bunch of rogue wolves on our hands."

I agree with his assessment, knowing it hits the mark. A deafening silence descends on our group, only the crackling of the flames breaking it.

"If it comes to it..." Lucas meets our gazes above the fire. "We may have to step in, fix things up."

I glance at Luz, ensuring she's asleep, before meeting his gaze. "Whatever happens, I'm in."

Finn nods. "And I."

We all turn to Tristan, the only one who hasn't answered. He jerks his head from his hands at the sudden silence and nods. "Sim, claro, me too. You know it."

"Bene, it is settled then." Lucas nods, and his eyes drift to Luz. "You made a bold decision tonight, and you have my respect forever. But I swear to all that's holy, Dom, if you hurt her, I will have your hide."

I chuckle, shaking my head. "As if. She has me wrapped around her little finger."

Chuckles answer me all around, but I'm too busy staring at my mate to pay attention to their friendly jabs. I got the girl, I got the pack, and for now, everything is quiet. What more could a wolf ask for?

As if the universe hears me, the ring of a cellphone interrupts our little get together. We all turn to Tristan, who snaps out of his thoughts and pulls his cellphone out.

He looks at the number, frowning, then answers. "Yeah?"

Whatever he hears on the other end has him jump to his feet, almost stumbling over and into the flames. "Dani? Where are you?" I watch as his hand clenches around the phone, almost breaking it. "Não se mova. I'll be there in a few."

He hangs up, running a hand through his hair. His gaze drifts over us, stopping on me and Luz. "I've got to go."

Before any of us can say a word, he takes off, leaving behind a hint of his agitated vibe. "Do any of you know who Dani is?"

Shrugs all around answer me. But as I stare in the fire, Luz wrapped in the cocoon of my arms, I remember Ileana's words, and wonder if my godmother was right after all...

∞ ∞ ∞

∞ Soartă ∞

"Accept the things to which <u>fate</u> binds you, and love the people with whom fate brings you together, but do so with all your heart."

-Marcus Aurelius-

Dominic

Luz is shifting around in bed, and I move from the window to her side. After the bonfire, I didn't have the heart to wake her up, so I let her sleep. Then I got permission from Lucas—who says you can't teach an old dog new tricks?—to take off for the night, and brought us both deep in the mountains.

A while ago, when I first settled into Rockland Creek and before my pack life, I enjoyed my solitude a little too much.

I purchased a cabin buried here, with a perfect view of the sunrise above the snowy peaks. It's the closest I can get to memories of Romania, my little haven of peace.

One I want to share with Luz, like everything else in my life now and in the future that awaits us.

The sun's almost rising now, and I've been up half the night with weird questions, but mainly, a deep-seated need to protect her. I want her to wake up and watch nature's best trick with me.

So I move to the bed, pushing aside her flaming hair so I can kiss her shoulder. "Wake up, draga mea."

Luz rolls to her back, wrapping her arms around my neck and pulling me in for a sleepy kiss. I chuckle against her mouth, nibbling on her lips until her gorgeous emerald eyes blink awake.

"Good morning."

My heart squeezes, then expands in joy at this simple moment. I kiss her forehead, and her nose, before picking her up—covers and all—and walking us both on the porch.

Luz's eyes are wide as saucers when she realizes we're not in my home, but rather somewhere else. "Where are we?"

"A little retreat up in the mountains." I kiss her again, unable to stay away from her delectable mouth. "I told Lucas we're taking a vacation to breathe and relax, after the events of the last few days."

Luz meets my gaze with a smile. "You don't have to manage me, you know. I'm okay with what happened."

"I know. But I needed this, being away with you." Luz snuggles deeper into my chest, and I shift her so she can see below us.

Her delighted gasp is the best reward, and she tries to move off me but my hands rein her in. "You're barefoot, and there's still snow everywhere."

Luz shakes her head, gaze unwavering from the mountains and the sun peeking over their tips. "Dom, this is gorgeous!"

I kiss her shoulder again, tightening my hold on her. "I hoped you'd like it."

"Like it?" She turns, grinning like a little kid. "I adore it!"

We settle back to watch the sunrise, my heart and soul content at having my mate so close. And still, the thoughts that kept me up all night come back.

Ah, what the hell. Might as well get this over with.

"And you're sure you're okay, with all of this?"

Lucrezia

I peer up at Dom, shaking my head at his question. "Am I *okay* with this? Dom, you..." How can I explain to him what he makes me feel? How none of this—the world I got dragged into—could ever push me away because of the love I feel for him?

The answer? I can't. So I do the next best thing and show him.

Long hours later, I'm close to falling asleep when he says, "There may be a war coming with Jared and his pack. Promise me... No matter how stubborn and independent you are, swear to me that you'll allow my protection. Don't go places without me."

I notice the worry that lines the corners of his eyes and press my fingertips to his furrowed brow, trying to smooth it out. "I promise, Dom. Anything you want."

His eyes sparkle, and he looks boyish and endearing. "Anything?"

When I nod, he grins. "Move in with me."

I gape at his request. We've barely started dating, and there's still so much I don't know about werewolves —and vârcolaci, especially.

Yet despite all the reasons against it, and my better judgment, I know I'd already made up my mind the moment he asked me.

I've already made all the crazy decisions, what's one more?

So I kiss my wolf with all I have, then pull back and nod my answer. The joy in his sky-blue eyes makes my heart sing, and I nuzzle into his chest, soaking up the heat he so unconditionally shares—like everything else about him.

And in the quiet house, this little piece of heaven, something amazing happens. Dominic Konstantin, my wolf, falls asleep peacefully while I watch over him.

EPILOGUE

Lucas was in his house, unable to sleep. In a last ditch effort to quiet his errant thoughts, he drank from a bottle of whiskey. And drank some more. And more. When he was more than halfway through, he started pacing in his living room.

Movement outside drew his eye, and he stood, heading to the backyard. "What the..." For an instant, he thought it was a hallucination.

The woman on his land had long, wavy brown hair with eyes the color of the sun. A robe of roses, lilies and dandelions wrapped her body. When she turned to him, her beautiful smile and lilting voice struck him silent.

"Ah, the alpha." A faint accent lined her words, not unlike Dominic's.

Recalling what Finn told him about his beta's godmother took a moment, but it still did not help clear his head. "Are you...?"

"I am Ileana Cosânzeana, fair wolf."

"And what the fuck are you doing on my property?"

She laughed. "I was sent on the wind, by the wind..." Her voice trailed off, and she stepped closer. "You have suffered, all of you. Your wolves are proud, but they should not be lonely. I have decided to help you."

Something akin to a growl escaped Lucas' lips. "We do not need help."

"A woman's touch, her presence in a man's life, is like the sun. You, of all people, should know that."

"Get out of my head, witch!" He tried to grasp her, but only touched air instead.

Ileana danced around, circling him. "Too late. Love is coming, for all of you!"

She drew away, still laughing, and disappeared past his gated fence.

Lucas stared at the whiskey bottle in his hand, then hurled it against the wall of the house. Its shatter disturbed the peace of the night, causing a dog to bark in the distance.

Yet as he stood there, panting over the shards of glass, nostrils flaring and fists clenched, a single phrase escaped past his gritted teeth. "Non ci credo, Ileana. Not unless it's over my dead body."

Preview of Book II

Second to Surrender — A Moonlight Rogues Novel

Tristan

I couldn't believe it when I got the call. *Dani...*

Merda! Images of dark brown hair, smiling hazel eyes, a mouth begging to be kissed run across my mind as I'm driving over the speed limit. Replaying the conversation in my head does nothing to calm my fast-beating heart.

Tristan, I'm in trouble. I'd asked where she was, and she said her bus was pulling into Rockland Creek in a few minutes.

I didn't stop to think, though in retrospect I should have. Other images hit me—of Izabella, with her hazel eyes and tempting mouth, an exact copy of Dani. They'd been twins, once upon a time when we were all young.

I push back the rest of the memories, the pain, the betrayal and heartache. It has no place in my head if I'm to help Dani. But as I pull into the parking lot of the bus station, I can't help my wayward thoughts.

What could have happened that drove her all the way here... away from her pack?

I get out of the car, locking it behind me, and wait.

Daniela

I didn't want to call on him, for obvious reasons. He's demanding, a leader, a soldier, and did I mention demanding? Plus, we have a history—and no, not in that way.

It's simple story, really. Boy meets girl. Boy falls for girl. Girl breaks boy's heart. Boy goes into the army. But girl never lets him go... until she drives him out of town upon his return.

Ok, so maybe it's not that simple. The girl, in this story, was my twin sister Izabella. Not that it matters because she's gone now. But I know it'll matter to Tristan... I just hope he can help me out.

Because there's no way I'm going back home to face off my crazy family. Hell-to-the-fucking-no.

I step off the bus, pulling my hair in a ponytail and fixing my backpack on my shoulder. I'd left in a hurry and didn't bring much with me. Hopefully, Tristan won't mind.

Already antsy at being so in the open, I tap my foot as I scan the surroundings. My eyes linger on a guy leaning against a Mercedes SUV, arms crossed over his chest, baseball cap pulled low over his brow.

I can't see much of his face, but his body—holy shit. I avert my gaze before my wayward hormones get the best of me. Life as a wolf is difficult—being an unmated one is even more so, making the females prone to bouts of insanity.

"Where the hell is he?" I keep looking around, but Tristan is nowhere I can see.

Then I hear my name called out and search for the voice. It's coming from Mercedes guy. And now he's walking towards me, his stride long and purposeful.

When he's close by, he shifts the hat on his head and I get a full view of his face.

"Tristan?"

My surprise is snuffed out by the anger radiating off him. "What the hell are you doing here?"

Continue Reading![1]

---

1. https://www.alexawhitewolf.com/second-to-surrender

Sign up for my readers' group **at**
www.alexawhitewolf.com/contact and receive a
copy of *Unconditional Love* for **FREE**, as well as
first dibs on cover reveals, discounts, giveaways,
prizes **and more!**

Cheers,

Alexa

Did you love *First to Fall*? Then you should read *Second to Surrender* by Alexa Whitewolf!

They say blood is thicker than water...But what if family's the source of your pain?

Tristan

I swore I was done with love, after my last failed relationship. Being a soldier means making the tough decisions, all for the good of the pack. So when a little miss full of attitude waltzes in, dragging a shitload of trouble with her, I want nothing more than to make that tough decision and kick her the hell out.

Then she turns those big, feisty amber eyes on me, and my wolf roars otherwise. Shit-of-fuck but now I'm screwed.... And her family seriously has a screw loose. As do I, if the nightmares plaguing me are any hint.

But I'm gonna have to put on my big boy pants cause there's no way I'm letting her walk out of my life - not when there's obviously more at stake, our history included.

Daniela

You'd think running away from a psycho family would swear me off relationships for good. Guess what? So did I. In fact, I specifically searched Tristan out because he's the type I'd never be with. Too much of everything, if you get my gist - attitude included.

So why is it when he starts acting all protector, I can't help but swoon? His dark secrets don't scare me as much as this sudden tornado within me. This was not in the plans... And I just might have to make a run for it before he finds out what I'm hiding and starts hating me.

But when his touch is so sweet, his need for me so obvious, can I really take off again? More importantly, will he let me?

Book II in a paranormal shifter series filled with werewolves of all kinds, feisty females who stand up to them, and enough suspense to make it interesting. Can be read as standalone.

Read more at https://www.alexawhitewolf.com.

Also by Alexa Whitewolf

Moonlight Rogues
Moonlight Rogues: Origins
First to Fall
Second to Surrender
Third to Tumble

The Avalon Chronicles
Avalon Dreams
Avalon Wishes
Avalon Nightmares
The Avalon Chronicles - Complete Series

The Sage's Legacy
The Dragon Medallion
The Dragon Manuscript
Relics of the Underworld
The Sage's Legacy - Complete Series

Standalone Novels
Blood Ties, Love Binds
Unconditional Love
Blazing in a Storm of Ashes (Coming Soon)

Watch for more at
www.alexawhitewolf.com

About the Author

Alexa Whitewolf is a dog-loving, caffeine-addicted, all-around traveling enthusiast. Author of three series of fantasy, paranormal and young adult, she spends her nights dreaming up new stories and her days fighting reality. She lives in Ottawa, Canada, with her husband and two mischievous furballs- Zeus and Achilles. Check out her website at www.alexawhitewolf.com !

Read more at https://www.alexawhitewolf.com.